DR. OLEA NEL was born in Cape Town, South Africa. After completing her training as a teacher in Andrew Murray's heartland of Wellington, she relocated to Australia to further her studies. Besides attaining a PhD in Linguistics, she also has qualifications in Information Studies and Theology. Having now retired from her position as a senior librarian at the National Library of Australia, she is able to pursue her passion for research, especially within the fields of church history and biography. Her aim is to share her findings with fellow Christians.

Andrew Murray:
Destined to Serve

A Biographical Novel

Olea Nel

Clairvaux House

Author's Note

I decided to write this novel in the first person because I felt that there was no better way to portray Andrew Murray's character and his inward responses to the challenges he faced during his first year of ministry. Fortunately, there were numerous letters to parents and siblings that enabled me to elicit his thoughts and feelings about most events.

While I have taken a few liberties when describing minor characters and the dramatization of certain incidents, the story as told here is essentially true to fact, including my descriptions of the main characters.

Maps
I've included a few maps, particularly for those readers who have not been to South Africa. To avoid confusion, I have opted to use town names instead of river names whenever a town was planned or established within a five-year timeframe from the beginning of Andrew Murray's ministry. I've also used the Dutch spelling that would have been employed during the 1850s.

If you find the place names on these maps too small to read with ease, please refer to the Map Page on my website at http://www.onandrewmurray.com. You will also find photographs there of some of the places and characters mentioned in this book.

Notes for historical buffs

Readers who are knowledgeable about the life of Andrew Murray will notice that my account differs from those of his original biographers Johannes Christiaan Du Plessis and W.M. Douglas in a few instances. This is because these authors did not have all the facts available to them at the time. Whenever an important discrepancy of this type occurs, I've indicated it in a note.

I have kept the use of Dutch terms to a minimum. Nevertheless, there are a few I've used consistently to indicate conversations in Dutch. For example, I've used the appellation *Meneer* (Mr.), *Mevrou* (Mrs.) and *Dominee* (Reverend) in this way. Because Andrew Murray was a Dutch Reformed pastor, he will have always been addressed as *Dominee* by his Dutch-speaking parishioners, and *Mr. Murray*, by his English-speaking ones. Please consult the Glossary for other terms.

Those with a knowledge of South African history will also notice that the term *Voortrekker*—to denote Dutch emigrants who trekked in groups across the Orange and Vaal Rivers—is never used. This is because that term was not in use during the 1850s.

Acknowledgments

A special word of thanks goes to my husband Peter for his un-flagging encouragement and patience while writing this book. I'm also indebted to my dear friend Mareta van der Merwe for being a fellow pilgrim along my writing journey.

I would also like to acknowledge with appreciation the help-fulness of Lori Jackson, Joyce Hall and Attie van Wijk, who gave up their valuable time to read through my manuscript and offer improvements. I'd also like to thank Geoff Alves for formatting my novel, as well as drawing the maps that illustrate the huge distances that Andrew Murray needed to travel.

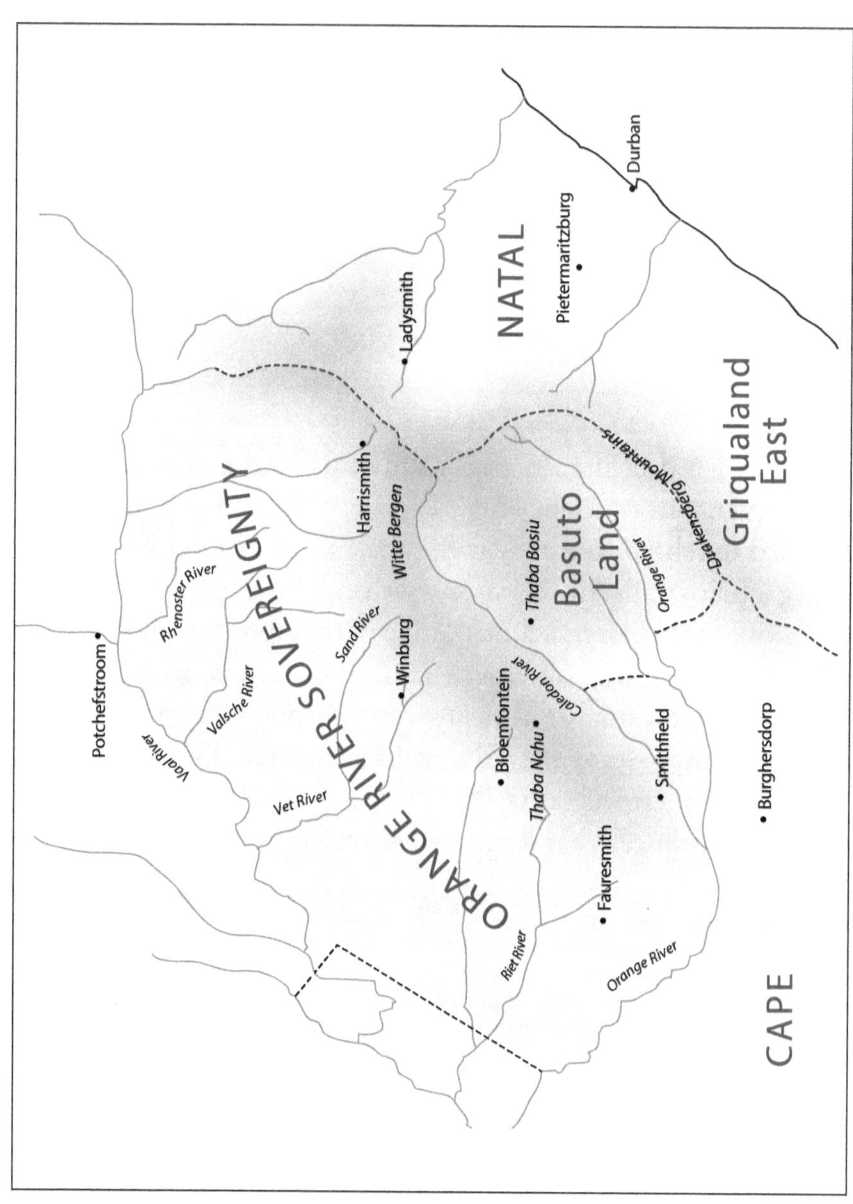

Orange River Sovereignty, 1848–1854

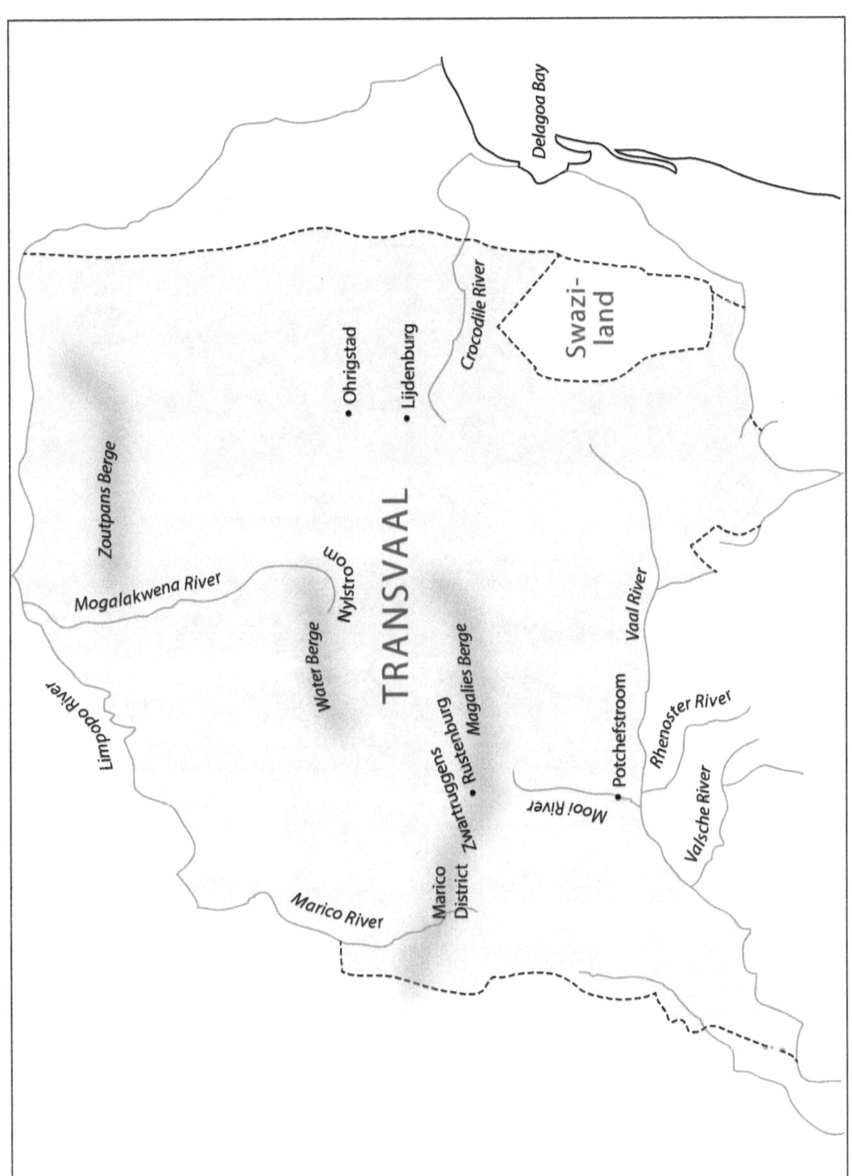

Transvaal, South African Republic, 1852

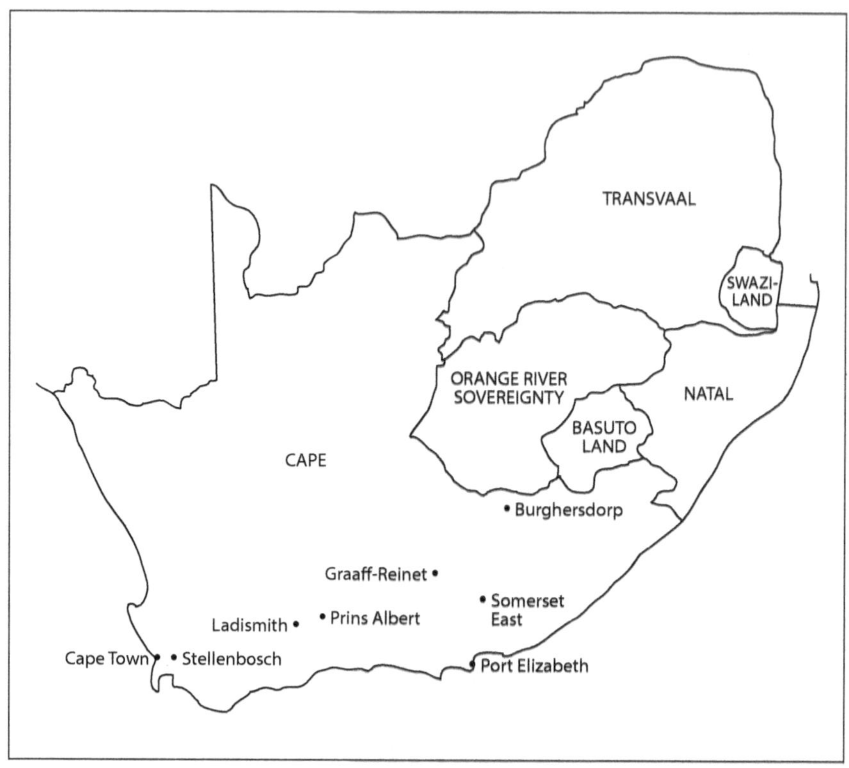

South Africa, 1850

Prologue
Clairvaux, Wellington

10 May 1915

I was waiting for an answer. I so wanted it be a "yes." There was no doubt that this three-letter word would change the whole direction of my academic output, and bring into public view the life and achievements of one of the Cape's greatest heroes of the faith.

I glanced over at the frail form of Andrew Murray who was seated in his favorite wicker chair. His eyes were closed, and his expression one of perfect repose. Despite his hollow cheeks and the step-like furrows on his forehead that ascended almost to his crown, he exuded an inner glow that defied description. It was as if he were wrapped in a cloak of holiness. And there I was, Professor Johannes du Plessis of Stellenbosch Theological Seminary, in just as much awe of him as everyone else.

Conscious of my nervous demeanor, I tried to strike a casual pose by resting my right ankle on my left foreleg—a posture I often adopted when chatting with students. But this ploy only belied my sweaty palms and oft-stroked moustache.

We were sitting on the back *stoep* of Clairvaux, the home Andrew Murray had built for his retirement in his beloved parish of Wellington. I had placed my chair diagonally across from him so as not to block his view of the narrow valley of vines. It still held the odd leaf of burnished red and gold that fluttered now-and-again in the autumn breeze. It was 10 May 1915, the day after his eighty-sixth birthday. It had struck me at the time that I should pay him a second visit to request that he release his personal papers into my safekeeping so that I might make a start on his biography. Someone had to write it. And to my mind there were only two candidates: Andries Dreyer, a missionary and church historian with at least nine book titles to his name, and myself. As it was a toss-up as to which of us was the better writer, I hoped that I would be the first to present my request.

While I perceived no difficulty associated with the release of the papers, I knew Dr. Murray might baulk at my expressed wish to visit him at regular intervals. Nevertheless, it would lend depth to his biography if I could ask him questions as well as hear him tell his own story.

While I was composing a few responses to the arguments he might raise, he opened his eyes and looked my way.

"My dearest Johan," he said, with a touch of mirth in his tone, "the thing is, I'm not dead yet."

"But Dr. Murray, that's exactly why I'm making this request. When I was editing the memoirs of some of our heroes of the faith—people like Helperus Ritzema Van Lier and Michiel Vos—so many questions sprang to mind. They had described the difficulties they had to deal with fairly well, but—"

"There were major gaps in the telling," said Dr. Murray, finishing off my sentence. "That's the trouble with memoirs of a spiritual nature. If you recall the depths of your despair, readers might hold you up as an example that provides them with an excuse to wallow in their self-pity. And if you describe your mountain-top experiences, that too might become a blueprint for some to emulate. In either case, you lay yourself open to the glorification of self."

"True," I said, "but biographies are different in that they are told by a third party in a more objective way. And the best ones enable their readers to learn from their hero's experiences."

He nodded, yet I could see by his raised brow that he was not entirely convinced. His ongoing silence was an obvious invitation to put my case.

"Readers want to know about the lows and the pitfalls, as well as the highs and the breakthroughs along the spiritual journey. In short, they want to be inspired to overcome and reach similar spiritual heights."

"But all that is covered in my books, Johan."

"Yes, but the question remains: How do your spiritual insights relate to your life's journey? Those are the issues I'd like to explore. And that is why I need your input."

He studied my face through hooded eyes that seemed to pierce through to my very soul. I realized I had just touched upon a major hurdle that was postponing a positive reply—his personal input. I knew he had flatly refused to write an autobiography, despite the pleas of senior colleagues and immediate family members. But a biography was different. I needed to make him see that. So I decided to clinch the argument with an insight that must surely find favor with him.

"Dr. Murray," I said, "I'm absolutely certain that a biography of your life will have an even greater impact if matched against the various stages of the spiritual journey you outlined in your writings."

A few moments of silence followed.

"You're very persuasive, Johan. But before I convey my decision, I need to tell you of a little conundrum I'm facing. Only yesterday, Andries Dreyer made the same request. And as you know, he has written a short overview of my life that was published in 1900. So now he considers it a foregone conclusion that he will be writing my biography. Nevertheless, I told him I would release my papers when I was ready."

At the mention of Dreyer, my hopes plummeted. I was certain that Dr. Murray's answer to me would be the same as he had given Dreyer. But to my surprise, he went on to say, "Now the question is: Why do you think you're the right person for the task?"

I had no idea what to answer, especially now that I was aware that Dreyer thought he had a prior claim. I'd also heard that Dreyer was a man after Dr. Murray's own heart. By contrast, I was a theologian with an intellectual bent who, at that moment, was in a spiritually dry place.

I shook my head while chuckling softly. Finally I said, "I can think of only one reason: My English is better that his."

Dr. Murray broke into a broad smile. "Ah, that's no small matter, Johan, especially if it's my expressed wish that my biography be written in both Dutch and English. But as I don't want to keep you in suspense any longer, I would just like to point out that all my papers have been catalogued by my daughter, Annie, in date order. You may take the boxes with you today if you wish."

"Am I hearing you correctly, Dr. Murray?"

"You are. It wasn't a decision I came to lightly. After Dreyer sounded me out yesterday, I laid the matter before the Lord. My answer was confirmed when you appeared this morning."

"But why me above Dreyer?"

"Several reasons. Dreyer is a man of great spiritual depth, and over the years we've each felt the freedom of sharing our spiritual experiences with each other. My fear is that he might be tempted to write a hagiography where I float two inches above the ground. Fortunately, that is not your temptation. If anything, yours is to be too objective. I'm sure you'll be scrutinizing every spiritual claim through that rational theological lens of yours. Not that I mind, though. In fact, my desire is for you to simply lay the facts before the reader."

"I can assure you I'll try my best in that regard."

"That is not to say that I won't reveal all the details of my spiritual walk to you. I'll probably let fly with my memories, knowing that you will sift the contents. At the same time, it is my heart-felt prayer that you will benefit spiritually from the telling. Regard it as an opportunity to go deeper with the Lord, Johan. Don't think I don't know that you're in a dark place at the moment."

I didn't answer, but looked down seeking comfort in the act of stroking my moustache. Poor Dreyer, I thought. He'd be most disappointed.

As if reading my mind, Dr. Murray said, "Another thing. Once I'm gone, tell Dreyer why I chose you over him. He'll understand. In any case, I have another project in mind for him: a history of our Missions Institute that details the countless blessings God has bestowed on both home and foreign fields through its graduates."

It was a triumphant statement and one I could readily agree with.

We sat in silence for a while—he, resting content with the decision he had made, I, contemplating the project ahead with heightened anticipation. Before long, he spoke again, obviously voicing the thoughts going through his mind.

"You've made your request at the right time, Johan, because I'll be available to you throughout the rest of autumn and winter. But when Spring comes, I intend to embark on another preaching tour."

"Surely not," I said, conscious of the frail figure before me.

"*Ach*," he said, dismissing my objection with a wave of his hand, "these days I travel in relative comfort in the train, so let's not dwell upon this topic. Come Johan, sit here on my left next to my good ear so that we can begin."

I dutifully followed his instructions and found myself facing the wind-swept vines and the low hill in the distance.

We got off to a slow start. He described how he was only ten and his brother John, twelve, when they were sent to Scotland to pursue a liberal education. Having kept up with his brother throughout their student years, they were able to graduate together with Masters' degrees from Aberdeen University. They had then proceeded to Utrecht to complete their theological degrees for ordination in the Dutch Reformed Church.

After he had completed a rather dull and factual account of his time as a student, I asked, "What was life like on a sailing ship as a ten-year old?"

"Strange as it may seem, Johan, I can't recall a thing, except that the wife of the missionary couple looking after us was blessed with the birth of a baby. And as for our departure from Cape Town, well, that is even more vague. It appears that the trauma of it was so great that I've blocked it from my mind. But," he said, leaning towards me so as to underscore the next point, "I remember our arrival back at the Cape as if it were yesterday. What a glorious day that was! But oh, how bold, impetuous, and lacking in wisdom I proved to be."

As he described sailing into Cape Town harbor, his right hand swiped and punched the air. He was once again on that sailing ship, reliving his homecoming.

I felt a tingle of rising goose bumps as I readied myself to accompany him on a journey that would take us across swollen rivers, along wagon tracks, and several ocean crossings to England and America.

I fingered open my briefcase at the side of the chair with one hand, and located my notebook and pencil. Thankfully, he hadn't noticed, so intent was he on telling his story. Soon I too would be drawn into the homecoming he was reliving. It was a world not far removed from my own in years, but oh, how different!

I

Table Bay

November 1848

On the evening before we were due to dock in Cape Town, our barque, the *Lady Flora*, began to pitch and toss as she sailed into a violent South Easter near Table Bay. The threatening storm had prompted Captain Eagles to issue the command for all passengers to be confined to bunks. This was no small matter, as we were all in the throes of readying ourselves to disembark on the following day. Trunks and boxes, which had already been packed and placed in the saloon, were now sliding back and forth—taking their turn to bang into the fixed planks that served as seats around the mess tables, and then to crash into the wooden cabins that encircled the saloon.

There were four bunks in our cabin. Two were occupied by John and myself, the others by Ian and Colin Grant, two brothers in their twenties who hailed from Edinburgh.

"I feel sorry for those blighters above deck," said John, expressing a concern we all felt.

"Amen to that," I said. "How they can climb those ratlines in this weather, Lord alone knows."

Ian, who professed to have some knowledge of sailing, tried to calm my fears. "Don't concern yourself with that, Andrew.

They are sure to have reefed the topsails by now."

He had barely uttered these words, when we heard a deafening crash above deck that was followed by another in quick succession.

Colin groaned. "I hope you realize that we may have lost both top masts."

"That often happens in a storm," said Ian. "Besides, topsails are always reefed while sailing into harbor, so not having them shouldn't hamper our progress at all."

Despite Ian's attempts to make light of what was happening above deck, we knew there was no chance of sleep that night. I dare say each person on board uttered a prayer with each sideways list, which threatened to keel the ship over, and each downward dip, which came perilously close to the *Lady Flora* plunging bow first into the deep.

Finally, at around 2.00 a.m., the storm abated. Shortly afterwards, we heard the anchors drop. We had arrived in Table Bay.

I was awakened in the morning by the swabbing down of the deck at 7.30 a.m.—an hour later than usual. I completed my ablutions in double-quick time, and donned my Dutch Reformed clerical garb that comprised a stiff-collared shirt, white bow tie, and black suit. I did not wait for the others to dress, but hastily left the cabin. After clambering over the trunks and boxes that lay scattered around the saloon, and bounding up the ladder leading to the main deck, I emerged into the morning glow of a perfect day.

To my right, rose the fabled Lions Head, a rocky outcrop that stood to the fore of a hill that looked uncannily like the silhouette of a lion at rest. The section of the hill that corresponded to the neck and rump ran parallel to the shoreline that stretched a mile or two to my left. Several small estates with impressive homes could be seen along the green belt that separated the hill from the shore. Within their tree-lined boundaries were flower and vegetable gardens, fruit trees, and myriads of wild flowers that grew in uncultivated areas. As yet, Table Mountain was only partially visible. I made up my mind to savor every minute as it came into view.

A short while later, I heard Captain Eagles give the order for the Bosun to weigh anchor. I turned to glance aloft, and noticed that both the fore and main top masts had snapped—just as Ian had surmised. Thankfully, the lower portions had not been damaged. I could see that their sails were already unfurled. We were apparently ready to set sail, and would no doubt be docking within an hour or two.

At that moment, I felt an urgent desire to have John with me. I was deeply conscious of how much I owed him. He had been my mother, father and brother all rolled into one—at times prodding me on, at other times, holding me back. It was therefore inconceivable that he should not be at my side to share the joy of our homecoming.

I doubled back to our cabin and poked my head around the door. There was John kneeling beside a small trunk in which he was scrounging for something between his clothes.

"What on earth are you doing, John? We're about to get underway at any minute."

"Found it," he said, flourishing a thin volume in the air. "I thought it advisable to have a book at the ready in my shoulder bag so I can whip it out during in-between moments. One never knows when the subject matter might serve as a handy topic of conversation."

"What a ridiculous notion," I said. "We've just spent seven years in Scotland and three in Utrecht—not to speak of the storm last night—and here you are suggesting that our descriptions might falter and our conversations flag. Well I never!"

Undeterred by my outburst, he rose from closing the trunk in a calm and dignified manner. I couldn't help admiring his dashing appearance, even in clerical garb. He was tall, good-looking, and even at twenty-two, endowed with broad shoulders that cut a manly figure. As he turned to face me, his jaw dropped.

"Good heavens Andrew! Your hair resembles a floating bunch of kelp."

Somewhat bemused by this description, I glanced at my reflection in the mirror. My hair was indeed a mop of crinkly waves. Given my slight build and medium height, I was sure I looked no more than sixteen or seventeen. To make matters worse, there was an unruly curl over my forehead and another over my right ear that reinforced my youthful appearance. I licked my palms and tried to smooth the waves down.

"Unfortunately, dear brother, I washed my hair in salt water yesterday, and now it won't lie flat. But given the fact that we'll be wearing hats when we disembark, no one will be any the wiser."

"I certainly hope so," said John. "At least you've made a decent effort with your bow tie."

We hauled his trunk into the saloon, where we found most of the passengers still sorting out their possessions. Although bleary eyed, all appeared to be in good humor. We smiled, exchanged greetings, and made the obligatory remark about the storm. We then slowly snaked our way to the deck ladder. Once on deck, we were relieved to find the ship rails still relatively free of passengers.

"Well I never," said Angus Ross, the junior officer of the deck, as soon as he became aware of my presence. He was looking rather dapper in his navy dress-uniform with its starched collar and gold-braided frock coat. Unlike other officers, he neither sported a moustache nor beard, probably because they were still wispy like mine. Over the four months on board, we had become amicable sparring partners, always competing for the clinching quip.

He looked me over with unfeigned amusement. "I didn't realize you were a *Dominus,*" he said. You look far too young with your boyish locks and cherub kiss-curl."

"I'm much obliged to you, sir, for this flattering description, especially as a few minutes ago my fetching hairstyle was described as a floating bunch of kelp."

He made a show of inspecting my hair. "What a tawdry description. I'm sure it would make even Neptune flinch. No *Dominus*. Your hair is more like a bobbing halo not quite in place."

I gave a mock bow by way of accepting his judgment. "Well my friend, seeing both you and Neptune have discredited that woeful description, I owe it to you to correct your usage of *Dominus*. The correct appellation for a Dutch Reformed pastor is *Dominee*. It's the equivalent of Reverend. And as you correctly noted, it is derived from the Latin term *Dominus*."

"Much obliged to you for the lesson, *Dominee*. If I had known of your exalted status when we met, I would have treated you with due deference."

"Officer Ross," said John, in an attempt to change the conversation, "do you know the name of the cove we are passing?"

"That I do, sir. According to the annals of Dutch nautical history, it has been known as Three Anchor Bay ever since the first Governor arrived here two centuries ago."

"You mean Jan van Riebeeck?"

"I dare say that was his name. Anyway, the story goes that

the three ships comprising his party dropped anchor just about here. But First Officer Van Reenen doubts this version of events. He's quite the expert on all things Dutch, you know. He claims it was the early Dutch sailors who named the cove because most Dutch ships that plied these waters in the seventeenth and eighteenth centuries usually dropped three anchors in its vicinity."

"Why was that?" John asked.

"Because one anchor wouldn't hold against the powerful undercurrents in the Bay."

"I take it then that we also dropped three anchors last night?"

"Believe me," Mr. Murray, "with Van Reenen's warnings of dire catastrophe reverberating in our ears, and his tale of eight ships going down during a storm in May 1837, we dropped the bow anchor, the best bower on the starboard, and our large sheet anchor—three all told."

We had just rounded a point and were admiring the tall lighthouse that stood on its headland, when a wreck wedged in a rock came into view.

This eerie sight was a sobering reminder of our powerlessness in the face of a major storm at sea. It was during this contemplative moment that Angus Ross handed me a folded leaf of parchment.

"To commemorate your time aboard ship and our short, but memorable, association."

To my surprise it contained a short poem. On nearer inspection, it appeared to be a hymn with a refrain. As I read the lyrics, my eyes welled with tears.

"Where did you get this, Angus? The words are so simple, yet so profound."

"A mate of mine who regularly sails to America gave it to me. As you can see, it was written by a Miss Priscilla Owens of

Baltimore[1] for her Sunday School class. I transcribed that copy especially for you."

I was so overcome by his thoughtfulness that all I could manage was a nod and a simple "thank you."

"There's a tune to accompany it, by the way. Van Reenen and my mate tried their hand at composing one. We then taught it to a group of sailors in a tavern at Gravesend before we left. And need I say, it was a rousing success."

He watched me closely to see my reaction.

"Well I dare say a tavern could be the best place to test the efficacy of a seafaring hymn—that is, if sung by sailors who appreciate its deeper meaning."

"That goes without saying. Yet, I must confess, the meaning of the words only struck home last night. And doubtless, because of the storm, their meaning will have greater significance for you too."

"How does it go?" I asked, eager to hear the tune.

I felt a sharp nudge from John, but chose to ignore it. I winked at Angus, who broke into a rakish grin and started to pump the planks with his heel to establish the beat. I knew he was an excellent tenor who never missed the opportunity of accompanying the crew in the rigging when they sang their sea shanties. So I was confident his rendition would do the hymn justice.

His voice rang out clear and strong, his diction crisp:

> Will your anchor hold in the storms of life,
> When the clouds unfold their wings of strife?
> When the strong tides lift, and the cables strain,
> Will your anchor drift, or firm remain.

When he reached the refrain, his voice rose in a gradual crescendo that finally reached fortissimo as he prolonged the last note of the third line. His tone then firmed as he emphasized the final words.

> We have an anchor that keeps the soul
> Steadfast and sure while the billows roll;
> Fastened to the Rock which cannot move,
> Grounded firm and deep in the Savior's love!

"Sing with me, Andrew—the first verse and the refrain."

John elbowed me again, knowing that I was inclined to sing off key.

"C'mon Andrew, the tune is easy enough . . . one, two, three."

We belted it out together, my head bobbing from side to side in time with the beat, while he conducted with a flourish and tapped the deck with his heel. A little distance away, Mr. Joseph Freeman of the London Missionary Society started to whistle along. It emboldened me to sing with even greater gusto.

"What a swash-buckling chorus," I said. "Thank you so much for this copy. It will always remain in my Bible as a reminder of our friendship."

While I was undoing the clasp of my shoulder bag to locate my Bible, I felt an uncontrollable urge to inquire after his soul. Quite unconsciously, I raised my forefinger, as was my habit when saying something important.

"Before you go, Angus, I would like to ask you something. The question is: what about you? Do you have an anchor to keep your soul?"

He inclined his head slightly. "I see that you are about your business, Andrew, so I had best be about mine."

He swiveled around and walked off with not so much as a goodbye. But he'd barely taken half a dozen steps, when he turned around to face me again. I noted the broad grin as he raised a forefinger in an obvious parody of my own gesture.

"Now the question is . . . will your ribcage hold?"

He laughed as he pirouetted back to face the way he was going. I watched as he traversed the deck with a jaunty step while whistling the chorus he had just taught me.

The blighter, I thought. But at least he hadn't taken umbrage at my question. I knew it had been my duty to pose it, and God's to decide where the seed would fall.

I opened my shoulder bag and slipped the parchment into my Bible. I then turned to see what had happened to John. He was leaning on the rail, his eyes focused on the water directly below.

"I hope you realize that you've just made a first class spectacle of yourself. And what's more, your behavior reflects on me. I know you're excited, Andrew, but you need to settle down."

Fortunately, I was spared John's prissiness when one of his shipboard friends came over to speak with him. This gave me the opportunity to join Mr. Freeman[2]. He had just stepped closer to open up more space at the rail for a few passengers who'd recently come on deck. He was an elegant man, athletic in appearance, with a full crop of silver hair. During the voyage, he had grown a full beard in preparation for his ox-wagon trek to visit London Missionary Society stations throughout southern Africa. John and I had conversed with him on several occasions, and had found him to be a sympathetic listener, both knowledgeable and astute.

"I gather your brother was not amused," he said.

"Well the thing is, I'm overly excited at the moment, while John is excessively anxious. So from my perspective, it's best to regard his present tetchiness much like the skimming of stones over water. The stones will sink and the ripples soon disappear."

"I can understand that. But what on earth is making him so anxious?"

"It's all to do with his church appointment. He'll be receiving it from the Governor via Dr. Abraham Faure within a day or so. And added to this is his concern about preaching his inaugural sermon in the *Groote Kerk*—the Great Church, as the Dutch like to call it. I believe it's at the top of Heerengracht Avenue, near the Dutch East India Company Gardens.

Freeman nodded. "I know it well. Dr. Faure gave me a tour of the building when I last visited Cape Town."

I was taken by surprise at this information because I hadn't expected Faure to be in contact with any official from the London Missionary Society.

"How do you know Dr. Faure?" I asked.

"Ah, now that's an interesting question. It might surprise you to know that Faure studied under Dr. Bogue at his Gosport Academy in England. And as you may know, Dr. Bogue was a co-founder of the London Missionary Society in 1795. So you see, we have a lot in common."

"But I thought Faure studied at Utrecht?"

"He certainly did, but only after completing two years at Gosport. He's quite a revivalist and missions enthusiast, you know. He especially admires the works of Jonathan Edwards and William Bates."

"Well that's certainly news to me. I'm really looking forward to meeting him now."

Freeman chuckled, obviously amused by my response. "Tell me," he said, "Won't you also be preaching in the *Groote Kerk*? You are ordained, aren't you?"

"Yes, that's true, but unlike John, I'm under age—only

twenty. That means I may preach, but not be appointed to a congregation until I'm twenty-two. So in the meantime, I'll probably be an assistant pastor in my father's congregation at Graaff-Reinet. I must say, I'm rather looking forward to it."

He stroked his beard as he pondered this information. "So let me get this straight . . . John's feeling nervous, but you aren't?"

"Well, I'm not really the nervous type, you see. In fact, I'm relishing the opportunity to preach in the *Groote Kerk*. I suppose it's because I have nothing to lose, whereas John feels he needs to make a good impression."

Freeman looked perplexed. I knew he was a man of great discernment, so I was anxious to know why. I was on the verge of asking, when he said, "Andrew, I feel there's something amiss here. All the emphasis appears to be on John, while you are in the background."

"That's true. But then I'm two years younger than he is."

"Nevertheless, John tells me you were able to keep up with him throughout your school years. It was also *you* who won the scholarship to Marischal College at Aberdeen University."

"Again, that's true, but the operative phrase, Mr. Freeman, is 'keep up.' John won the prizes at school. John passed his Master's degree with Honorable Distinction. And John was considered to be one of the brightest and best theological students at Utrecht. He also caught the eye of the professors, while I went almost unnoticed."

"Because of your youth, perhaps?"

"Could be."

"Yet John tells me the Hague Committee agreed to ordain you at twenty, despite the ordination age being twenty-two."

"Ah, Mr. Freeman, that's another case in point. I'm sure they took one look at John—his dignity, his charm—and thought some of it might rub off on me."

He laughed while shaking his head. "No, my dear fellow. Besides them recognizing your obvious disposition for being a pastor, it was simply sound common sense."

He laid his hand on my shoulder and looked me in the eye. "The time has come for you to step out from behind John's shadow and the prod of his elbow."

I sighed heavily, knowing that what he was suggesting was easier said than done.

"I've tried that, especially when making friends and introducing myself to superiors. You may not realize this, but John is very shy and diffident in that regard. But then, when I introduce John to my new-found acquaintances, he is the one who makes the favorable impression, leaving me standing once again in his shadow."

"I don't believe that for a moment, Andrew. You have charisma, intelligence, and a love for souls—strengths that will make a most effective pastor. So think on that, and don't sell yourself short. Your time has arrived."

He had said it with conviction, but my experience to date indicated otherwise. I would still be playing catch-up for another two years. And then there was the obvious drawback of my youthful looks and playful temperament. Yet, in spite of these reservations, I smiled to acknowledge his flattering words. He nodded back as if to underscore his remarks. He then turned to watch the passing scene, leaving me to think matters through.

I reflected upon my time in my uncle's home in Aberdeen. He was a Presbyterian pastor who had laid great stress on the role of the eldest son. He had favored John over me, and had expected him to excel in all he did. His only expectation of me was that I keep up. I had therefore been free to be myself—to laugh and to have a good time with my cousins. I realized now that John had not had that luxury because of the expectations placed upon him.

The sad thing was that by the time we arrived at the Academy of Utrecht, John's drive to excel had become all-absorbing. It had also been accompanied by the fear of not being able to live up to his own expectations. This drove him to apply himself even harder. Although I too kept to a strict timetable, I tended to cruise through my work, just happy to score acceptable results.

Poor John, I thought. He had sacrificed so much for academic achievement and the acknowledgment of others. He had also been burdened with the added responsibility of overseeing my studies while at school, and keeping me in check ever since.

As I pondered these facts, I realized that John deserved his superior status. And if the truth be known, I wanted to keep mine as younger brother—at least for the time being. The path I would tread now lay clearly before me.

Noting a change in my posture, Freeman turned to face me again. "So?" he said. "Are you now prepared to take your place alongside John?"

"I think there's another issue at stake here."

"And what would that be, dear fellow?"

"First, let me say that the notion that my time has finally arrived is quite intoxicating. I feel exhilarated by the mere thought of it. But if that be true, then it's also my opportunity to help John in his time of need. He encouraged me through ten years of study, so it's only right that I should now support him."

I could tell from Freeman's expression that I had just veered off in a direction he had not anticipated.

"And what would supporting him entail?" he asked.

"I've decided to do everything in my power to help boost his confidence and waylay his fears. I will also try to meet all his requirements for dignity and decorum to put him at ease."

Although I had spoken these words with sincerity and emphasis, my tone must have sounded out of character, because Freeman looked decidedly amused.

"Well, you had better start by not bouncing down the gangplank," he said.

"My pace will be slow and dignified, Mr. Freeman. Slow and dignified."

The vision that these words conjured up resulted in both Freeman and myself bursting into laughter—mine a little too raucous for my liking. Out of the corner of my eye, I could see John turn to glance our way.

"Would you believe it," I said, "John has heard us laughing and is coming over."

It struck me then that my resolution to act with decorum had already floundered on the rocks of my laughter. In the meantime, Freeman was desperately trying to muffle his. I was delighted to observe a touch of the boy in him. It seemed to indicate that he understood me well enough.

"You two appear to be in high spirits," said John, looking first at Mr. Freeman and then at me.

"Ah, who wouldn't be on a day such as this, Mr. Murray. Do join us," said Freeman, not missing a beat.

John seemed to be over his pique, and I was back in the fold. All was now right with the world.

At long last, the *Lady Flora* rounded the hind part of the "lion's rump", and Table Mountain came fully into view. It had been like a slow and intoxicating unveiling of each cliff and crag that ran down its sheer face.

I took in the broad sweep of its level plateau that was a few miles long and over three thousand feet high. It was flanked by

Devil's Peak to our left and the back side of Lions Head to our right. The town itself lay in the natural amphitheater created by these dramatic backdrops.

Mr. Freeman spoke first. "There's a grandeur and sublimity about the Cape that I'll never tire of. I passed this way in 1830 and 1836 on my return journey to Madagascar. On both those occasions, Table Mountain was covered in dense cloud that poured over its edge. It is said that this table-cloth effect is created by the South Easter—the same wind that caused the storm last night."

John lent back to address Freeman over my shoulder. "My father's best top hat blew off during a South Easter while he was attending the synod here last year. Poor man. It must have been rather undignified for him to chase after it. Apparently, the wind was so strong that he had to let it go."

It was already after nine when the wharf came into view. Even from afar, we could see that it was crowded with horse wagons, open goods carts, and a variety of hooded buggies and chaises. Freeman had just extracted a small spyglass from his inside pocket and was adjusting the focus.

"Speaking of hats," he said, "I can see a huddle of three top hats and one straw dress hat. Two I have the privilege of knowing. One is my friend Dr. John Philip, who has come to fetch me. The other is Dr. Faure, who has obviously come to welcome you. I'm afraid, the other two are unknown to me. Perhaps you know them," he said, passing the spyglass to me.

"I'm sure my Uncle William Stegmann is wearing the other top hat. You may have heard of him. He's the pastor of St. Stephen's. But I can't tell who's under the straw one. Here, you take a look, John."

He put the spyglass to his eye, and without hesitation said, "It's our brother Willie. I'm sure of it."

He handed the spyglass back to me, and this time I recognized the young man to be Willie.

During my years abroad, I had retained fond memories of him as my favorite playmate. Although only a year younger than I was, he had lost out on going to Scotland because of financial constraints on the home front. I couldn't help thinking how unfair it was that one's position in the family should dictate one's educational opportunities. From what I could gather, he was now working in a merchant warehouse in the city.

While I was thrilled that he was able to get off work to welcome us home, I realized that I would have to be sensitive to his feelings. This would mean that I could not relate my experiences with my usual descriptive flair and unbounded exuberance in his presence. I'd have to show constraint. And that could prove a major challenge.

I was about to focus on Uncle William, when my thoughts were interrupted by Freeman.

"About the name St. Stephen's, I didn't know that the Dutch Reformed Church named their congregations after biblical characters."

"As far as I know, they don't," I said. "It's actually the name of a mission church for freed slaves. It was started by Uncle William, a Lutheran pastor, and Dr. Adamson, a Presbyterian one. There are also a number of helpers from the *Groote Kerk*."

"How interesting," said Freeman. "And are they able to work together amicably?"

"Very much so. One of the reasons is that Uncle William was sent to live with my parents after they were married. This arrangement came about because he was fretting for my mother, his sister. You see, their mother had died a few years earlier. When he was old enough, my father sent him to Scotland to further his education. He lived with my Uncle John, a Presbyterian minister—just as we did. So with his Dutch Reformed-cum-Presbyterian background, he is able to work quite happily alongside these denominations."

Because I was keen to evade further questions about Uncle William, I decided to steer the conversation back to the naming of St. Stephen's.

"Would you like to know how St. Stephen's received its name? It's rather an interesting story."

"By all means."

"Well, according to my father, the mission church grew in leaps and bounds until there were too many attendees to fit into St. Andrews Presbyterian Church. To overcome this problem, Uncle William transferred the services to a theatre on Riebeeck Square known as the *Komediehuis.* As several parties were opposed to a church for ex-slaves being established there, they stoned the building. So it was no surprise that Uncle William and Dr. Adamson should name the church after St. Stephen, the first Christian martyr who was also stoned."

"What about those who were opposed to the mission? Are they still causing problems?"

"Not at all. You see, the Lord sent a powerful revival, which meant they were fighting a losing battle."

"Well I never. How marvelous are His ways!"

"But that's not all. Several of the young men from the *Groote Kerk* who had experienced this revival at first hand decided to become pastors. Abraham Faure's son, Hendrik, is one, while our best friends Nicolaas Hofmeyr and Johannes Neethling are two others. All three are presently studying theology at Utrecht."

"And on that happy note," butted in John, "we had better say our farewells."

Freedman laid a hand on each of our shoulders. "May the Lord's blessing go with you."

"And with you," we chorused in turn.

We rushed back to our cabin to don our hats and straighten our bow ties. We had just completed our grooming, when John said, "Listen Andrew, I need you to do me a favor."

"Certainly. How can I help?"

"Would you mind preaching first in the *Groote Kerk*?"

I stood there stunned. Surely he must realize that if he wanted to be regarded as a sought-after graduate, he simply had to be the one to preach first.

"You haven't thought this through, John. You are the one who's expected to preach first, as you are the one who's old enough to be appointed to a congregation."

"But you don't understand. Hendrik Faure told me that reporters from *Het Volksblad* and *De Suid Afrikaan* would be present to review the sermon. And I'm sure my congregation— whoever they are—will be eager and poised to read their every comment."

"John, you're an excellent preacher. Besides, reporters from these papers will be there whether you preach first or second."

"I know. But it will be easier on me if I went second."

"Just the opposite, dear brother. You'd be working yourself up into a right lather by then."

"Please Andrew!"

"Well, what reason would you give? You couldn't very well say that it would be easier on you to go second, as that would imply that you are letting me go first because it's more diffi-cult. Besides, Dr. Faure would think you are abrogating your duty—which of course you are. And there's also the possibility I could deliver a first class sermon that puts yours in the shade."

His lips twitched into a shadow of a smile while he considered my last argument. I knew by his expression that he thought there wasn't the slightest chance of this conjecture coming to pass.

"We're about equal, Andrew, although I must say you're far too lively in the pulpit."

"By the same token, brother, some might think you're too formal."

"Fine, I accept that view. Now let's get back to my request. Will you do it?"

"With a heavy heart, John—not because I don't want to help you, but because I think it will place you in a subordinate position to me. The only possibility of you being seen in a more favorable light is if I deliver a poor sermon. And I pray God, that won't happen."

He gave me a hug and patted me on the back. "I'll be forever grateful, Andrew."

"By the way," I said, "what reason will you give for going second?"

"Don't worry, I'll think of something."

I walked over to my bunk and ever so gently lifted a box that contained a present for my mother. I was ready to go.

"Is that the Spanish doll you bought for Ma in London?"

"Yes. What of it?"

"It will be smithereens after last night's storm. That's why I advised you not to buy it."

"No it won't. It'll be as good as new because I slept with the box between my knees last night. So there you are."

He rolled his eyes as we exited our cabin. He was back to being his old self, smiling and saying his goodbyes with an air of poise and confidence. I walked behind him, determined not to judge, but to work on my own shortcomings.

2

Cape Town

When we finally came on shore, we were welcomed with beaming smiles and a round of handshakes. No doubt there would have been hugs and cheek-kisses as well if our hats hadn't got in the way.

After the expected comments about our looks and dress, I could see that Dr. Faure was ready to get down to business. He was a thickset man with snow-white sideburns that descended down his jawbone until they merged with his beard. But the most prominent feature was his bushy eyebrows that grew in ever greater profusion the closer to the temples they got.

After we had fallen silent, he said, "In my official capacity as *Actuarius* of the Synod and first minister of the *Groote Kerk,* I couldn't resist coming to the ship to welcome back two of our Cape-born sons. It has been many a year since this has happened. And on a personal note, my son Hendrik has written to tell me all about you two. So I feel you are family."

He turned to John and handed him an envelope. "This is no doubt what you've been waiting for—your appointment letter from Governor Sir Harry Smith."

John turned it over and gazed at the seal. He seemed undecided whether to break it open.

"I'll put you out of your misery, John. Your congregation is Burghersdorp. It's on the northern border of the Colony, not far from the Orange River. It also falls within the Presbytery of Graaff-Reinet, which means you'll be able to spend time at home during Presbytery meetings."

John's face lit up, and his posture, which had been rigidly upright until then, relaxed. He could not have asked for a better appointment as a novice pastor.

"Now to business," said Faure, still addressing John. "I'm sure your father will have told you about our centuries-old tradition of inviting recently-arrived Dutch Reformed pastors to preach at the *Groote Kerk*."

"Yes, we were forewarned, so we've already prepared our sermons."

"Excellent. I'd like you to preach in my place this Sabbath, while Andrew can preach for Mr. Heyns on the following one."

John cleared his throat. "I was wondering if I couldn't swap places with Andrew to let him go first. We've already discussed this on board ship."

"A magnanimous gesture on your part, I'm sure. But it's expected of you to preach first."

"Yes I know, Dr. Faure. But Andrew's voice is stronger than mine, so going second will allow me the opportunity to assess the acoustics and judge to what extent I'd need to project my voice."

Faure fell silent and studied John for a few moments. We were standing in a circle—John and my brother Willie facing Faure, while I stood across from Uncle William. I was watching for cues that would signal their responses to John's request. Uncle William, a jovial man with a round face and rosy cheeks, who had been beaming with happiness ever since greeting us, now looked puzzled. Willie, whom I had always known to be warm and supportive, turned his head my way and raised a questioning brow. As for me, I wanted to sink into the ground with embarrassment. At the same time, I noticed that John was too buoyant from the news of his appointment to be aware of these signals.

"There's naught to fear, John," said Faure. "The acoustics are excellent. But no matter how weak or strong your voice, the ideal result is always achieved by projecting it as best you can."

He then turned to me. "And what about you, Andrew? Are you ready to rise to the challenge?"

"It will be an honor, Dr. Faure."

"I'm pleased to hear it. Now regarding your appointment, you'll be assisting your father in Graaff-Reinet until you turn twenty-two. And seeing you are his namesake, I would like to tell you something about him that will make you proud."

"I'd be delighted to hear it," I said, wondering what detail of my father's life was yet to be revealed to me.

"You may be aware that when your father arrived at the Cape in 1822, he had only been able to spend ten months in Utrecht to learn Dutch. But what you probably don't know is that he rose to the challenge of preaching in Dutch in the *Groote Kerk*. He was the only Scot to have done so on initial arrival, both then and now."

"Well, well," said Uncle William. "My brother-in-law is certainly a dark horse."

"That he is," said Faure. "That's why I'm taking the opportunity to tell this tale."

He cleared his throat before continuing. "As you can imagine, the Governor, who was Lord Charles Somerset at the time, was so impressed that he decided to publish this fact in the *Cape Gazette*. The news of it even reached Scotland, where it was published in the *Edinburgh Christian Instructor* of 1823. I have a copy, because the article makes mention of me."

He paused for us to grasp the significance of these facts.

"Pa took over from you at Graaff-Reinet, didn't he?" I asked.

"That's right, I inducted him. I had only been pastor there for four years when I was called to be third minister of the *Groote Kerk.*"

"It must have been extremely difficult for Pa at first?"

"Believe me, the unsettled nature of the frontier posed a challenge for every pastor who'd ever been appointed there, especially as the district of Graaff-Reinet equals the size of Portugal. That is why Governor Somerset took over five months to select the right person to take my place. On closer acquaintance with your father, he decided that he was eminently suitable. You see, he was looking for someone who was astute enough to deal with a congregation of disgruntled stock farmers who were continually being subjected to cattle raids and ongoing frontier wars with African tribes. And need I say, Andrew Murray Sr. has certainly met that challenge for over twenty-six years now."

I blew out an audible breath while I considered the overwhelming task my father had faced on arriving in Graaff-Reinet.

Faure chuckled as he studied my face. "You certainly have a great deal to live up to young Murray, but I'm sure the Lord will be your support and stay as you face your own trials. In the meantime, make the most of your two-year apprenticeship to your father."

While Faure had been speaking, John and I had noticed that our trunks and boxes were being offloaded. The ensuing lull in the conversation enabled us to excuse ourselves in order to point them out to Uncle William's workers. They had been waiting patiently beside his goods cart. Once our luggage was loaded to our satisfaction, we returned to find Dr. Faure still chatting amicably to Willie and Uncle William.

"My goodness," said Faure. "I was so busy telling stories that I forgot to let you know that I've arranged for both of you to deliver your inaugural sermons at our second Dutch Reformed Church in Wynberg. My brother, Dr. Philip Faure, who is pastor there, is visiting the Dutch emigrants across the Orange and Vaal Rivers at the moment. He is being accompanied by Dr. Robertson of Swellendam. Unfortunately, there's been a major skirmish between the British and our Boer emigrants at Boomplaats—just north of the Orange River. So they've gone to help settle things down."

John looked startled by this information because Burghersdorp lay just south of the border. Neither was I immune from the possible consequences of Philip Faure being away. I was desperately hoping that I wouldn't have to act as full-time pastor for him until he returned. My home in Graaff-Reinet beckoned, and I wanted to get there as soon as possible. John, of course, couldn't be expected to stay behind in Cape Town because of his recent appointment.

"Now John," said Faure, "you'll need to preach at Wynberg this Sunday because Andrew will be preaching at the *Groote Kerk*. As the village is situated on the outskirts of Cape Town, a deacon will fetch you on Saturday afternoon and drop you home again on Monday. The same will be the case on the following weekend for you, Andrew. Your uncle here tells me that he has no objection to these arrangements. Fortunately, they don't clash with his plans for you to preach at St. Stephen's on alternate Sunday evenings."

He tipped his hat and made to depart. "By the way, you're both invited to dinner tomorrow evening at six. We'll discuss these plans in greater detail then. And it goes without saying that my wife and daughter, Geertruide, are particularly keen to meet you to hear how Hendrik is faring in Utrecht."

Without further ado, he alighted his four-seater Cape cart. I watched with interest as the Colored driver flicked his whip over the horses' heads, and the cart pulled smoothly away. We were well and truly back in Africa.

With Faure gone, I spent a moment taking in my surrounds. In my estimation, no other country I had visited could boast the vibrancy of the Cape. It echoed through the cracking of whips and the Cape Dutch slang spoken by Colored drivers and wharf workers. Some were singing as they worked, others were shouting instructions interspersed with jokes and colorful banter. Just to think that a little more than a decade before, most had been slaves.

It was in 1838, after a few years as so-called apprentices, that they'd finally been manumitted from slavery. It was also in 1838 that Uncle William and Dr. Adamson had started the mission church of St Stephen's, and John and I had left for Scotland. And it was during that same year that the last of the emigrant farmers had trekked across the Orange and Vaal Rivers to establish independent states.

I recalled how my little friends had boasted that they were going on trek, while I had boasted, in turn, that I was going to Scotland. Now I was back, but they would still be somewhere across the border in the back of beyond.

My reverie was broken by a call from Willie. "I will be taking you in my cart, Andrew, while John will be going with Uncle William."

I realized that Willie was still holding the box with my mother's present that I had passed to him before seeing to the luggage. Not having seen him for ten years, I now realized that he resembled me. He was also slight of build and had similar coloring and features. The main difference was that he was gentle and reflective, while I was bold and impulsive.

He handed the parcel back to me, then went to collect the quarter-sack of hay he had placed before his horse to keep it from wandering off.

"Here Andrew, hold the horse's bridle while I grab the reins. He's a good horse, but inclined to start off prematurely if he's been standing too long."

I felt like a novice. I should have known to do this without being asked. I watched how he deftly handled the reins and soothed his champing horse with a few words of sweet-talk. He was a true son of Africa, experienced in its ways, while I had a great deal of catching up to do. At least my ship-board tan matched his—a good start, I thought.

From the dock area, we wended our way up Portswood Road, passing several dilapidated cottages belonging to fisher folk. We then drove through the midst of a group of boisterous children, who squealed as they scattered to let us pass.

Willie was the first to break our companionable silence. "What's in the box?" he asked.

"It's a Spanish doll for Ma that I bought at a market in London. It's a replica of the one she has in her cabinet. This one, though, has a scarlet dress with black lace, whereas hers, if I recall, is dressed in royal blue."

"How can I ever forget it," said Willie. "When our sister, Maria, was a little girl, she used to gaze at it and beg Ma to be able to play with it—even when she was quite old. But Ma always refused. I think it was because she had inherited it from her mother, and feared it might break. So what she did to pac-ify Maria was to arrange her hair in a bun—exactly like that of the doll's—and allow her to put on her party frock with the flounces. She would then hug Maria and say, 'You look just like her my darling, and just as pretty.' That never failed to delight her."

"Maria must be seventeen now."

"Yes, and just as passionate and emotional as ever. I some-times think there must be some Spanish blood coursing through her veins. It's within the bounds of possibility, you know."

"Hmm, I'm not too sure about that."

Well, we know that Ma comes from German, French and Dutch stock. And as you are aware, the Spanish ruled the Low Countries in the sixteenth century, so some Spanish blood could have slipped in somewhere. If not, it's a certain throw-back to our French connection."

We both sniggered at the thought.

"Now listen here Andrew, I don't want to dampen your en-thusiasm in relation to this gift, but red is not exactly Ma's color. Caste your mind back. Her Spanish doll stands on the central shelf of the Delft cabinet. Every piece of pottery there is blue on white. A doll with a red dress would simply look out of place there. So why don't you give it to Maria. She'll cherish it."

My heart sank at his words, even though I recognized the truth it conveyed. It was just that I had gone to so much trou-ble to get it home in one piece, not to speak of my recurring reverie of seeing my mother's delighted smile on opening it. But now, as I considered the matter, I knew he was right.

"Thanks for the advice, Willie. You're obviously far more perceptive than I am."

❧

We had just reached the Main Road, forcing Willie to slow down to let a cart pass before turning left towards town.

"Tell me," said Willie, "why didn't John want to preach first at the *Groote Kerk*? I felt he was letting himself down. In any case, Faure certainly thought as much. That's why he told us that story about Pa. As for me, I certainly hope to rise to the challenge when I return from Utrecht."

At first, his throw-away line about Utrecht didn't register. The reason was probably because the name Utrecht slipped so often off the tongue in conversation with John.

"What did you just say?" I asked.

He flicked the reins in an act of pure delight—his face beaming. "I thought you'd be surprised. I'm off to Utrecht to study for the ministry."

"But you told me in a letter that Pa thought you didn't have a calling."

"Ah, but that was before coming to Cape Town and hearing Uncle William expound the Gospel in the demonstration of the Spirit and with power. And that's not all. I was present at a service at St. Stephen's when a revival broke out. Man, I tell you . . . the Holy Spirit moved in a wondrous way. It was also at this service that I received the call to become a pastor."

"So when are you leaving?"

"In March, with Servaas Hofmeyr. He's the brother of your friend Nicolaas. Another fellow, Andreas Louw, also received a call at the same service. Unfortunately, he has to postpone his trip to acquire Latin and to polish his Standard Dutch."

"So how's your Latin? All the lectures are still in that language, you know."

"Not too bad. I'm really thankful Pa sent me to Swellendam where there was a Latin teacher. But I definitely need more tuition. That's why I'll have to stay in Cape Town until I leave."

"So you're not going home for Christmas?"

"Afraid not. I need to save all the money I can. In any case, we'll have a few weeks together while you're in Cape Town."

From the street sign, I could see that we had reached Somerset Road—not that the name registered any meaning for me. But I was determined to memorize the route we had taken, and to learn as much about the street layout of Cape Town as possible.

We were nearing an imposing building with a series of high, oblong windows interspersed by pilasters. I was about to ask its name, when Willie pre-empted my question.

"Look over there to your right, Andrew. We are approaching St Andrew's Presbyterian Church. I'll drive around the block to give you a better look. Then we'll head off to Uncle William's home in Schotsche Kloof[3] via Chiapini Street. It's situated on the "lion's rump" overlooking Table Mountain. The views are simply spectacular."

As we drove around the building, I commented, "Well, it's certainly classical Georgian, but there's no belfry or steeple."

Willie laughed. "I think it had a lot to do with lack of funds at the time. You have to remember that when Dr. Adamson established the Presbyterian Church here in 1827, the English-speaking community was small with only a few Scots among them. He was also the first to live in Schotsche Kloof after he persuaded the Governor to build a loop road to make it viable for a Cape cart to make its way up the higher slopes. Apparently, only a mosque and a few cottages belonging to Muslims existed at the foot of the hill."

"But why didn't he just choose land on even ground?"

"Far too expensive. Schotsche Kloof was the cheapest land available that was close to St. Andrew's. And it goes without saying that as soon as the road was opened, more Scots built their homes in the area—hence the name Schotsche Kloof."

I fell silent thinking of all the difficulties Dr. Adamson must have faced. My thoughts then turned to my preaching and visitation schedule.

"A penny for your thoughts," said Willie.

"Oh, I was just thinking of Dr. Adamson as well as all the things I need to do while here."

"Well please place Uncle William on top of your list. You simply must hear him preach, even if it's only at a mid-week service. He's the most Spirit-filled preacher I've ever heard. Do you realize that no less than six of us have received calls to be pastors through his ministry. There's Nicolaas Hofmeyr, Johannes Neethling, Hendrik Faure, Andreas Louw plus Servaas and myself. And of course, there could be more."

As I considered the fruitfulness of Uncle William's ministry, I couldn't help thinking how wonderful it would be if I, with the Lord's help, could match it. Willie was right. I needed to learn as much from Uncle William as possible.

"Thanks for the advice. I'm really looking forward to getting to know him better."

"I'm afraid you won't have much time for that because Aunt Elizabeth has just had a baby boy at her parent's place in Stellenbosch."

"That's wonderful news! Uncle William should have told us at the docks."

"The thing is, it's been a difficult birth, so she'll be remaining in Stellenbosch with the family until the christening."

"Oh well, I suppose it's the best solution under the circumstances."

"*Ja*, but that means that Uncle William will only be in town for Wednesday and week-end services until she has recovered. You were very fortunate that he was in town to be able to welcome you today. He was due to depart for Stellenbosch early this morning, when a neighbor, who's a shipping agent, came to tell us that the *Lady Flora* was sailing slowly along the coast, and would be docking later in the morning. I then rushed to the other side of town to tell Dr. Faure."

"He must be doing an awful lot of travelling. From what I remember, Stellenbosch is quite far from Cape Town."

"About twenty-five miles."

"So when will he be back?"

"Saturday afternoon. He's due to deliver the evening service for those who can't be there on Sunday. And that's when you'll be able to hear him preach. He's also hoping that you or John will be able to preach at the two mid-week services on Wednesday in his stead."

I could tell from Willie's expression that he expected a positive reply, if not an enthusiastic one. All I could think of was how John and I would be able to fit in visiting family and friends if we were supposed to conduct mid-week services in addition to Sunday ones.

"Oh well, I suppose that's the least we can do," I said.

We had just turned off Chiapini into Wales Street, when there, to my surprise, stood a long row of picturesque cottages that lined both sides of the road. They were built mainly in the Dutch style with straight parapets, horizontally divided doors, and elevated *stoeps*. The street was also buzzing with activity. And what was more, all the women were brightly dressed in floor-length garments that ranged in color and hue. As we approached, they waved to us, as did most of the men who were out and about.

"They're Muslim," I said, in surprise.

"Yes, this is the area above Cape Town known as the *Bo-Kaap*. English speakers usually refer to it as the Malay Quarter.

In 1838, when the slaves were emancipated, the Government built cottages for the Muslims here because they wanted to be in walking distance from the mosque."

"I see. So that means we have to drive through this quarter to get to Schotsche Kloof?"

"That's right. The Muslims live on the lower slopes, and we on the higher. And that's just how Uncle William likes it. You have to remember that these are the people he's working amongst and aiming to win for Christ. The other positive outcome is that it's mostly Scottish and Lutheran Christians who live in this area. The reason is that St. Andrew's plus the Lutheran Church, as well as St. Stephen's, are all on this side of town."

By now, we'd left the rows of adjoined cottages behind, and were ascending the open hillside. On the slopes above I could see substantial homes with large gardens and grassed terraces on which a few horses grazed. Despite the interesting journey and beautiful views, my mind was working solidly on trying to formulate a doable visitation schedule for the weeks ahead. John and I would need to visit my mother's family as well as Aunt Elizabeth in Stellenbosch. We also needed to deliver the presents from the Utrecht students to their families.

"I don't want to sound forward, Willie, but it would be helpful to know if any special events have been organized on behalf of John and myself?"

"Afraid not, brother. You see, you've arrived at a bad time, what with Aunt Elizabeth staying over in Stellenbosch. As for events, the only one on the horizon is the christening of Uncle William's newborn son Charles."

We were now driving along the horizontal section of the loop road that overlooked the city below and the wide expanse of Table Mountain on the opposite side. Willie pointed out the parsonage of St. Andrew's, and then drew my attention to the single-story home up ahead.

"It's roomier than you think," he said. "It has five bedrooms, a decent-sized study, plus a large lounge and dining room that overlook Table Bay. So I'm sure you'll enjoy your stay here."

It was certainly an attractive-looking house, especially with its L-shaped *stoep* that ran along the entire ocean side of the house. It looked warm and inviting, and I could see myself sitting on the *stoep* of a morning reading my Bible and enjoying the ocean views.

As we pulled up to the front entrance, I waved to Uncle William and John who had arrived a few minutes earlier. It was such a pity, I thought, that Uncle William had to depart for Stellenbosch so soon after our arrival. Come to think of it, it seemed strange that he would choose to spend so much time with Aunt Elizabeth when she was being looked after by her family. She, or the baby, were obviously not doing so well. Willie was not telling me the whole story.

"Before you see to the horse, Willie, just tell me quickly . . . is there anything I need to know, because I don't want to put my foot in it?"

He stared at me for a moment, then shook his head. "What a question to ask on your first day back, Andrew. It may have escaped your notice, but there's only been ten years of lost family gatherings and interpersonal relationships to make up for. Just take it one step at a time, and let the unfolding occur naturally."

He flicked the reins and headed to the outbuildings behind the house. I stared after him, feeling foolish and naïve. In fact, I was feeling very much like a country bumpkin instead of a sophisticated young man from Europe that I was supposed to be.

To cap it all, I now had to take off my hat to expose my mop of seawater-engendered waves. Oh well, if nothing else, it would be good for a laugh.

3
The *Groote Kerk*

Willie and I arrived at the *Groote Kerk* about an hour and a half before the service was due to begin. We had followed the track leading from Uncle William's home to the foot of the hill where it met Longmarket Street. From there it was an easy stroll downhill until we reached Heerengracht, the main street of Cape Town. Just a block away to our right, stood the *Groote Kerk*.

On arrival there, we found the doors locked. So I took the opportunity of viewing the building from a suitable vantage point in the center of the street. With not a soul in sight, the stillness of the morning lent the building a majestic air. Although nothing like the grand cathedrals of Britain and Europe, its façade was no less pleasing against the backdrop of a modest Cape setting.

The building was beautifully proportioned with high Gothic windows separated by pilasters. To our left, I noticed a baroque belfry-cum-clock tower with a tall spire.

"It's not the original building, of course," said Willie. "This one was completed in 1841, so it's relatively new. The adjoining belfry is all that remains of the old church."

I gazed at the building, thinking of all the pastors who had delivered their inaugural sermons there. And here I was, about to do the same.

"You know, Willie, I don't know what the people will think if they know what I truly am. Just pray with me now that I will not be tempted to preach myself by attending too much to the beauty of language and thought."

I had barely uttered these words, when Willie placed his arm around my shoulder and squeezed it tightly. "Just offer your sermon up to the Lord, Andrew, and He will speak through you."

There we stood in the middle of Heerengracht with heads bowed, offering up our prayers. I was only too aware of my littleness and the need for God's mercy and grace.

At Willie's prompting, we decided to try the doors to the back entrance. We were walking down the side street adjacent to the *Groote Kerk*, when a hooded cart passed us and turned left into the small square behind the church. As we arrived there, we saw Dr. Faure alight from his cart.

"Welcome to you both," he called in a chirpy voice. "What a glorious morning. Come, it's still early. I'll show you around."

Faure led us up the main aisle to the front door so that I could view the inside from the perspective of a visitor entering the church. Unlike many of the cathedrals in Europe, the *Groote Kerk* was light and airy, with flickers of sunlight dancing across the vaulted ceiling.

Faure smiled as he followed my gaze. "I see that you're admiring our spanned ceiling. It's unsupported you know, and therefore quite rare. The builder, Hermann Schutte, also fashioned those magnificent plaster rosettes."

I strained my head upward, following in the direction that Faure was pointing. The rosette in question had eight dark petals that overlaid a white base of fern-like fronds. It reminded me of the intricate flower patterns I had seen on crocheted doilies that were so popular in Scotland.

"Beautiful," I murmured.

"But our masterpiece," said Faure, "is the pulpit that was carved by Anton Anreith and the carpenter Jan Greeff in 1789."

We followed him down the aisle towards the pulpit. Along the way, he closed a door to one of the pews that had been standing ajar. It shut with a click that echoed through the church.

"As you can hear, we have latched doors to our pews. Unfortunately, one can hear them click open and shut from inside the consistory. It's rather noisy, but one gets used to it."

We were half-way down the aisle, when he stopped abruptly and turned to face me. "I don't know if Willie has told you, but we have a system of renting out pews to families within the congregation. It takes the place of a tithe, and helps to supply the church with regular funds. On the whole, it's an excellent system, but Willie, here, disagrees."

"Of course I do, Dr. Faure. The reason is that the system runs counter to the teachings of the New Testament. It's based on wealth and social standing, and feeds upon people's pride."

"*Ja,*" said Faure with a wink. "That's why it works so well. But it's not as bad as it was a century or so ago. Nowadays the newcomers have to be content with the pews they are given. There are also the wealthy *Oumas* and *Oupas* who no longer want to crook their necks gazing up at me on high. Then there are the Willies of this world who insist on sitting in the free seats that have been allocated to the servants and the poor at the back."

"Just so," said Willie, with a slight bow.

"Oe! But then," said Faure, in a theatrical voice, "no sooner has Willie sat down, when there's a tap on his shoulder. It's someone from the Hofmeyr clan who's inviting him to come up higher and sit with them near the front. And what does

Willie do? He walks to the front with a swagger, leaving others to wonder who this important fellow might be."

Poor Willie. His face had turned scarlet, and his eyes were caste to the ground in utter consternation.

Faure chuckled as he turned tail and proceeded down the aisle, speaking over his shoulder as he went. "Never mind, Willie. We all know you are humble. That's why you receive all the invitations to sit at the front. But let me say this. It'll be interesting to note how you deal with your prideful congregation when you become a pastor one day."

We now stood in front of an ornately-carved wooden pulpit that towered over the sanctuary. The base rested on the shoulders of two lions, each holding one paw aloft in which was a wreath of olive leaves. These obviously represented the crowns we would one day receive at the Judgment Seat of Christ. The other paw of each lion stood upon a parchment-like scroll that signified the Word of God.

"Impressive, isn't it?" said Faure. "The lions are carved from stinkwood, and the pulpit and canopy from Burmese teak. But now let me point out something that most visitors miss. The scroll actually opens out. Go and take a look behind the lions, Andrew."

I had expected to see a quotation from the Bible, but instead, there was a carved depiction of the New Jerusalem alongside the old.

"I think it best if I remain silent, Dr. Faure, as anything I might say would be an understatement."

"My sentiments precisely."

Faure turned to Willie and patted his arm. "I'm afraid this is the point where you need to retire to one of the back seats. I would like to pray with Andrew in the consistory before the elders and deacons arrive. Your turn will come soon enough."

Willie looked my way, his eyes locking with mine. He didn't have to say a word because I knew he would be upholding me in prayer throughout the service.

I followed Faure through the door behind the pulpit.

"We had best put on our robes before we pray," he said. "I'll lead the way to the back room."

On arriving there, I took out my white bib and academic gown from the calico bag I'd been carrying all morning. Both items were newly purchased in Holland in readiness for this occasion and the years of ministry I hoped would follow.

As I viewed my frame in the mirror, I asked the Lord to subdue my nerves and quieten my jostling thoughts. It was time to focus on Him and the Word He had led me to preach. It was based on the text from 1 Corinthians 1:23: "*We preach Christ crucified.*"

May it be true, Lord, I prayed. *And may I not preach myself.*

Before I knew it, the church service was over and Faure was ushering me to the front door to greet the departing congregation. I felt pleased with the execution of my sermon. The words had come easily, and I had been able to make regular eye-contact with the congregation. But whether the message had touched people's hearts was another matter entirely. Hopefully, I'd be able to gauge from the remarks made at the door. But shortly after Faure and I had moved into handshake mode, my high spirits began to plummet. The last thing I had expected was to receive regular comments such as the following:

"*Ach Dominee*, you look so young."

"I think you must be very clever."

"Your parents must be so proud."

"A good sermon for someone so young."

"What lively preaching."

"I look forward to hearing you again in a few years' time."

And so it went—on and on—banal comments with no bearing on the sermon.

My mind drifted back to the service at St. Stephen's the evening before when Uncle William had preached a dynamic sermon on thanksgiving. Time after time, I had heard members of that ex-slave congregation exclaim how God had spoken to them, or how they had found a certain aspect interesting. I soon realized that no such remarks would be forthcoming from the *Groote Kerk* congregation. Surely a point or two had enlightened their understanding? Or was it that my expectations were unreasonable, given the length of the queue and the desire of most to get home?

At long last, the line of hand-shakers had dwindled until only one family remained. They had obviously waited until last in deference to the elderly gentleman in their midst. He was leaning heavily on his walking stick as he shuffled to the door. He had a full crop of white hair and sported a neatly-trimmed goatee. His demeanor, together with the cut and quality of his suit, suggested someone of standing in the community. He was flanked by his family, two of whom were endeavoring to assist him. I watched with interest as he indicated that they should go. He had obviously done this sort of thing before, because they readily complied with his request.

"*Môre Oom* Barend," said Faure. "It's good to see you back at church after such a long absence. I take it you would like to speak with *Dominee* Murray alone."

Oom Barend nodded and then turned to me with right hand extended. "Barend de Vries," he said.

As Faure had addressed him using the honorary title of "uncle," I decided to do the same. "Please to meet you *Oom* Barend."

At this point, Faure left us, and the sexton who had been waiting to lock up, turned, and walked towards the consistory. Willie, who had been standing a little distance behind *Oom* Barend, took his cue from these departures and indicated that he would be exiting through the other entrance. I couldn't help wondering how long this door-side chat would take.

Oom Barend favored me with a broad smile that lasted several seconds. "You know *Dominee,* as I was listening to you preach this morning, you reminded me so much of *Dominee* Helperus Ritzema van Lier. He arrived here as a twenty-two-year-old to take up the position of third minister in 1786. I was also twenty-two at the time, and a regular attendee here, so I remember his arrival as though it were yesterday."

"How wonderful it is to meet someone who knew Van Lier in the flesh," I said. "My only knowledge of him is through his collection of sermons I came across in Utrecht. I must say, I was most impressed."

In actual fact I was more than impressed. For there in the foreword of Van Lier's *Collection of Simple Teachings* I had not only found the topic for my inaugural sermon, but also his view on preaching that I had decided to adopt as my own. I vividly remember reading his words: "Even if it is permissible to dazzle my listeners with eloquent, poetic language—and I had the ability to do so—I hope never to forget that I must not preach myself, but Christ crucified."

"You know *Dominee,*" said *Oom* Barend, interrupting my train of thought, "at the time of Van Lier's arrival, this church was at a low ebb. But within six years, there was life and vitality. He had literally revolutionized the place. You should have heard his inaugural sermon. It touched our hearts and at the same time hit us like a hammer. It all came back to me as I listened to you preach."

"Can you recall the topic of his sermon?" I asked.

"It was similar to yours. You based your title on 1 Corinthians 1:23: '*I preach Christ Crucified,*' whereas he based his on 1 Corinthians 2:2: '*For I determine not to know anything among you save Jesus Christ and Him crucified.*' I marked it in my Bible with the date, you see."

His words left me feeling stricken. What if he thought I'd plagiarized Van Lier's sermon, or, at best, based it on his? What if it were in his collection of sermons all along and I'd overlooked it? I just couldn't recall seeing it there. I tried to hide my unease by keeping my intonation in check.

"What an amazing co-incidence."

The words were barely out of my mouth, when I realized that it just wouldn't do to cover things up. So after a moment's hesitation, I said, "You know, *Oom* Barend, I don't recall seeing that sermon topic in his collection."

"You're quite right. It wasn't there because he felt it did not meet his own sermon criteria."

"I see. So what did you think of my sermon?"

"I was just coming to that. I don't want to sound critical—that's not my intention—but I'm of the mind that you could become an excellent preacher if you decided to adopt his approach."

"To tell you the truth, I thought I had."

"Ah, but like him, you have overestimated this congregation. Half the men are unlettered, while the women have barely any education. And in country areas, you'll find the situation far worse."

I knew what he said was true. I also knew I was receiving the feedback I craved.

"Please continue *Oom* Barend. I need to hear this."

"Well, as you are aware, Van Lier believed in short sermons with a clear message to be delivered in simple language with great vitality. He used to say to me, 'Barend, it serves no purpose to speak to the congregation in sophisticated tones of worldly wisdom and showy eloquence. All that type of preaching does is to detract from the simple message of the Gospel.' So what did he do? He shortened the services as well as the prayers."

"Really? And he was able to do that while still a young pastor?"

"I assure you, no one could deflect him from this objective. In no time, he had assembled about sixty helpers to evangelize the slaves in their homes—something unheard of in those days. He also organized the church into home groups for Bible study and prayer. I tell you, the Holy Spirit used him mightily because of his close walk with God. In fact, he can be regarded as the forerunner of missionary endeavor at the Cape. It was through him that the Moravians were welcomed back. And it was undoubtedly through his influence that the South African Mission Society was established by his protégés in 1799."

I found these details interesting because they helped to place his sermons in context.

"Tell me, *Oom* Barend, has anything been published about his ministry?"

"Not his ministry, as such, but his powerful conversion."

"You mean the publication of his six letters to John Newton that were translated from Latin into English by William Cowper?"

"That's the one. Have you read it?"

"No, but I came across a Dutch version in Utrecht. I flicked through it, but didn't have time to read it. I'll certainly make an effort to locate a copy now."

I thought our conversation was over, when *Oom* Barend leant heavily on his stick and inclined his head towards me. "But then the unthinkable happened," he said. "Van Lier died

at the age of twenty-eight—only six years after his arrival at the
Cape."

"My goodness! What a tragedy!"

"I've often asked the Lord why He needed to take His faithful servant. But as your Uncle Stegmann is wont to say, 'We
shall only know the full story one day in glory.' How is your
uncle, by the way?"

"Very well, thank you. Aunt Elizabeth has just given birth to
a baby boy a week or so ago."

"*Ach*, I'm thrilled to hear it because he's been tried in the
school of suffering for so long now—what with the death of
his first wife shortly after the birth of his son George, and then
the death of all those children one after the other. These deaths
must number six or seven now?"

All I could do was nod. I now knew what Willie had been
hiding from me. Just as well, I thought. Had I known, I might
have found it difficult to have been my natural self with Uncle
William.

"But you know," continued *Oom* Barend, "although we do
not know the whys and wherefores, it has deepened your uncle's walk with the Lord. The Holy Spirit always accompanies
his preaching, and the revivals keep on coming. But I think
the greatest crop of fruit that has resulted from this 'fellowship
of the cross'—as he likes to call it—is that the ex-slaves see his
trials and flock to his services. They know that his sermons on
suffering are born out of his own experiences. They also realize
that the Lord has made himself known to your uncle in a deeper way through them."

I remained silent as I reflected on Uncle William's ability to
mirror the Lord's love in the midst of these trials. I think *Oom*
Barend may have sensed my awe, because he laid his hand on
my shoulder and searched my face.

"When I came here this morning," he said, "I thought I'd be hearing your older brother preach. But when I learnt it would be you, I was disappointed at first. But then I recalled how the Lord often chooses the younger over the older. This thought was ratified when you announced the text of your sermon. I knew then that God had given me the strength to be here for a purpose."

A tingle went down my spine in anticipation of the spiritual counsel I was about to receive.

"My advice to you is this: The spiritual power that was evidenced in Van Lier, and now in your Uncle, is a gift of God that can only come to fruition via a close communion with Him. Seek that walk, and the Holy Spirit will accompany your preaching mightily."

As I watched *Oom* Barend join his family, I thought about his parting comments. Like most newly ordained ministers, I had already received this advice on numerous occasions—both before leaving Utrecht, as well as during our final visit to Scotland. But what made this occasion different was the knowledge that my inaugural sermon had not impacted the *Groote Kerk* congregation as I would have wished. There was also the realization that I was not spiritually capable of taking the *Groote Kerk* by storm, as Van Lier had done; or being used of God to kindle a revival fire, like Uncle William was doing. It was a challenging realization, and one that needed to be addressed. But how to go about it was the question.

My reverie was interrupted by Willie and Servaas Hofmeyr, who had re-entered the church by the other door. I realized that I'd better make haste if I wanted to be in time for lunch at the Hofmeyrs'.

4
Bound for Home

December 1848

Our stay in Cape Town finally drew to a close after three-and-a-half weeks. During that time, we managed to fit in a preaching round of morning and evening services for Mr. Morgan at St. Andrew's, and Mr. Miller at the Free Church of Scotland.

Our last week was spent in Stellenbosch visiting *Oupa* and *Ouma* Stegmann plus other members of our extended family. I'm afraid, matters did not always run smoothly in relation to the names we employed to address some family members.

Oupa Stegmann, who had been baptized Johan Godlieb Stegmann, made it clear that he expected us to call him *Oupa* Godlieb. We also learnt that Uncle William's real name was Georg Wilhelm Stegmann. But because the family now spoke Dutch, we were advised to address him by the Dutch equivalent of his second name. So instead of Uncle William or *Oom* Wilhelm, it had to be *Oom* Willem. A further embarrassment was in store for us when we learnt that Aunt Elizabeth had been christened Maria Clementina Elizabeth Sandenbergh, and that her side of the family knew her as Maria. Fortunately, commonsense prevailed when it came to our young cousin

George Willem Stegmann Jr., who thankfully answered to the name George.

When Friday, 1 December arrived, the whole family congregated at St. Stephen's for the long-awaited christening of Uncle William's new-born son Charles Graham. I could see that John relished the opportunity to officiate at this joyous occasion. And to everyone's surprise, little Charlie seemed content to be cuddled by him.

The following day was Saturday, and time for our departure by coastal ship to Port Elizabeth, where my father was due to collect us by horse-wagon. Dear Willie had organized it all. He had explained that the six-day return journey from Graaff-Reinet to Port Elizabeth was far easier on my father than the arduous twenty-day return journey to Cape Town. This would also mean that we would spend less time travelling by horse-wagon.

As we waved Willie goodbye, I knew it would be years before our paths would cross again. But by then, he would be a *Dominee*, just like us.

Our arrival in Port Elizabeth did not hold the same excitement for us as when we sailed into Table Bay. If it were not for the fact that my father would be there to meet us, it would have been an anti-climax.

The dock area was crammed with huge wagons drawn by long spans of oxen, some twelve, fourteen and even sixteen deep. While several horse-wagons were also present, Cape carts were few and far between. The sounds that wafted up to the deck were also different from those we heard in Cape Town.

There was the cracking of whips and a strange-sounding click language being spoken by numerous Africans who were apparently from a Fingo tribe who lived in a large village nearby.

Our eyes scanned this scene for the presence of our father who would be standing alongside a horse-wagon. I pondered on the fact that both the wagon and horses would have been lent to him by the farmers in his congregation. It was a quicker conveyance than the unwieldy ox-wagon that travelled about three miles per hour. From memory, a *schoft* for a horse-wagon—the distance one travelled before the horses were outspanned—was also three hours, but a horse-wagon could cover around fifteen to eighteen miles on a relatively good wagon route. By contrast, an ox-wagon could only travel nine to ten miles within a three-hour *schoft*.

Thankfully, Graaff-Reinet was one of the main staging posts on the way to the hinterland. It was situated about 130 miles from Port Elizabeth, making it a three-to-four-day journey by horse-wagon. Nevertheless, Willie had warned us that our trek would probably take five days because of the rest day on Sunday and the services Pa was bound to hold on farms along the way.

I couldn't help feeling sorry for those travellers who would be lumbering into the interior by ox-wagon. I remembered how our parsonage had become a center of rest and refreshment for all the missionaries who had passed through Graaff-Reinet when John and I were still at home. My mind went back to the visits of Mr. Moffat and Dr. Livingstone, as well as some of the French missionaries such as Pellissier, Roland and Casalis. As a young boy, I loved to watch how the Bechuana and Basuto drivers outspanned and watered the oxen in our spacious yard. Perhaps it wouldn't be too long before I'd be able to observe a similar scene when we again entertained a party of missionaries.

My thoughts were interrupted by a nudge from John. "There's Pa. He's just taken off his hat and is using it to wave to us."

I looked to where John was pointing, and sure enough there stood my father. I hadn't recognized him because of his simple travelling shirt and broad-brimmed hat. I could see that he was graying at the temples, but that this mark of maturity was balanced by his trim figure and clean-shaven face, which made him appear much younger than he was.

Dear Pa, he had followed every step of our development and educational journey through his regular correspondence. His letters had always been filled with fatherly advice and loving words of Godly wisdom. And now I would be privileged to enjoy his company again.

It's impossible to describe the charged emotions that welled up within me as I greeted my father face to face. He took turns to hug us several times, squeezing us close, while speaking each of our names and then murmuring, "Welcome my boy! Welcome!"

Try as I might, I couldn't contain my tears. To my embarrassment, they flowed freely, the salt clinging to my cheeks as I tried to wipe them dry with the back of my hand.

After an interval of silence, during which my father took time to study us both, he turned to John and said, "My, but you're a handsome fellow, John! Your build and bearing is of someone far older in age. And as I wasn't expecting such maturity, I didn't recognize you at first."

He then turned to me, his lips breaking into a broad smile. "Well now, Andrew . . . your youthful looks and slight build will serve you well as my apprentice. It will help the congregation realize that you have not reached the required age of being appointed to a congregation of your own. Just think, you'll be able to hone your preaching skills and make the inevitable pastoral mistakes while still my assistant."

When he saw my deflated expression, he patted my arm playfully and said, "Not to worry, dear boy. You'll soon fill out and mature in the next two years. And by that time, you'll be an experienced pastor. Regard it as God's merciful provision."

After introducing us to the Hottentot drivers, who had been especially hired to manage a span of eight horses, we turned to the task of placing our trunks and boxes in the covered wagon. This was by no means as simple as it looked, for they had to be neatly stowed below the two *katels* made from wood and wickerwork that served as our seats by day and beds by night.

I noticed that bedding had already been placed on both *katels*, with extra blankets and pillows folded in a pile for the person who would be sleeping under the wagon. And that person would undoubtedly be me. The Hottentots, as I recalled, preferred to sleep alongside an open fire under the stars.

Even before the whip had cracked and the wheels had started to turn, I was already eyeing the huge food basket that I knew would hold our favorite cakes and sweetmeats. I also noticed the bags of *boerbeskuit*— rusks the Dutch farmers like to dunk—and the strips of dried meat and sausages at the back of the wagon. John, who had noticed them too, exchanged glances with me.

My Father laughed. "All in good time," he said. "Let's commit this journey to the Lord in prayer."

As Willie had anticipated, it had taken us three days to reach the farm where Sunday services had been scheduled. Pa had planned our journey so that we would arrive home on Monday morning before morning tea. This meant an easy three-hour *schoft* from the farm into town.

When Monday morning arrived, we set out at six, having shaved and donned a clean change of clothing in readiness for meeting the family. Although the weather was pleasant and the morning air refreshing, this proved to be the worst leg of the journey.

We were now well and truly in the semi-desert of the Great Karoo. The land was flat and looked parched and dry, despite the thunder storm the afternoon before. There were no trees and hardly a green bush to be seen between the stubbles of gray scrub that covered the landscape. In the distance, the Sneeuberg Mountains beckoned.

Not long now, I thought, because I knew that amongst its foothills lay Graaff-Reinet. And there, too, would be the Sundays River that looped around the town like a horseshoe. It brought with it life-giving water that made the town a virtual oasis in the surrounding desert. But at that moment, the Sneeuberg range seemed like a mirage that was forever receding.

We were travelling at a steady pace, each thinking his own thoughts, when my father said, "John, dear boy, I need to ask you a favor. It's about Charles."

"I'm listening, Pa."

"There's a wee problem. The thing is, our school here in Graaff-Reinet hasn't had a teacher since Mr. Paterson left to become a missionary. And since Charles is bright and wants to become a pastor, I've had to send him away to a private boarding school in Swellendam. There's an instructor there who's able to teach Latin, you see. It's been rather a drain on my purse—what with you two in Utrecht and Jemima at Mrs. Pears in Somerset East."

"I think I know what you are about to ask, Pa. You'd like me to instruct Charles."

"Not only in Latin, I'm afraid, but also in the subjects that will prepare him for Utrecht. He'll be sixteen this February, so it's important that he receives the proper instruction. The fact of the matter is, I need to help Willie with his tuition and board. It's the right thing to do."

"Absolutely," said John. "Does Charles know about this arrangement?"

"Not yet. I wanted to sound you out first. As you need a holiday, and so does Charles, it would be appropriate to make a start at the end of January. And then, when you go to Burghersdorp in May, I'd be much obliged if you'd take him with you."

John seemed taken aback by this request, and so was I. He'd be starting out in ministry, and wouldn't want the extra responsibility of supervising Charles. What was more, I'd be available in Graaff-Reinet to follow on from where he had left off. John was also thinking along these lines, because he expressed the same thought to my father.

"I want to do all I can to help, Pa, but I'd like to point out that Andrew is able to instruct equally as well."

"That may be the case, John, but Charles needs a teacher who's more mature—someone he'll respect as his senior. Andrew's disposition is far too lighthearted and playful. Besides, I have an important job for him to do other than being my assistant."

John responded with a knowing nod, while my father looked my way and smiled. He was obviously trying to soften the blow related to his assessment. I folded my arms and smiled back, thereby indicating that I wasn't deterred in the slightest. After all, supervising and keeping others in order was John's forte.

And ever since receiving comments about my youthful looks at the door of the *Groote Kerk*, I'd become accustomed to the fact that I looked young for my age. In any case, it wouldn't be too long before I matured and broadened out.

In addition, I'd also come to realize how similar John and my father were in outlook and disposition. Both were measured, thoughtful and serious, although there was a warmth and tender side to my father that John didn't possess. I, on the other hand, thought of myself as good-humored, direct, and full of beans.

I was wondering what job my father had for me, when he addressed John again.

"You know, John, having Charles with you at the start of your ministry won't be such an imposition as you think. On the contrary, I'm sure it will be a great help, especially when you need a prayer partner or someone to share your experiences with. I know, because I'm speaking from experience here."

As it didn't appear that he was going to elaborate, I decided to draw him out. "Please don't stop there, Pa. It's quite embarrassing that we know so little of your own experiences."

"Very well then. . . . When I arrived at the Cape in 1822, and set out for Graaff-Reinet, the Governor, Lord Charles Somerset, asked me to take William Robertson under my wing. He was only seventeen at the time, and had been appointed as teacher to the free school to be set up here. He lived with me in the parsonage for over two years. During that time, we were a great support to each other. Then, after five years, he returned to Scotland to study for the ministry. Now he's Dr. Robertson, and pastor of our church in Swellendam."

"Isn't he the one who's visiting the emigrant Boers across the Orange and Vaal Rivers along with Dr. Philip Faure from Wynberg?"

"One and the same, Andrew. And he's due to pass through Graaff-Reinet at the end of January. My word, am I looking forward to enjoying a leisurely chin-wag with him!"

He looked John's way and said, "That reminds me, John . . . seeing that Burghersdorp is so close to the Orange River Sovereignty, try to ascertain as much as possible about the situation there from Dr. Robertson."

He sighed, then closed his eyes and adjusted his sitting position to make himself more comfortable. He looked contented, now that he had settled a concern that had obviously been weighing on his mind.

By contrast, my excitement was rising with every hoof-beat. I was also anxious to know what job my father had in mind for me. I waited until he opened his eyes again.

"Pa?"

"Yes my boy?"

"Could you tell me about that special task you've set aside for me?"

To my surprise, my question brought on a broad smile and a twinkle in his eye. "It's right up your ally," he said. "I want you to spend time with Georgie. He's three-and-a-half, has boundless energy, doesn't want to sleep in the afternoons, and is leading everyone on a merry dance, including me. He's even more boisterous than you were at his age."

John nudged me while winking at my father. "Poetic justice, I'd say. It's time you were on the receiving end of some lively behavior."

"It's no laughing matter, John," said my father. "I've been wracking my brain not knowing what to do. The nursemaid can't discipline him anymore, and your mother is inclined to give into his whims. Your sister Maria has stepped into the gap, but is far too strict and teacherish. I think it's because she's overworked, poor girl. She instructs James, Isabella and Kitty in the mornings, and for part of that time, Georgie wants to join them in the school room. So she has to prepare activities for him until your mother or the nursemaid takes him out to play. Then after lunch, when everyone else is having a nap, she joins your mother in the sewing corner of the dining room to help her make clothes for the children. As Georgie won't settle, she's the one who usually gets up to discipline him. Now she has taken it upon herself to teach him pucker English. That's all very well, except that the wee tike can't move or say anything without being corrected or scolded."

"Hmm, so how can I relieve the situation, Pa?"

"Play with him when you have a moment. Tell him stories. Take him off your sister's hands in the afternoons when everyone takes a nap. I fear I'm partly to blame because I haven't given him the fatherly attention he craves. I'm just too busy. And as you have the energy and the disposition, I'd be most grateful if you'd step into the breach."

"I'll do my best, Pa. In any case, I can't think of a more delightful prospect than to play with my brothers and sisters. It's been a long time coming."

At a rare attempt at humor, John said, "Well Pa, I hope you know what you're doing by entrusting Georgie to Andrew's oversight?"

"Oh, I've every confidence in his ability on that score. I dare say it's because both he and Georgie are two sprouts from the same branch of the family—your mother's, of course."

5
Graaff-Reinet

As we approached Graaff-Reinet, fond memories of my youth came flooding back. Some of its marked features, which had simply melted into the background then, jumped out at me now with striking clarity.

To my left, I caught sight of Spandau Kop, a hillock that formed a picturesque backdrop to the town. And straight ahead, I could see the steeple of our Dutch Reformed Church that stood erect and tall, like a sentinel for Christianity that invited all beneath it to drink of the living water.

As we entered the town, I couldn't help noticing the rich pinks and reds of the flowering Oleander trees that lined the streets. They were interspersed by lilac Syringas as well as orange and lemon trees. In the center of the street, I noticed that the water in the irrigation furrow was flowing swiftly—a sure sign that there'd been a thunderstorm the day before.

As we travelled on, we passed a few public outspan places where large teams of oxen were being fed and watered.

"How many of these rest places do we now have around town?" I asked.

"About thirty or so," said my father. "They seem to be multiplying by the day. And now that Britain has annexed the land across the Orange River, there are bound to be more ox-wagons passing this way. Just look over there. One of our entrepreneurs has opened an inn next to that outspan place."

"Surely he wouldn't get many customers? Most would simply camp in their wagons."

"On the contrary. I believe it's always full. That's because after two or three weeks in an ox-wagon, you simply crave to sleep in a bed. Just ask William Robertson and Philip Faure when they arrive back from their three-month trip."

My excitement rose as our church came into view. In the distance I could also see the old Drostdy building with its attractive Dutch gable where we'd be turning off. Before the British arrived, it had been the courthouse and administrative hub of Graaff-Reinet. It overlooked the entire length of Parsonage Street to our home at the far end.

As we drew closer, my father said, "Remember the old Drostdy building? Well, our friends Jeremias and Elsie Ziervogel purchased it last year. Since then, it has become their home—and a beautiful one at that. Your mother and Elsie are able to visit each other more regularly now."

Our wagon slowed almost to a stop to enable the driver to make a smooth turn into Parsonage Street. The first building on the right was a small church that we had passed daily as children.

Pointing to the church, my father said, "I'm sure you remember the Mission Church established by Dr. van der Kemp of the London Missionary Society. Well, old Amos, my driver, went to school there. That's why he can read, write and speak a little English. Mr. Campbell is now the teacher there." Almost in the same breath he said, "And by the way, this building we're just passing now is where William Robertson set up the first public school. It was converted into a public library last year."

My father's patter continued unabated for the length of the

street, but I had eyes for no other building than the parsonage up ahead. It was one of the most beautiful H-styled, six-gabled homes in the colony. There were also large cellars below the main house that corresponded with the rooms above. Some of these were partitioned off as additional bedrooms when the house was full of visitors. As young boys, we loved to play hide and seek in them.

The horses slowed again as we turned right into Murray Street and then left into the side street that led to the wagon entrance behind the parsonage. In my mind's eye, I could visualize the extensive yard area with its outbuildings, stables, vegetable garden, orchard, small vineyard, a plot of oats for the horses, and another of lucerne for the cow.

Only minutes to go, I thought.

Amos saluted us as we passed through the gate. He was about eight years younger than my father, but his brown, periwinkle-like curls were now speckled with gray, and the furrows above his brow had deepened, giving him a wizened look. As a boy he had taught me to ride, had scolded me, had joked with me, had prayed with me, and had even coached me when I'd needed to recall the divisions of a sermon my father had just preached. For without that knowledge—which my father tested before Sunday lunch—I wouldn't have been allowed to join my parents and guests for supper that evening. And as a young boy, I definitely didn't want to miss out on that opportunity. I suspected that this custom still prevailed in our home.

After closing the gate, Amos rushed to the front of the wagon to help my father alight. He then turned to greet me. He clasped my hands in both of his and shook his head in wonderment that I was home again.

"*Ach*, it's good to see you back, *Kleinbaas. Nxt*, just look at you. You have grown to be exactly my size."

And being the first class opportunist that he was, he placed his hand over his mouth as if to register surprise. "I'm sure your clothes will fit me now."

I kept a straight face, and pretended to compare our sizes. I knew he was testing me to see whether I, as a newly ordained *Dominee*, would be standing on my dignity. After a minute or two of holding my composure, my twitching lips finally gave way to laughter.

"Never fear, Amos. I've got a present or two for you."

He let out a high-pitched yelp and clapped his hands. "*Ach*, it's good to see that *Kleinbaas* hasn't changed."

Without further ado, he turned to John. "*Oe*! And look at *Kleinbaas* John. He looks like a real *Dominee*. But then there can only be one *Dominee* in the house, and that is *Kleinbaas's* father—not so *Dominee*?"

"Quite right, Amos," said my father. You will continue to address me as *Dominee* and John and Andrew as *Kleinbaas*."

Amos drew back his shoulders and stood erect. He looked highly pleased with himself now that my father had re-established the pecking order that had prevailed when we were boys. From his perspective, we were still sons of the house with the token title of "small boss." From our perspective, this form of address simply gave him the recognition he deserved for his overseer role when we were young. It was the perfect compromise.

It was not long before squeals of excitement could be heard coming from the back *stoep*. Our brothers Charles and James were the first to make an appearance and bid us welcome.

"It's all about plaits, ribbons and bows up there," said Charles. "We're expecting visitors, you see, so the girls are dressed in their Sunday best. They're just waiting for Ma to lead the way."

I remembered him as a boy of five. Now, he was taller than I was, and could have passed for eighteen or nineteen. After we had hugged and answered questions about the welfare of our brother Willie and the Stegmann family in Cape Town, he introduced us to our brother James. He was a fair-haired boy of eleven who had suffered from a severe bout of rheumatic fever at the age of seven. I noticed that he still looked pale and sickly, which accounted for him being taught by Maria at home.

Charles waited until we had exchanged a few words with James before pointing to the pergola near the boundary wall. It was covered by a luxuriant vine that spilled over its edge. Below this canopy was a large table already set for morning tea and coffee.

"It would be best if you three got out of the way and went to sit over there. I'll help Pa and Amos unpack the wagon and see to the horses."

He made a grab for my box and the case we had filled with gifts for the family, but I stopped him in his tracks. "Don't worry about these. They contain your presents."

Stopping to eye them for a moment, he said, "Well then, you might like to hide them under the table. The girls won't be expecting to receive their gifts so soon."

I marveled at his maturity and self-assured manner. I wasn't sure if I would have had the forethought to put my sisters' interests first. *I'll enjoy getting to know him,* I thought.

No sooner had we hidden the box and the suitcase, than my mother and sisters appeared on the steps of the *stoep* behind us. Bringing up the rear was the nursemaid with Georgie, followed by two kitchen maids carrying coffee, milk and *boerbeskuit.*

My gaze focused on my mother. Except for her thickened waistline, she looked hardly a day older than when I had waved her goodbye. She was dressed in a striking turquoise frock that set off her fresh complexion and rosy cheeks. She wore her hair parted in the center and twisted into bunches at the side. It was not only the height of fashion, but also softened her face and contributed to her youthful looks.

On seeing us, she stopped, took a series of deep breaths, then lifted her skirts and hurried to greet us. She didn't speak, but going from one to the other, she held our faces between her hands and kissed us on the mouth, the cheeks and the forehead, before starting the process all over again.

"I need to sit down," she said at length. "My heart is beating so fast I can hardly breathe. *Ach liefie*," she said to Maria, "you introduce John and Andrew to Georgie and the girls."

My attention was now drawn to Maria. And there, in a word, stood my Spanish doll. Her dark hair was parted in the center and drawn back into a bun at the nape of her neck. Despite the severity of the look, it suited her complexion and high cheekbones.

The color of her dress also added to her Spanish look. It was russet-red with deep folds that reflected various colors in the dappled light—now orange, now red, now brown. It reminded me of the changing colors that could be seen on the Karoo's rocky outcrops just before sunset.

After John and I had greeted her with a peck on the lips, she lined up the other siblings according to age. "Now greet John and Andrew with a kiss, then tell them your full name and age. Don't be shy."

John went first and I followed. This gave each of us the opportunity to ask questions and make personal comments.

First in line was a pretty, fair-haired girl dressed in pink.

She wore her hair in plaits that encircled the top of her head. She reminded me of the typical *Fräulein* I'd seen in Germany. Following Maria's example, she greeted me with a peck and then stepped back into line. It was far too regimented, I thought.

"I'm Jemima," she said. "and I'm twelve going on thirteen. I'm afraid I don't remember you."

"Well, I remember you," I said. "You were like a little doll at two."

Not being able to think of anything else to say, I moved on to the next girl. She was also fair-haired, just as pretty, but dressed in blue.

"I'm Isabella, and I'm nine, and I'll be turning ten in February. Maria made my dress, you know. She even rolled my hair under at the back—just like Mrs. Pears. I believe it's the height of fashion in England at the moment."

"Bella, that's enough," said Maria. "Andrew doesn't want to hear about hair and fashion."

"Not at all," I said. "I'm your brother, so I'd love to hear about the things that interest you."

I smiled at Isabella and then at Maria to try and break the tension. It was such a pity that Maria's voice had taken on the sharp edge of a castanet. Why doesn't she just relax and be more sisterly? I thought.

I moved on to the next sister in line. I could see she was bursting to tell me about herself. She wore a pretty pinafore dress in peppermint green that was tied with a large bow at the back. Her hairstyle mirrored that of Isabella's, but was rolled less tightly to give the impression it was loose.

"I'm Kitty," she said, "and I'm seven. My real name is Catherine, but Papa's the only one who calls me that. Yesterday I was able to say all my Bible texts, so *Dominee* Pears, who was preaching for Papa, said I could sit up at table when our visitors come this morning to greet you."

"Kitty, that was supposed to be a surprise," said Maria.

Kitty put her hand to her mouth. "Sorry," she said. "I didn't mean to tell."

"Not to worry Kitty. John and I guessed as much when we saw you all in your Sunday frocks."

Kitty gave a hop and beamed a smile. "Maria is wearing her confirmation frock. It's made of silk."

"My goodness," I said. "That must have cost a pretty penny."

"Not really," butted in Isabella. "It was in *Ouma* Hoppe's chest when she died. Mama says we'll all be able to wear silk for our confirmations."

"What lucky girls!"

By this time, John was already seated at the table with my mother and was helping himself to coffee and *boerbeskuit*. He had obviously given Georgie short shrift, so I decided to make up for it.

The first thing I noticed about Georgie was his mop of auburn hair and his sturdy little legs. Although he was holding the nursemaid's hand, he was standing astride as if ready to make a getaway. He was watching my every move as though sizing me up, which I'm sure he was doing.

"This is our new nursemaid Katrina," said Maria in Dutch. "She joined us three years ago."

I nodded a greeting and then focused on Georgie. I was going through the motions of asking his name and age, when he suddenly blurted out: "Mrs. Ziervogel is coming."

"Mrs. Ziervoggel? What a funny name."

"Nooo! Mrs. Ziervogel."

"Ah, now I have it. Mrs. *B*iervogel."

"Nooo! Mrs.—

"Andrew, you have no idea what he's like," said Maria. "He's sure to greet her using those names. And worse still, he'll let her know that you called her that."

"She's a real lady and frightfully fussy," added Isabella.

I looked down at Georgie, who was looking up at me with a twinkle in his eye. I returned his mischievous gaze with a wink. "You won't tell Mrs. Ziervogel, will you?"

Georgie gave me a toothy grin. I could see that he was enjoying this game, especially now that I'd given him permission to do just that.

I turned to face the girls. "Who else will be coming?" I asked.

"Three other Ziervogels," said Isabella. "There's John's friend, Carel; your friend, Jacobus; and Maria's friend, Maria-Anna."

I kept a straight face and pretended to be deep in thought. "Yes, I remember Annamarie."

"Nooo! Maria-Anna," said Georgie, still delighting in the name game.

"Please don't call her Annamarie," said Jemima. "She hates being called that because Carel teases her with it. We call her Maria-Anna to distinguish her from our Maria."

"I see. It sounds as if I'll have to mind my p's and q's at morning tea. What will there be to eat, by the way?"

"It's a surprise," said Jemima. "And it's all your favorites. There are also lots of extras in the kitchen for the other guests who will be dropping by from time to time."

"Jemima baked it all," said Kitty. "She's very clever in the kitchen."

I turned to Georgie and said, "Come, let's visit the dining room and take a look."

Well! Did the castanets begin to clap!

"He'll run amok in there," said Maria. "And when he sees the decorated table, he'll start crying and stage a performance to want to stay for morning tea. And poor Katrina will have to deal with the aftermath."

I turned to Georgie, whose bottom lip had started to quiver. "I suppose it *is* a surprise, so we'd better stay here with Mama and Papa."

He was about to burst into tears, when his expression suddenly changed and his eyes opened wide. I noticed that Kitty's mouth was agape and that maid Katrina was trying to keep a straight face. I turned around to see what was happening. There was John with coffee splattered all over his suit jacket. I watched as he grabbed the wet hand towel that had been neatly folded on a plate, and vigorously tried to wipe off the tell-tail signs. He'd obviously been dunking his rusk when a piece had broken off and plopped into his full cup of coffee.

I couldn't resist the temptation to point out the obvious. "Most undignified," I said. "Can you imagine if that happened in the presence of Mrs. Ziervogel?"

The others were too well-mannered to comment. As for me, my playful streak was starting to rise to the surface. John's rusk episode had also offered the golden opportunity for me to get my hands on some of those sweet treats languishing in the kitchen. And I knew exactly how to go about it.

"Hmm," I said, "I'm afraid I'll have to pass up the *boerbeskuit*. I don't want to get any splatters on my new suit. Is there anything else I can tuck into before Mrs. Ziervogel and Maria-Anna come for morning tea?"

"There's plenty of milk tart," said Jemima.

I puckered my nose in apparent distaste. "Milk tart? Oh dear, I don't like the English variety. It's too custardy. I was hoping there'd be some *melktert*—you know, the milky one with the fluffy egg-whites folded in."

"That's exactly how Jemima makes it," said Isabella. "She got the recipe from *Ouma* Van Reenen in Stellenbosch. And at the church bazaar, her *melktert* was voted the best in Graaff-Reinet."

"So is it milk tart or *melktert*, Jemima? There's a difference you know."

"Definitely *melktert*, Andrew."

"In that case, I'd love to sample a slice."

"I'll bring some *koeksisters* as well. Mama says you used to love them."

Before I could respond, an agitated Maria was already expressing her consternation.

"You know, Jemima, I've worked really hard to settle Georgie down, and here you are bringing out *koeksisters* that you know will make him more lively."

"It's for Andrew, not Georgie."

"And do you think for a moment that Andrew will be able to eat it without giving Georgie a piece?"

"*Ach* Maria," said my mother, "it's a special occasion. Let Georgie enjoy a piece. He only has it once in a blue moon."

I could tell that Jemima didn't want to cross Maria. Nor did she want to disobey my mother. The maid Katrina, meanwhile, was giving me pleading looks, and I couldn't blame her. For as a child I'd also become overactive when eating this super-sugary treat. But at that moment, the mere thought of it made my taste buds salivate. I could just picture the plaited dough being fried in a deep pan of hot oil until it was golden brown, and then dipped into a cold, sugary syrup.

When I tuned in once more, Jemima was trying to placate Maria. She seemed a sensible girl with a balanced approach. "I don't think you need to worry Maria, because the *koeksisters* won't be very sweet. It's summer, so the syrup isn't cool enough to be absorbed by the dough. It won't be anything like the *koeksisters* we make in winter when we place the bowls of syrup in the frost to cool."

I could see that Maria wasn't convinced. I could also tell that my mother was becoming impatient with her reluctance to budge.

"Jemima," said my mother, "time is moving on and the Ziervogels will be here in half an hour. Poor Andrew is still waiting to sample those special treats you've made for him. So hurry up my girl and bring enough for your father and John as well."

Maria looked utterly deflated. Her objection to the *koeksisters* had been overruled in the presence of her younger siblings. And as this state of affairs was partly my doing, I decided to come to her aid. The last thing I wanted was for her to feel that her views no longer counted just because John and I had arrived home.

"Before you go, Jemima, just a quick question. Are there any *koekbrothers*?"

"Beg your pardon?"

"You've made *koeksisters*, but what about *koekbrothers*?"

Her amused expression told me that she knew where I was going with this. "No such sweet exists, Andrew, There are only *koeksisters*."

"But they have plaits," I said, "just like yours. They are also far too sweet and are called 'sisters,' so I don't think they are suitable for big boys and men—only for girls and church sisters, of course."

I looked down at Georgie. "I'm afraid *koeksisters* are out of the question. We have to remember that we are not girls with plaits. We need something healthy to eat—something that will make you strong and me grow a beard. Now what can that be?"

I began to massage my chin as I pretended to ponder this question.

"*Boerbeskuit*," said Georgie.

"What a clever boy. You're absolutely right," I said. "But the only thing is, it could plop into my coffee like John's did, and splatter on my new suit. No, for the moment, it has to be something else. Will you help me out here, Georgie?"

He nodded.

I hunched down on my haunches and said, "Open your mouth quickly, so I can examine your teeth."

He dutifully obliged, while I peered into his mouth and tapped a tooth or two. I then turned to Jemima and said, "What we need is *melktert* for milk teeth. It's the best treat for a growing boy—and for a man who wants to grow a beard."

Isabella and Kitty burst into applause, while Maria smiled at me in appreciation. On realizing that the impasse was over, a relieved Jemima ran off to do my bidding. Behind me, I could hear my mother say, "It's good to see that Andrew's just as fun-loving as ever."

I never heard John's response. I expected it was a judicious silence.

Fifteen minutes later, we were all seated around the pergola table. Georgie had gone to look at the horses with Katrina, while the rest of the family were busily opening their presents. I heard a little gasp from Maria as she lifted the Spanish doll out of the box. She gazed at it in wonderment, turning it this way and that.

"Would you mind terribly if I give her a new dress?" she asked. "I have some lovely silk offcuts that would suit her perfectly."

"Not at all. She's yours to do with as you please."

"I think I might even look like her. Ma used to say as much when she compared me with her doll in the Delft cabinet. And when I became too passionate or upset, she'd say, 'All you need now are some castanets.' I suppose you think so too?"

I kept my voice light. "Well, it had crossed my mind."

She looked my way, and then let out a deep sigh. "I feel it's only right to warn you that I'm very sensitive and get easily upset."

"And I need to warn you that I'm full of fun and laugh too much."

"Oh dear, what a pair we make."

"Well, I won't hold it against you if you don't hold it against me."

She studied my face to see if I were joking or being serious. I grinned back and winked.

"It's our pact then," she said.

And from that moment, we became the best of friends.

6

Interpreting the Cues

January 1849

It was a Thursday afternoon towards the end of January, and I was again under the pergola with Georgie. He was sitting contentedly on a high chair by my side, having just helped me pick a basket of figs. As the fig trees had been planted next to the boundary wall on the far side of the lucerne plot, they were out of bounds to the children. So climbing under the nets to help me pick the figs had been a first class adventure for him.

I was helping him peel one, when we heard a couple of horses trotting along Murray Street.

"Now who ventures out on a hot afternoon like this," I said, half to myself. "They must be daft like us."

You can imagine my surprise when they turned into the side street and stopped at the wagon gate. I could hear their indistinct chatter as they fumbled with the latch before leading their horses through. Amos had heard them too, and had come out of his quarters to investigate. One of the riders was Carel Ziervogel, but I did not recognize the other.

"Good-day *Kleinbaas* Carel," said Amos. "Now let me see. Your friend here looks familiar. Who can he be? Please help me out a little."

"Don't you remember me, Amos? I'm Manie Pretorius, Charles's friend. You always insisted upon calling me by my real name Emmanuel."

"My goodness. When I saw *Kleinbaas* last, he was just a little boy. But look at him now. He must be six-foot. Just remind me. How old is *Kleinbaas Emmanuel* now?"

"Seventeen. Just a year older than Charles."

"And which Pretorius is *Kleinbaas's* father again?"

"Willem Sterrenberg Pretorius. He's now an elder of the church in Bloemfontein in the new Orange River Sovereignty. He's the cousin of Commandant-General Andries Pretorius who fought against the Zulus at Blood River. He used to bring me here to play with Charles."

Amos's face lit up. "I know who he is now."

"Anyway Amos, you'll meet him again this evening because he's accompanying Drs. William Robertson and Philip Faure, who have just been on tour beyond the Orange and Vaal Rivers."

"*Ja*, but they let us know two weeks ago that they'll be arriving tomorrow evening."

"That was the original plan. But instead of taking a rest day yesterday, they decided to push on to Graaff-Reinet to be here this evening. That's why I've ridden ahead to tell you."

Amos now looked alert and ready to spring into action. "*Kleinbaas* Emmanuel must be hot and tired. Come, he can clean up in the washhouse. I'll take care of the horse."

"He's a bit frisky, Amos."

"*Ach*, I have a knack with horses, so leave him with me. But first, *Kleinbaas* needs to understand something. *Dominee* says I mustn't use nicknames, only baptismal names. So sorry, I'm not allowed to call *Kleinbaas* by his nickname, Manie, only by his real name, Emmanuel—God with us."

He looked at Manie and smiled, knowing full well why Manie preferred his nickname.

"Don't worry *Kleinbaas*. We all let God down sometimes. He'll forgive you."

While I now knew why Manie was back in Graaff-Reinet, I was still wondering about Carel Ziervogel. It wasn't like him to be out riding this time of the afternoon. Nor did it seem that he had ridden far. There were no signs of tiredness or perspiration. His shirt also looked freshly ironed.

I watched as he knee-haltered his horse near the water trough, then draped his tie and jacket over his arm. Next, he took off his hat and ran his fingers through his fair hair that was neatly trimmed at neck length. He was a dapper fellow who sported a short boxed beard with a becoming soul patch just below the bottom lip. From observation, he was greatly admired by all the young ladies.

The stillness was suddenly broken by Isabella who came tearing down the back steps to see who had arrived. She greeted Carel, and then alerted him to Georgie and my presence under the pergola.

Carel had obviously told her about Manie, because she then went over to speak to Amos's wife, Magriet, who had appeared in the doorway of their quarters. By this time, Carel had strolled over to the pergola.

"Good gracious, Carel. What are you doing out and about in this heat?"

"I'll tell you later," he said. "Is John at home?"

"Afraid not. He's visiting Maria-Anna at your place."

"My goodness. He's a fast worker. He's been dropping in to see her every other afternoon. So it must be getting serious, hey?"

"I'm afraid I have no idea. As you've probably guessed, John plays his cards very close to his chest in these matters."

"Same with Maria-Anna. She knows that John's my best friend, so won't tell me a thing. Nor will my mother or the maids. So now I also keep dumb about my activities—except in the case of my father, of course. It always pays to keep him informed."

I was sure he was going to tell me more, when we both spied Isabella striding towards us—her expression business-like.

"Andrew, I thought it best to let you know that Magriet and I have come to the decision to let the man from Bloemfontein have one of John's old shirts that was hanging in the wash-house. Magriet says it's been recently washed, and that John has been keeping it for gardening. Do you think John will mind?"

"Not at all, especially as he's unlikely to do any gardening."

"We had to do something, you see, because the man's shirt was smelly and dripping with sweat."

"Very perceptive of you, Isabella. Now go and tell Pa that Charles's friend Emmanuel Pretorius is here from Bloemfontein."

"Before you go," said Carel. "I have a message for him too. Tell *Dominee* to expect a visit from Carel because he's just become engaged to be married."

I was half-way out of my seat to congratulate Carel, when I noticed the expression on Isabella's face. Her forehead was puckered due to the lift of her eyebrows, and her mouth had dropped open as if dumbstruck. Something was obviously amiss.

"You're engaged to Anna—Elizabeth—Ritchie?" she said, stressing each of the names in turn.

"That's right. Aren't you going to congratulate me?"

"But she's only fifteen and not confirmed yet. Papa will never marry you unless she's confirmed. And Maria-Anna and your mother think she's far too young for you."

"Isabella that's enough," I said. "How dare you question Carel's actions. Now apologize for your unspeakable rudeness. Don't you realize that you're also insulting Mama and Papa? They were engaged when Mama was only fifteen, and married just after her sixteenth birthday. And Papa was far older than Carel here. He was also nearly double Mama's age."

Isabella blushed to the roots of her hair. She seemed to shrivel under my unwavering stare. Her shoulders began to shake and her chest heave as she let out a sob.

By contrast, Carel was looking decidedly chuffed with himself. I realized I'd just given him the necessary ammunition to use against any criticism he might encounter at home. And it also went without saying that my father was unlikely to voice any objection once Anna Ritchie was confirmed.

Carel took hold of Isabella's hand and stroked it gently with his thumb. "Isabella, please sit down a moment, and wipe away your tears. I'm not at all angry with you because you're just the right person to help me out of a tight spot. Would you like to do that?"

Isabella nodded in response to Carel's soothing voice and engaging smile. It was obvious that she would now be putty in his hands.

"Isabella, sweetie, my problem is this. I don't want my marriage to clash with Maria-Anna's and John's. So I need to have some indication of their plans. Unfortunately, Andrew is unable to tell me what they are because, being a *Dominee,* he has to keep them to himself."

I was intrigued by Carel's deviousness and how he was able to turn the situation around to his benefit. He obviously believed that I knew more, but in actual fact, I was just as curious as he was.

"Well," said Isabella, pausing a moment to give this matter due consideration. "I overheard Jemima saying that Papa warned John that he was raising Maria-Anna's hopes by going to visit her so often. John then replied that he'd already made up his mind. Then Papa said that he shouldn't declare himself until he had gained a few months experience in Burghersdorp. According to Jemima, John agreed and thanked Papa for his advice. I also know that your housemaid, Caroline, told our maid, Magriet, that Maria-Anna still wanted a year to get her trousseau ready."

"I see," said Carel, looking more pleased than ever. "That's very helpful information. I can now set the date for my wedding after Anna's confirmation and John's induction. That will leave plenty of time for Maria-Anna to organize her wedding. So what do you think? Are congratulations now in order?"

Isabella wiped away a stray tear, hopped off the stool, and gave Carel a peck. I followed this up with a hearty hand shake.

When Isabella was out of earshot, Carel said, "Phew! Am I pleased I accompanied Manie here this afternoon. It's turned out to be a God-send because I now have all the information I need to smooth my road to marriage in June. It has to be this June, you see, not the next. I don't want to have to wait another year. I'm almost twenty-four."

"What does your father think about your plans?"

"He likes the girl, but it's my mother and Maria-Anna who think she's still too immature for marriage. They want me to wait another year. Her parents, on the other hand, are delighted, and can't foresee any problems, especially as she's due to be confirmed next month. All I have to do now is get my mother and sister on side. And thanks to you and Isabella, I have it all worked out. As a matter of fact, if your father's study door is open, I'll declare my intentions to him now."

He got up, put on his tie and jacket, ruffled Georgie's hair, and said, "You've eaten enough figs for today, Georgie. There'll be no space left for *melktert*." He then turned to face me.

"You'll make a good *Dominee*, Andrew. But take a leaf out of my book. Gather the facts, know what you want to achieve, then negotiate your way to a mutually agreeable resolution. Better still, let the opposition think they've come off best. If you don't, you'll be the one to lose out."

I followed his gaze across the yard to where a refreshed-looking Manie was speaking to Amos.

"By the way", said Carel. "I believe William Robertson is an excellent negotiator, and, according to Manie, so is his father Willem Pretorius. Now I wonder why he's come all this way to Graaff-Reinet? It might be to your advantage to find out."

I was about to ask him what he meant by this, when I saw Manie heading our way. Carel waved a quick goodbye, gave my shoulder a squeeze, then strode towards the steps leading to the *stoep*.

For the life of me, I couldn't see how Willem Pretorius's visit could have anything to do with me, or even the Graaff-Reinet Presbytery, unless Manie dropped some clue while chatting with Carel on their way here. If so, knowing what it was would give my father and me the necessary time to think it through and commit it to prayer. With this thought in mind, I decided it was time to get some practice in decoding the cues.

Manie approached me with hand outstretched. "*Dag Dominee*," he said. "Sorry I took so long. After freshening up, I went to check on my horse and speak to Amos and Magriet."

Manie placed his hat on a stool and drew up a comfortable chair. His dark hair was still wet after being freshly washed, and he smelt of soap and talcum powder beneath John's draw-string shirt. He had left it half undone to reveal his tanned chest. His look and demeanor was of an honest farm boy who had been brought up well.

Eyeing Georgie, he lent forward to greet him. "And what's your name?"

Georgie met his gaze for several moments, then started to shake his head.

"Andrew's not a *Dominee*. John is."

Manie looked at me, then back at Georgie. "Really? And here I was thinking he's a *Dominee*."

"He laughs and plays with me," said Georgie.

"Oh, I see. And who's ever heard of such a thing—a *Dominee* who laughs and plays with little children. I'd like a *Dominee* like that. Wouldn't you?"

Georgie nodded.

"So John doesn't play with you?"

"No, cause I'm naughty."

"What about your Papa?"

Georgie thought for a moment, then shook his head. "No, cause he's busy. But sometimes he lets me sit on his knee."

Manie turned to me. "Out of the mouth of babes and sucklings, hey?"

I wasn't sure whether to feel embarrassed for myself, or for John and my father. But one thing was clear: Georgie had observed that a *Dominee* was someone who conducted himself in a certain manner. Manie's questions, however, had deliberately drawn answers from him that had favored me. Under the circumstances, I felt obliged to set the record straight.

"It's not as bad as it sounds, Manie. John can't be expected to play with Georgie because he's taken on the task of instructing Charles in Latin and a host of other subjects. And as for my father . . . well, you can imagine how busy he is. But like all his children, he'll give Georgie due attention when he's a little older."

"Speaking of Charles," Manie said, "I'm really looking forward to seeing him again. Is he home?"

"Afraid not. He's taken our brother James to Barend Burger's farm in the Sneeuberg Mountains for a few days. Their absence will enable my mother to billet Drs. Robertson and Faure in their rooms. They'll be back on Tuesday."

Manie played several four-finger scales on the table while considering this news. "That's a pity, as I wanted to warn him of the request my father's about to make for his catechetical services."

"Catechetical services? Good gracious. He'll only be sixteen next month. Not only that, he has to study in preparation for Utrecht."

"*Ja* man, my father knows all that. But these are exceptional times. The thing is, while other parts of the Sovereignty have settled down, the hot heads of Winburg are still upset about the British takeover. They are the ones who requested that my father's cousin Andries Pretorius should come across the Vaal to lead a commando against the British. But what upset them even more was when Drs. Robertson and Faure failed most of the young people from the Winburg area who wanted to be confirmed. They didn't have sufficient knowledge of the Heidelberg Catechism, you see. The upheaval this caused forced Dr. Robertson and Pa to hatch this plan to help settle things down."

"How long do they want Charles for?"

"Only six weeks."

"Six weeks! That means about two-and-a-half months if we factor in travelling time. I can't see my father agreeing to such a long stay. Two weeks, perhaps, but not six."

"That will be a pity because Dr. Robertson says he can't think of anyone better for the job than Charles. He's also worked out a plan to ensure that Charles will be in Burghersdorp in time for John's induction. He's very persuasive you know."

"So I've heard."

Manie fell silent for a moment, then said, "How do you think Charles will react to this request?"

"He'll probably jump at the opportunity, especially if he can get out of having to read the demanding Latin of Seneca and Cicero. It's my father's reaction you have to worry about."

As I considered this turn of events, I couldn't help wondering if Willem Pretorius had any other request up his sleeve. It seemed a long way to come solely to ask for Charles's services. In any case, it would be William Robertson who'd be the most likely person to discuss this matter with my father. Perhaps Carel was right after all. And if he was, it wouldn't hurt to do some prodding.

"Tell me Manie, did you fight against the British at the Battle of Boomplaats?"

"No, I wasn't allowed to because I'm still living under Pa's roof. But my brother Petrus did. Pa said that as an elder of the Church he wasn't there to fight, but rather to negotiate on behalf of our Church if the Boers weren't able to expel the British. He also persuaded the elders of the other three churches to do the same."

"So what did Andries Pretorius think of that?"

"Strangely enough, he acknowledged Pa's arguments, mainly because there are no pastors beyond the Orange and Vaal

Rivers. But he didn't like the fact that Pa warned my brother to pull out of Boomplaats if the numbers were against us. In answer to that question, Pa quoted Luke 14:3 about the king who had to consider whether he was able with ten thousand to wage war against a king who came against him with twenty thousand."

"So Petrus fought at Boomplaats, did he?"

"No, he pulled out. But he fought at the Bloemfontein skirmish before that."

Manie's cheeks ballooned as he blew out a breath. "I'll have to go back to the beginning. Let me explain. You see, there are several tribes living beyond the Orange River. There are the Basuto, the Bushmen, the Korannas, the Rolong, the Tlokwa, and some Griquas. And all of them are continually warring against each other. We Boers have tried to stay out of their squabbles because we've suffered enough during the frontier wars here in the Cape. But your new Governor, Sir Harry Smith, decided to poke his nose into their affairs by deciding to impose a western style rule of law and order upon the territory."

"How did he do that?"

"Well, in 1846 the British built a small fort named Fort Drury in Bloemfontein. They said it was simply an outpost to settle tribal disputes. Then at the beginning of last year, Sir Harry Smith decided to visit the fort. It was while he was there that he issued a proclamation saying that the region between the Orange and Vaal Rivers was now British territory. He then declared that it would be called the Orange River Sovereignty."

"So what happened next?"

"A group of stock farmers near Winburg called upon *Oom* Andries, who lives across the Vaal River, to be their Commandant-General. The reason is that he's a great strategist and also a God-fearing man. He won a major battle in 1838 against the Zulu chief Dingane near the Ncome River in Natal. At the time, he had only 464 men, while Dingane had 5000 warriors. But he and his men prayed to God and made a covenant with Him that should He give them the victory, they'd always commemorate that day. And as you may have heard, God gave then an overwhelming victory. It is said that the river ran red with the blood of the Zulus who had lost their lives—about 3500, I'm told."

I nodded. "I believe the place is now called Blood River."

"That's right. Well anyway, *Oom* Andries was able to form a commando of about a thousand men. The first thing they did was to expel the Resident, Major Warden, and his garrison of 400 men from Fort Drury. This was the skirmish in which Petrus took part. Then in August, they heard that Sir Harry Smith had crossed the Orange River with a large number of troops. So *Oom* Andries decided to ambush them at the farm Boomplaats. But when they got there, they were shocked to find that Sir Harry Smith's troops numbered around 1200. There were also about 250 Griquas. If that weren't bad enough, our spies also reported seeing six small cannon. It was at that point that my brother and more than half of the commando decided to pull out. They reasoned that going ahead would only result in a bloodbath and an unnecessary loss of life."

"So how many men were left?"

"Between three and four hundred."

"And Andries Pretorius still decided to fight?"

Manie Nodded.

"But that was madness. What on earth prompted him to go ahead?"

"In short, he didn't count the cost. And according to Petrus, his disgust at the annexation ran too deep for him to think clearly. But if you want to hear a long sermon on that topic, just ask Pa."

Manie smirked, knowing full well that it would stretch the patience of the best of listeners.

"So what happened at Boomplaats?" I asked.

"Well, Major Warden told Pa that Sir Harry Smith was banking on the fact that we'd be sensible and send a delegation to sue for peace. And, because he was convinced that would happen, he rode out in front of the advance guard in his dress uniform. From what I heard, his white trousers and the gold braid on his blue jacket so bedazzled the eyes of our men that they couldn't shoot straight. They only grazed his leg and wounded his horse's nose."

"It was a wonder he wasn't killed."

"And it was a wonder that our commando lasted for four hours. But what could three-hundred-or-so men do against six field cannon?"

"Were many killed?"

"Official figures put it at seventeen British, six Griquas and nine Boers."

"What about the wounded?"

"According to Dr. Drury, thirty-eight British were severely wounded, but only five on our side."

Manie's voice had slowed when recording the dead and wounded. He was obviously still upset by the needless loss of life.

"I take it that the commando was forced to retreat in the end?"

"*Ja*, but not until everyone had realized that the situation was hopeless. It was only then that *Oom* Andries gave the order to retreat to Winburg. But he didn't stay there for long because he knew that the British would be after him. So he fled to his farm across the Vaal. The British now regard him as an outlaw and have placed a £2000 bounty on his head."

"Phew! That's a lot of money. Isn't he afraid someone might give him away?"

Manie gave me a look of disgust that I could even pose the question.

In the silence that followed, I became conscious that no one had thought to bring him a drink. I suspected that the excitement aroused by the news of Carel's engagement was the reason for the hold-up in the kitchen. I noticed too that Georgie could hardly keep his eyes open. I was about to suggest that we go inside, when I suddenly thought better of it. If there was anything I should know, now was the time to find out.

"So tell me Manie, what's the situation like in the Sovereignty at the moment?"

"To tell you the truth, we've done an about face. Every church place is now trying to curry favor with Sir Harry Smith in the hope of receiving preferential treatment."

"Just stop there a moment. What do you mean by a church place?"

Manie paused to consider his answer. "Well," he said, "as there are no church buildings beyond the Orange River, it's any place where a church service is scheduled to take place. It can be on a farm, or in the veld. In can be a temporary site chosen for a special occasion, or a permanent church place. In the Sovereignty we have four permanent places that are regarded as centers of a particular region. They are Bloemfontein, Winburg, Rietpoort and Riet River."

"I see."

"Well as I was saying, the leaders of these centers are now trying to curry favor with Sir Harry Smith in the hope they'll receive funds for teachers and some Government aid for the building of their churches. For example, Winburg has just named a small village to the east of it, Harrismith. And would you believe, the farmers in the districts of Rietpoort and Riet River have also named their church places after him. Both are still in the veld, mind you, and the layout of their towns haven't even been planned yet. The church place at Rietpoort is now called Smithfield, and the one at Riet River, Fauresmith. As Pa says, 'We've experienced the stick, now it's time to vie for the carrot.'"

I noticed that Bloemfontein hadn't been mentioned, and wondered if they too were trying to curry favor with the powers that be.

"So what is Bloemfontein doing to earn a carrot?" I asked.

Manie's face lit up and his gestures became animated. "Man, I'm happy to tell you that we were the first to be offered a carrot. When Drs. Faure and Robertson passed through Bloemfontein on their journey north, they formally established our congregation and inducted Pa and Jan van Zyl as elders[4]. After they'd left, Pa and Van Zyl arranged for the laying of the cornerstone of our church to coincide with their return journey. It took place as planned on 6 January. And who do you think we asked to do the honors?—none other than the Resident Major Warden. At the ceremony, he promised to support our building program and also agreed to serve on the building committee together with his aide, Mr. Allison. And best of all, the Colonial Government has promised to pay the salary of a minister when he's appointed."

I was careful to downplay my reception of this news by simply offering a smile to acknowledge the headway Willem Pretorius and Van Zyl had made in establishing the Bloemfontein congregation.

So there it was—just as Carel had anticipated. Reading between the lines, it was clear that Bloemfontein was seeking their own pastor. And as I was the only candidate already on African soil with barely fourteen months to go to my twenty-second birthday, it was bound to be me. In fact, none of the Cape students in Utrecht would be back for another two to three years.

I rose from my chair to indicate that it was time to move inside.

"Come Manie," I said. "You must be dying of thirst. As luck would have it, I think there's likely to be a scrumptious tea party because Carel has just announced his engagement."

I lifted a droopy-eyed Georgie into my arms and kissed his forehead. I was thankful that I still had eighteen months to prepare for my new pastorate. After what Manie had told me, there was no doubt that it would be Bloemfontein. In the meantime, I'd cherish my time at home.

7
The Call

February 1849

The visit of Faure and Robertson sped past rapidly. We hung on their every word as they told of their travels through the Orange River Sovereignty and the territory beyond the Vaal River. They told us that the latter territory was now being referred to as the Transvaal.

We marveled at the fact that they'd held 113 services at 17 church places, and had baptized 920 children and confirmed 628 young people—barely six months after my father and P.K. Albertyn had conducted similar services on their tour. In spite of their many references to church places, I found it strange that neither man had mentioned the laying of the church cornerstone in Bloemfontein.

It also struck me as odd that my father had neither invited John nor me to the meeting he had scheduled with Faure and Robertson on Saturday afternoon. He had simply poked his head around our door and voiced his approval at seeing us hard at work on our sermons.

Before leaving he'd said, "I think it best if the two of you remain here to polish your sermons. It'll be a big day for both of you tomorrow, especially with our guests in the congregation."

Later that afternoon, while enjoying afternoon tea with the rest of the family, I heard Willem Pretorius arrive, and the door of my father's study close firmly behind him. As Faure and Robertson were still with him, he'd arranged for a private afternoon tea—apparently nothing unusual when discussing church matters with important guests. Nevertheless, I'd marveled that no-one in the family had expressed interest in knowing what the lengthy deliberations were about.

It also appeared that John had taken my father's comments about polishing our sermons at face value. This probably stemmed from the fact that my father was a stickler for thorough preparation. Our sermons had to be written out in full and then committed to memory, with only a few headings to guide us when we came to delivering them.

On Sunday, I was to deliver the morning sermon followed by the application service in the afternoon, while John was to deliver a shorter sermon that evening.

Judging from the comments I received at the door—not least from Faure and Robertson—it seemed that my messages had been well received. It was little wonder then that I was in a relaxed mood as we congregated in the dining room for supper that evening.

We had just risen from the table and were saying our goodnights, when William Robertson tapped me on the shoulder.

"I wonder, dear fellow, if I may presume upon you to accompany me down Parsonage Street?"

"I'd be delighted to," I said.

"To be truthful, Andrew, I'm hankering to stroll down memory lane. Over the past few days, I've only been able to catch a glimpse of the little school where I used to teach. I'd love to gaze at it unhindered and be taken back to my teaching years. I was only seventeen when I arrived here, you know."

Although his request sounded reasonable, I couldn't help thinking it could also be a ploy to discuss Bloemfontein. But due to my buoyant mood, I brushed this thought aside for the time being in favor of humoring him. I decided to pose a question that would grant him the excuse to reminisce on his early working life as a teacher.

"How long were you here in Graaff-Reinet?" I asked.

"About five years. It was during my fourth that I received a call to the ministry. The following year I returned to Scotland to pursue my theological studies."

As we chatted, I was able to inspect his features close up. Although he was only forty-four, he seemed much older. It was probably his stocky build and receding hairline that accounted for it. Unfortunately, the full beard he'd grown during his tour up north didn't help to lessen this impression. It was almost pure white, as was the hair at his temples. But the physical feature to which one was magnetically drawn was the fluffed out bunches of hair on either side of his forehead. In my boyish imagination, they looked just like cows ears that were ready to flap this way and that at any moment. Nevertheless, one lost sight of this unusual hairstyle as his strong personality and commanding presence came to the fore.

As he finished telling me about the school and its gradual acceptance by the local farmers, I steered him towards the front door. It wasn't long before we had crossed over Murray Street and were strolling down the middle of Parsonage. We walked in silence while delighting in the full moon that lit up the white facades of the buildings we passed.

Although I adopted a nonchalant demeanor, my thoughts were continually churning over the question of whether he would use this opportunity to sound me out about a call to Bloemfontein. Fortunately, I didn't have to wait long. On reaching his old school, he finally raised the issue.

"You know Andrew, while I was travelling through the Sovereignty, I met several of my past pupils who had attended this school. And each and every one begged me to find teachers and pastors for the Sovereignty. The spiritual situation there is quite dire, you know."

I remained silent, not trusting myself to speak.

"What would you say to becoming the pastor of Bloemfontein' in May this year? We could set the date for your induction early so that you could still attend John's induction in Burghersdorp."

"May *this* year?" I said. "I'm afraid that's an impossibility because I won't be twenty-two until May *next* year."

"I'm aware of that, but these matters can be negotiated, you know—perhaps not for the Colony, but certainly for the Sovereignty."

"But it's a matter of church law," I said. "It can't be changed willy nilly."

"I agree. Nevertheless the Hague Committee, who ordained you on your twentieth birthday, has already done so. And who can argue with the highest ecclesiastical authority in the Dutch Reformed Church?"

"But that was due to special circumstances—the Cape being so far away."

"And aren't these special circumstances as well? Just think, Andrew. There are twelve thousand Dutch-speaking souls in the Sovereignty and another eight thousand in the Transvaal who have been crying out for a pastor since they started leaving the Colony about fourteen years ago. And here you are, an ordained minister of the Gospel, wanting to twiddle your thumbs in nice, comfortable Graaff-Reinet with its beautiful parsonage, its church with its silver goblets for Holy Communion, and its newly installed steel pillars in case of fire, not to mention a congregation who's had the privilege of hearing the Word preached every Sunday since 1792."

I was pleased I was standing in the shadow of a tree so that he couldn't see the consternation on my face. He was being grossly unfair, and I wasn't going to let him get away with it. I kept my voice low and steady.

"I do not recall ever having said that I didn't want to go to Bloemfontein, Dr. Robertson. I was simply expressing my concern about obeying church law."

"I understand your concern. Nevertheless, you do well to remember that church law has been devised by men, and can therefore be tinkered with, as the Hague Committee has already done. And secondly, this call has been endorsed by Philip Faure, the moderator of the Synod; your father, who is chairman of the local Presbytery; and yours truly, the chairman of the Synodical Committee."

"That's all very well, Dr. Robertson. But doesn't Sir Harry Smith have the final say?"

"True. But in my opinion, he'll heartily agree because there's a host of factors in your favor that do not rest upon church law. You see, Bloemfontein is presently an English-speaking town with a large detachment of the Royal Artillery stationed there. But there's also a small detachment of the Cape Corps who are Hottentots—or Coloreds, as they refer to them these days. And they only speak Cape Dutch. So it's hopeless sending an English-speaking army chaplain to Bloemfontein who isn't able to speak the Cape lingo. But then there's you—the perfect answer to the religious situation in the Sovereignty."

"With due respect, Dr. Robertson, I think you're gilding the lily a bit."

"Not at all. Although you'll be inducted as a Dutch Reformed pastor, you'll also be acting as an army chaplain and pastor to the English-speaking community. And best of all, you'll be trusted by British and Dutch alike. And if there happens to be some misunderstanding, you'll be able to use your influence to reconcile the parties."

I started to laugh. And try as I might, I couldn't stop. My over-active imagination had taken over. The scene that Dr. Robertson's words had suggested just didn't accord with reality. And as it played out in my mind, it became a rollicking farce.

My laughter finally came to a halt when I saw a lit candle appear between the half-open drapes in the neighboring house. I quickly beckoned to Dr. Robertson to follow me onto the *stoep* of the library. There was a bench there on which we could sit and talk this through.

"Dr. Robertson, it's me you are speaking to—Andrew Murray Junior who's only twenty, but looks no older than seventeen. I couldn't possibly hold down a position like that. I'm far too immature."

"My dear boy, your youthful looks will be in your favor. There'll be few expectations from someone they consider to be so young. And think of the experience you will have gained after one year."

"That goes without saying. But you yourself have just put your finger on my major handicap. You called me a boy. And while I can see that there are benefits in appearing young, from my perspective it's a major drawback. I don't want my congregation to make allowances for my youth. I want them to treat me as a fully-fledged minister who's been called by God to be their pastor."

William Robertson laid his hand on my shoulder and breathed a deep sigh. I was expecting him to counter my argument, but instead he nodded.

"I apologize for that slip. It was unforgivable. But you know, Andrew, we all enter the ministry with a weakness in one area or another. Take your father for instance. He had to overcome a huge language and cultural barrier when he arrived here. Take your brother John. He's diffident and shy, as well as being preoccupied with what people might think. Then there's you, a born leader and preacher with an innate ability to relate to people. You're also bold and forthright. But as you have pointed out, the major hindrance to your ministry—for the moment at least—is your youthful looks and immaturity. Isn't that so?"

I nodded.

"Now tell me, Andrew, how many years did it take for your father to surmount the language and cultural difficulties he had to face? Three years? Five years? Ten years? And how long do you think your brother will take to get over his personality limitations? Five years—even ten, perhaps. And what about your friends in Utrecht? When they return, will they have the privilege of being able to preach on a regular basis and learn the ins and outs of the ministry like you are doing?"

"You needn't say any more, Dr. Robertson."

"No, we need to face the hindrances you've identified fairly and squarely. Like you, I can foresee that your youthful looks and immaturity could be a stumbling block. It might simply be an issue of perception for some, while for others, it might be a question of whether you have the necessary leadership skills. During the first few months, you may even find that strong elders like Willem Pretorius and Jan van Zyl will try to wrestle the reins of leadership from you. But honestly, Andrew, with your superior education and theological knowledge, how long do you think it will take before everyone accepts you as their spiritual leader. A year perhaps, or even less?"

It was my turn to nod. He'd helped me see that I was far more qualified for the ministry than I'd initially realized. And like my father and the other pastors who'd gone before, I'd need—with God's help—to overcome the barriers that were peculiar to me and my own pastoral situation.

As I sat there, with head bowed and my arms leaning on my legs, I knew in my heart what God wanted me to do. I also realized that it would be selfish to remain in Graaff-Reinet when there was a crying need for a pastor in the Sovereignty.

I was now ready to accept the call.

"I'll be honored to go to Bloemfontein this May," I said. "I've been aware for several days that such a call could be in the offing, but always thought it would be for May next year. But I see now that God wants me there sooner rather than later. So tell me, Dr. Robertson, do you really think Sir Harry Smith will endorse it?"

"Never fear. He'll jump at it. But pray about it tonight and then convey your decision to your father in the morning. If you still see your way clear to accepting the call, we'll invite Willem Pretorius to dinner tomorrow evening and announce it to the family then. Your father will tell your mother beforehand, of course."

I let out a sigh. "She won't be happy about it because she's been looking forward to my being home for another year."

"Don't I know it. And I fear she'll put the blame squarely on my shoulders. Believe me, Andrew, negotiating with a man is one matter, but with a woman, quite another. I'm afraid I still have much to learn on that score."

☙

My mother was her cheerful self the whole of Monday—that is, until just before our evening meal. It was obvious that it must have been while my parents were dressing for dinner that my father had finally found the opportunity to tell her of my call to Bloemfontein. This hadn't given her much time to digest the information or acquaint herself with the details.

When she came into the front parlor to announce that dinner was ready, all were conscious that something was amiss. Instead of the gracious smiles, for which she was known, and the pointed enquiries about the welfare of her guests, all she could muster was a perfunctory greeting for Willem Pretorius.

As she and my father led the way into the dining room, I noticed Pretorius exchanging glances with William Robertson and Philip Faure. He then turned to me and in a conspiratorial manner whispered, "I detect that your mother hasn't accepted the news of your call very well. Do you think she'll voice her objections after we've completed family devotions?"

"I'm sure she will. So you had better brace yourself, because my father won't come to your aid. He'll never try to sway her in front of visitors. Nor will she do the same. She's usually putty in my father's hands, except when it comes to protecting her children."

"*Ja*, my wife's the same. But is there any risk that your father might change his mind?"

"With him, yes. With me, no."

Because we were bringing up the rear, he was able to give me a light slap on the back to indicate his approval. I marveled at his youthful appearance and the fact that he'd been elected elder at the relatively young age of forty-six. To my mind, he could have passed as Manie's brother rather than his father. But unlike Manie, Willem Sterrenberg Pretorius didn't come across as an unlettered farmer, but rather as a suave and intelligent townsman. He certainly cut a manly figure with his broad shoulders, well-groomed hair, and neatly trimmed goatee. I think it was a surprise to us all when he appeared at the front door dressed in black tailcoat, starched collar, and top hat.

We entered the dining room and stood behind our chairs while we waited for my father to say grace. I noticed Maria, Jemima and John exchanging questioning looks, as did the servants who were positioning themselves along the wall nearest the kitchen. I pretended not to notice, and kept my eyes lowered.

As soon as we were seated, my mother started to fidget. She first straightened her fork, then her knife, then smoothed the edge of the damask tablecloth in front of her before repeating the routine all over again. Her consternation seemed to be mounting by the minute. It was a relief to us all when dinner was brought in. Unfortunately for her, it would not be until after family devotions that she'd be able to voice her disapproval. This was because my father, who followed the Puritan tradition, would only allow conversations based on Christian themes and biblical topics during mealtime.

Finally, the long-awaited moment arrived. My father cleared his throat and tapped his water glass to summon our attention.

"I've a very pleasant announcement to make," he said. "Andrew has just accepted a call to Bloemfontein this May. This will enable him to commence his ministry at the same time as John. And although he'll be slightly under age, it's expected that Governor Sir Harry Smith will approve the appointment."

"That's wonderful news," said John, who was the first to congratulate me. "You've kept abreast of me all these years, so it is only fitting that we begin our ministries at the same time."

"Here! Here!" said William Robertson, whose exuberant approval was followed by congratulatory remarks from Philip

Faure and Willem Pretorius. Meanwhile, Maria and Jemima, who had by now guessed the reason for my mother's sullenness, began to mirror her disquiet. Jemima managed a nod and a token smile, while Maria looked positively forlorn.

"I certainly hope the Lord will bless your ministry," she said, "but we were so looking forward to having you here for another year. It seems as if you've been stolen from us."

"Nor can I help expressing *my* disapproval." said my mother. "Church law is there for a purpose—a good, sound purpose. It's there to protect both the congregation and the candidate. In this case, you've only thought of the congregation, but not the candidate."

My mother straightened her back, pursed her lips, and looked straight down the table at William Robertson and Willem Pretorius. My father, meanwhile, had averted his gaze and was studying the inside of his teacup. Because he loved her so much, I knew that he'd let her voice her displeasure, and then, when alone, would calm her fears and console her with kisses—or so Maria had once explained the process to me.

From my mother's perspective, William Robertson and Willem Pretorius were the obvious ones to tackle because they were the prime initiators of my call. And because she was the lady of the house, and they the guests, they would have to produce arguments to defend their position in a manner that would take her distress into consideration—something, I guessed, neither of them were used to doing.

After a charged pause, my mother continued. "Andrew is still a growing boy who needs time to mature. Yes, he's kept abreast of John all these years, but that took effort. Now he needs time to catch up mentally and emotionally. It's not fair to take that away from him. And then there's all this conniving with the Governor to get his approval."

"But *Mevrou,* "said Pretorius, "As I understand it, he's due to start as your husband's apprentice in May. In fact, it seems as if he's already begun. So instead of helping out in Graaff-Reinet, where there's already a pastor, he'll be ministering in Bloemfontein. All that has changed is the location."

"And another thing," said Philip Faure. "If he starts in Bloemfontein the following May, he'll have triple the work."

"I can't see how," said my mother.

"Let me explain. Remember how we told you about all the wedding, christening and confirmations services we conducted only six months after your husband's tour, well that will triple within sixteen months. It'll be much easier on him if he goes this May."

"I would also like to add," said William Robertson, "that Bloemfontein falls within the Graaff-Reinet Presbytery. So he'll be home for all Presbytery meetings."

"And *Mevrou,*" said Pretorius, I promise to take good care of him. I'll be fetching him in my own horse-wagon when the time comes. But the good news is that I've just ordered a sturdy, four-seater Cape cart from the wagon-makers here in Graaff-Reinet. It should be ready well before May. So *Dominee* and Andrew can ride in that. I'll bring a young Hottentot driver with me for the cart when I come. Manie and my personal driver will be responsible for looking after his household goods in the horse-wagon."

My poor mother knew she was outnumbered and outflanked. Her shoulders seemed to droop as she accepted the inevitable. She looked across at Pretorius and smiled. "*Meneer* Pretorius, I'm delighted to hear about the Cape cart. Would you mind if I accompanied my husband and Andrew to Bloemfontein? It's only right that I be there for Andrew's induction."

"Of course. The cart's at your disposal—"

"I'm afraid that's out of the question," interrupted Robertson. "The roads are far worse than those in the Colony. And besides, there's no parsonage, as yet, in Bloemfontein. Andrew will have to share a house with another male—probably a military officer."

"He's right, my dear," said my father.

My mother looked unconvinced. "But what's the difference between my going to Bloemfontein and travelling the ten-day journey by horse-wagon to Cape Town every five years when you attend the Synod? What are you not telling me Andrew?"

William Robertson cleared his throat, thus indicating that he would deal with this question. I held my breath as he began to offer an explanation.

"My dearest Maria," he said. "The long and the short of it is that besides Bloemfontein, Andrew has to be inducted into the other three congregations in the Sovereignty as well. We have tentatively set the induction schedule so that the first one takes place at Fauresmith on 29 April, followed by Bloemfontein, Winburg, then Smithfield on three consecutive Sundays after that. This will leave a week for Andrew and his father to reach Burghersdorp for John's induction on 27 May."

"I don't understand. Why must he be inducted at the other church places as well?"

"Because he'll be their acting pastor or *consulent* until they call a pastor of their own."

"Does that mean that he'll have to conduct the quarterly communion services at each of these places in turn?"

"Yes, I believe that's the case."

"But that's ridiculous, William. That means he'll be the pastor of the whole of the Sovereignty numbering about twelve thousand Boers, while John, here, will only have a congregation of a thousand souls—two thousand at most."

"That's correct. And what a wonderful calling that is."

"So let me see. . . . He's too young to become a pastor in the Colony, but not too young to become a bishop in the Sovereignty. Can't you see the ridiculousness of it? You are being blinded by your own arguments, William."

I could tell that my mother was ready to dig her heels in. Meanwhile John, who was sitting opposite me, had folded his arms as if to register his opposition to the whole Sovereignty idea. The last thing I wanted was for him to openly side with my mother. I also wanted to take her focus off the fact that I'd be serving four congregations. With this in mind, I jumped up, bounded to the foot of the table and put my arms around her shoulders.

"Ma, I don't think it's wise for you to accompany Pa and me to the Sovereignty. It will be a long journey of more than a month, and a cold one at that. And to be honest, having you there will be a distraction. I'll be so anxious about your comfort and the need to introduce you to the people, that my attention will be on you rather than them. It's far better that you and Maria accompany John to Burghersdorp and help him unpack."

She massaged my arm for a few moments before looking up and giving me a wan smile. "I'm so sorry my boy. I should be congratulating you instead of expressing all these reservations. Please forgive me. It's just that what's expected of you is so unreasonable. You'll only realize that once you're there."

"I understand, Ma. But as overwhelming as the circumstances might appear, God will make a way if I'm obeying His will."

She heaved a deep sigh, "I dare say you're right."

She patted my arm, but I could tell that she was unconvinced and would probably remain so until my first Presbytery report. The men, on the other hand, were all smiles.

My mother now turned her attention to John. "What about you, John? Poor Andrew won't have anyone at his induction. Surely you'll attend?"

"I can't see how that's possible, Ma. Frankly, it'll be too much of a rush. As much as I would like to, I feel that my duty lies with my congregation. I also regard the days leading up to the service as a time to spend with God in prayer and contemplation. You need to realize that I'm a man more suited to teaching and building the kingdom with a trowel than a knight in shining armor galloping hither and thither brandishing a sword."

My mother seemed quite taken aback by the vehemence of John's assertion. To show her disapproval, she subjected him to a withering stare. Fortunately, William Robertson made an effort to lighten the mood in order to dispel any hurt I might be feeling.

"Well Andrew," he said, "I take it that you and your father are the knights in shining armor—a most worthy metaphor."

"In that case, I must be knight's maiden," my mother said.

Jemima clapped her hands in delight. "I can just picture it, Mama: you being swept up into Papa's strong arms and galloping away into the blue."

My mother broke into a smile, while the rest of us burst into laughter. Unfortunately for John, I don't think he expected his knight to be associated with the spiritual one described in Ephesians 6:11-17. As a matter of fact, I had the sneaky suspicion that he'd really been alluding to Don Quixote of La Mancha, the hapless knight in the novel by Miguel de Cervantes.

Be that as it may, the tension had been broken, and although I was disappointed that he wouldn't be attending my induction, I could well understand his motives for not wanting to do so. To my surprise, so could Willem Pretorius.

"You know *Mevrou,*" he said, "it's a gift to know one's limitations and to have the courage of one's convictions to say so. It's a lesson I wish my boys would learn. I'm always telling them to count the cost before they agree to a proposal."

"I'm sure you're right," my mother said. "It's just that I want what's best for both John and Andrew."

Pretorius stood and bowed in the direction of my mother. "Well *Mevrou,* you've certainly outdone yourself on that score this evening. Thank you for a lovely dinner and a most insightful discussion."

Turning to me, he smiled, then added, "When I come to fetch you in April—subject to the Governor's approval, of course—make sure you're wearing your full armor and have sharpened that sword of yours so that you'll be victorious in the Lord's work."

I returned his smile, then walked around the table to shake his hand.

"Just a quick word before you go, Elder Pretorius. I'm afraid I'm facing a significant hurdle. As a knight, I need a horse."

For the second time that evening I was relieved to hear laughter around the table, including my mother's.

"You don't own a horse?" he said, in mock indignation. "Never fear, I'll get you a good one at a bargain price when we arrive in Bloemfontein."

8

My Journey Begins

April 1849

Dr. Robertson had wasted no time in negotiating my official call to Bloemfontein with Sir Harry Smith. In actual fact, he'd sent off a letter to both Sir Harry and Abraham Faure while still in Graaff-Reinet. Towards the end of February, he let me know that Sir Harry had already endorsed my nomination, and that Abraham Faure would be sending my official letter of appointment very shortly. This duly arrived on 13 March.

I now had only six weeks to visit friends as well as pack my possessions and collect the various household essentials needed for Bloemfontein. Thanks to my mother's organizational skills, most of the furniture, linen, and crockery had either been supplied by her or given to me as gifts from members of the Graaff-Reinet congregation.

A few days prior to my departure, which was set for Monday, 23 April, Willem Pretorius arrived with his roomy wagon drawn by a team of ten horses. No sooner had he arrived, than he collected his brand new four-seater Cape cart. It received a hearty seal of approval by one and all as we admired the tasteful upholstery and tested it for comfort. Thankfully, it would serve as our main means of conveyance to the Sovereignty and Burghersdorp—a far more comfortable option than the wagon.

He had also brought along two wagon drivers who would alternate between driving the cart and the wagon. Manie, who was keen to hone his skills with the reins, would act as backup wagon driver.

The day of my departure arrived far more quickly than anticipated. Just after dawn, our family assembled in the front parlor together with the servants. By any measure, it was proving to be a somber leave-taking filled with tears and sad goodbyes. Needless to say, I was all too conscious that I was about to take my first step into adulthood as well as a foray into the unknown.

On my left, I was clasping Georgie's hand, and on my right, Isabella's. I swung their arms playfully as we waited for my father and John to arrive. They had insisted that I stay with the rest of the family while they helped Amos lead the team of horses out of our side gate and around into Murray Street.

Isabella looked up at me, her eyes welling with tears. "Are you really going to be a *Dominee* in Bloemfontein? Why can't you stay with us forever and ever?"

"What! Would you have me make a little heaven for myself here and never want to leave it?"

Thankfully, at that moment the cart and the horse-wagon pulled up outside the front door. For Georgie and Isabella, this was a scene not to be missed. I couldn't help smiling as I watched them rush to the front window.

A few minutes later, my father and John entered via the front door, which they then left open. Outside, we could hear the cheers and guffaws of over fifty young men who'd decided to form a guard of honor that would accompany us out of

Graaff-Reinet. For them it was a time for laughter and rejoicing. Not only was I about to embark on my ministry, but their compatriots across the Orange River would finally have a pastor.

As the parlor was brightly lit, the men could view our family gathered there, although they couldn't hear what was being said. As soon as my father laid his hand on my head to pronounce the blessing, the commotion outside subsided as the men, one after another, removed their hats and bowed their heads. After the blessing and prayer for travel mercies, my father announced that we would sing the hymn: "O God of Bethel."

"As you know my children," he said, "it's become a tradition in our family to sing this hymn whenever one of our number leaves home. Ten years ago, your mother and I together with Willie, Maria and Amos sang it when John and Andrew left for Scotland. And now it's time to sing it again. Maria tells me that you've been practicing it, so let's lift up our voices to the Lord. Please provide the note, Amos."

Amos sounded the note in a clear, tenor voice. But when we began to sing, we could only muster a chorus of paltry strains due to our collective sadness and the tears that flowed freely. For me, this was the defining moment of my leave-taking, and a memory that I would cherish during the lonely years of toil ahead.

My sadness, however, soon gave way to excitement as I stepped outside and acknowledged the whoops and cheers of my waiting comrades. With a final wave to the family, my father and I took our seats in the cart. The driver flicked the reins, and we were on our way—the horse-wagon following behind.

If my farewell could be described as a climactic event of heightened excitement, then my arrival at Fauresmith—the first induction place—could be likened to a dip in the pool of despond. By the time we neared the farm where the induction was to take place, the rain had well and truly set in. The track we followed was deeply rutted, causing the wagon to sway precariously from side to side. Even the Cape cart, which was much lighter, churned up the mud.

Because of the inclement weather, only the elders, deacons and families from surrounding farms attended my induction. Fortunately, we were all able to squeeze into the front parlor of the farmhouse, where a most welcome fire was crackling in the hearth.

The rain did not let up until Tuesday morning, the day of our departure. Over breakfast, Elder Theunis Smit requested that I return at the beginning of June to conduct a series of sermons and to discuss the building of a temporary church.

"It'll have to be during the third week of June," said my father. "That's the earliest he can make it. He can conduct a service on Tuesday evening, three on Wednesday and one on Thursday. That should be sufficient to cover the services associated with communion as well as any baptisms and weddings. He can organize a confirmation service later in the year."

My head was reeling as I thought of the sermon preparation that lay ahead. Mercifully, my father had seen to it that I'd have two full weeks for that purpose. But why not wait until spring to hold the communion services? It could even snow in June?

"Won't it be too cold to camp out?" I asked.

"It'll be freezing," said Smit. "But we'll make camp fires to keep cozy. We'll also be meeting at the farm *Skietmekaar* (shoot each other) where there's a farmhouse with a large parlor and a wide stoep that can be closed in. All you have to do is arrive here, and we'll take you there. The people will come. You'll see."

❧

9
Bloemfontein

Our seventy mile journey to Bloemfontein was a slow affair along muddy tracks. As I needed practice with the reins, I took over driving the cart on the second day. To keep me company, Manie joined me on the box seat in front, while our Basuto driver joined his companion on the wagon.

Although I had few expectations regarding the countryside, I did not expect the topography to be so uninteresting. In fact, there were few standout features. We seemed to be driving through one undulating plain after the other, with a few rocky hills strewn here and there to break the monotony. On the other hand, we were delighted by the sight of herds of wildebeest, quagga, blesbuck, springbuck, ostriches, as well as a profusion of hare. In the distance, we also caught sight of a leopard and a pack of African wolves.

"Those wolves are very dangerous," said Pretorius, holding his gun at the ready. "They hunt during the day, you see. And believe me, they surpass most of the other predators hands down when it comes to skill and tenacity. I've seen them attack and kill large buck quite easily. Fortunately, the lions tend to hunt at dusk, which means that we can pen our sheep before then. And that reminds me, young *Dominee*. Always see to it that you're back in Bloemfontein before the sun sets, because there are several prides in the vicinity of the village."

It was just after three when we approached Bloemfontein. The village—if you could call it that—was situated on a small plain surrounded by a range of low-lying hills. It looked rough and ready with about forty to fifty houses scattered here and there without plan or forethought.

Manie nudged me, then said, "Besides the natural features of the landscape, what do you notice first?"

"I suppose it's the fort on the hill."

"And what do you notice first when you drive into Graaff-Reinet, or most other towns in the Cape, for that matter?"

"The church steeple, of course."

"Exactly. Pa says it's high time we changed the emphasis of this village from a fort to a steeple that proclaims God's presence. And your coming is the first step to achieving that goal."

"Thank you, Manie. Now tell me quickly. In which direction should I go?"

"To get your bearings, look towards the fort. Just below it are the barracks for the soldiers. There are about three hundred men there now. About two hundred are Cape Riflemen, while the other hundred are Hottentots of the Cape Corps. Now glance across to that large, oblong building in the middle of the plain. It's the schoolhouse where you'll be holding church services until our church is built. It stands alongside the fountain surrounded by flowers—hence the name Bloemfontein. Close by are the houses for the officers. They've all been built on plots that have access to water. You'll be staying with the regimental doctor Sergeant Drury until the parsonage has been built. I'll direct you there."

"By the way," I said, "has the church council bought a plot for the parsonage yet?"

Manie responded with a broad grin. "No, they are waiting for you to help them choose one."

Although I was disappointed at hearing that, after further reflection, I decided that their slowness could work in the church's favor. Knowing my father, he'd be sure to negotiate the purchase of the best plot available.

Before long, we'd arrived at Drury's house.

"Pull up over there, just behind that cart," said Manie. "I think that's Karel Burger speaking to Dr. Drury. By the looks of that large wooden tray at his feet, he's been delivering some herbs. Dr. Drury is interested in bush medicine, you see, and so is *Mevrou* Burger. She was very sick there for a while, so they left their two sons to take care of the farm while they moved into the village to be close to Dr. Drury. They now provide the garrison with vegetables and herbs."

"That's interesting. So Dr. Drury prescribes medicine for Boer families as well, does he?"

"Oh yes. Even my mother swears by him. She refers to him as *Prickly Aloe* because he's so bristly and direct. But like the aloe in the veld, you'll only find what's good below the spiky surface."

I regarded Dr. Drury with heightened interest. He was clean-shaven and dressed in the dark blue uniform of the Cape Riflemen. He was tall and angular, with a long patrician nose that seemed to be accentuated by the thin streaks of gray hair that were brushed back to one side. I judged him to be in his late fifties.

As I considered the fact that he was only a sergeant, I realized that he must have joined the army as a non-commissioned officer late in life. Interesting, I thought. I wonder how he came to be stationed here?

By contrast, Karel Burger was a thickset man with broad shoulders and a full beard. He was wearing well-worn farm clothes spattered with mud and flecked with grass stains. He was gesticulating wildly, probably to make up for his deficiency in English. The two men were so engrossed in their discussion, that it was only after we had alighted from the cart and were approaching the house that they finally turned towards us.

We were still a little way off, when Burger pushed back his hat and inspected me with a mocking squint. "So what have we here," he said, as if to himself. "My goodness, if it isn't a girl."

I could feel the fire rise in my cheeks as my consternation took hold. Although I was used to parishioners in Graaff-Reinet commenting on my youthful looks, to be called a girl was in another league entirely. A girl! How could he call me that to my face?

I could tell from his smirk that he was enjoying my embarrassment. I decided not to give way to feelings of being denigrated. After all, I'd defused many a bully's intent in the schoolyard with bravado and humor. And I could do the same on this occasion.

Locking eyes with Burger, I chuckled loudly and extended my hand.

"So what have we here?" I asked. "Fancy that! If it isn't the self-appointed comedian of the Sovereignty."

I left Burger looking confused and floundering for words as I turned to greet Dr. Drury. It appeared that the latter was none the wiser as to what had passed between Burger and myself. This was not the case, however, with the rest of our group. I noticed that Pretorius and Manie made a point of ignoring Burger, while my father gave him short shrift. Their response had left him in no doubt that his jest had been in bad taste.

On noticing their reaction, poor Drury was left wondering what had occurred. I decided to leave it to my father to enlighten him. As for me, I realized anew what a handicap my youthful looks could prove in establishing my pastoral authority.

With formalities over, Drury got down to business. "There's plenty of storage room in the wagon-house around the back for furniture and boxes. There's also sufficient space in your bedroom for trunks and suitcases. So without further ado, let me show you to your room, Mr. Murray."

He led the way into the house, while the others returned to the wagon to unpack my belongings. The first thing I noticed was that the house was built according to the English style, with two bedrooms at the front and a large sitting and dining room in the middle. A door opened into the kitchen from the dining room, while my bedroom was accessed via a passage leading off the sitting room.

When we reached my room, Drury opened the door with a flourish.

"It's smaller than the front bedrooms," he said, "but there's still adequate space. As you can see, there's an extra bed for your father and enough floor room to place mattresses for guests."

"You're most kind in letting me use this room."

"Not at all, Mr. Murray. Mr. Stuart and I are looking forward to your company. He's the occupant of the other bedroom, by the way. He's also the local magistrate and—you'll be pleased to know—a God-fearing man and a good Scott."

I nodded to be courteous, although my apprehension had just risen on spying a large table covered with little bottles.

Following my gaze, Drury said, "I'm afraid I keep my medicine bottles in here. So from time to time I might be called upon to invade your privacy. I hope you don't mind?"

"How could I, seeing I'm the one who's the real intruder. I'm sure you'll be relieved when the parsonage has been built."

"Don't fret yourself on that score. Out here you need to take things as they come. I hope you'll regard this home as a refuge from the fray."

"You sound as if you're speaking from experience, sir."

"Without doubt. And another thing . . . you'll find that you'll be tested in ways you least expect. But with each test will come experience, and with each failure, a lesson learnt. May you rise to the challenge, Mr. Murray. And may the Lord grant you the ability to do so."

As I followed him to the wagon to help with the unpacking, I pondered upon his words. Unlike the persuasive ones spoken by Drs. Robertson and Faure, Drury's words struck me as a more accurate depiction of what I would be facing. Nevertheless, when it came to his home being a refuge from the fray, only time would tell. I was sure he wasn't called *Prickly Aloe* for nothing.

After Pretorius and Manie had left for their farm in the wagon, we joined Dr. Drury in the sitting room.

"What a pleasure it is to be able to converse with you both. More times than I can care to mention, I've simply longed for civilized conversation. Mr. Stuart feels the same way, but unfortunately won't be able to join us because he's on his rounds up country."

We had barely sat down when Drury's servant arrived with tea and biscuits. It struck me then that I should find out how matters worked in relation to meals in that household.

"Does your servant do most of the cooking?" I asked.

"Goodness, no. With the exception of breakfast, we order our meals in from one of the officer's wives who used to be a cook at a country estate in England. Her meals are excellent, by the way, and the charge inexpensive—only £1 per month. But this evening I insist on you being my guests in exchange for some scintillating conversation. I have a host of topics in mind to explore."

"In that case," my father said, "I'd better pose my question first."

Drury looked up from pouring our tea. "I think I know what you're about to ask. So fire away."

"I heard from Dr. Philip Faure that you used to be a well-known doctor in Cape Town. So why join the army and be stationed in the Sovereignty?"

"I came at the behest of Sir Harry Smith. After practicing medicine in Cape Town for a few years, I decided to embark on an inland tour to further my knowledge of herbal medicine. When Sir Harry heard of it, he persuaded me to become regimental doctor to the garrison out here. That way, I could render medical services to the men, while at the same time pursuing my research into bush medicine."

"Most interesting. And do you think you've achieved your aim?"

Drury sat back in his chair, cup in hand. "Yes, I'd say so. At any rate, I feel I've accomplished most of what I set out to do. I'll therefore be returning to England sooner rather than later."

"A happy prospect for you, I'm sure."

There was a lull in the conversation while we sipped our tea and nibbled our biscuits. When Drury felt the time was right, he leant forward to show his earnestness.

"There's been a question niggling me for some time now. And seeing we do not have additional company, I regard it as an opportune moment to pose it. Can you explain, Mr. Murray, why large companies of Boers decided to pack up their belongings, sell their farms, and leave the Cape Colony for the lands beyond the Orange and Vaal Rivers? From what I've been told, some were even members of your own congregation in Graaff-Reinet."

My father sighed and closed his eyes while weighing up where to begin.

"There's a multitude of reasons. But they can be boiled down to the following issues: Many suffered terrible losses during the frontier wars. What made it worse was that the various governors formulated contradictory policies on the frontier. They also abolished the Boers' traditional administration system, thus leaving them without any form of representation. It is little wonder they felt ostracized and politically sidelined. But what hurt most was the high-handed way in which they were treated by the Colonial Government. The latter let it be known that they regarded them as inferior to the British."

"Hmm, we British can certainly be an arrogant lot when it suits us. And of course, the need of the Boer to retain his self-respect can be a powerful motivational force. I'm beginning to understand a few things now. Please continue."

"Well, another reason for their discontent was the acute lack of labor that they blamed on Ordinance 50. According to this ordinance, Hottentot farmhands were now able to roam at will, taking the cattle they'd earned as wages with them. As you can imagine, the lack of vagrancy laws inevitably led to constant cattle thieving and insecurity on the frontier. In the meantime, their opposition to Ordinance 50 led to inevitable run-ins with the missionaries and a bad press overseas—not all true, I might add. There were several other issues as well, but the prime one, as I see it, was the dire shortage of farm land for their sons."

"I see. But do any of these reasons have a direct bearing on the present situation in the Sovereignty? That's what I want to know."

"Ah, Mr. Drury. Now you're talking."

My father placed his cup on the rough-hewn table at his side, crossed his legs, and made himself comfortable before addressing this question.

"There's one vital issue that the Sovereignty needs to deal with, and that's the growing shortage of land. But the real issue behind this is lack of education."

"I don't follow, Mr. Murray. Of course education is important, but how do you make the leap from the shortage of land to the lack of education?"

"Well, take the average Boer family in the Sovereignty, for instance. They have large families averaging about twelve children, half of whom are sons. With no educational prospects, there are no other outlets for them except farming. So when there's no more land to go around, the Boer will want to expand into African territory. And you know what that means. And need I say, the same situation holds for the African tribes."

"Say no more, Mr. Murray. This is happening right now in the Sovereignty. Major Warden has drawn up maps with clear boundary lines, but the Africans complain that they don't want a line to hem them in. There are therefore constant squabbles between the various tribes as well as between them and the farmers—be they Boer or Brit."

"What a sad state of affairs, Dr. Drury. To my mind, it's no good trying to maintain peace over land issues if nothing is being done to address the underlying cause of the problem. The Colonial Government needs to develop a basic education policy that will enable more of its male citizens to embark on careers other than farming. And as a first step, it needs to appoint

Dutch teachers for the four church places in the Sovereignty. It is my firm conviction that the appointment of these teachers together with additional pastors, will go a long way to averting further wars down the track."

"Well said, Mr. Murray. And on that note it gives me great pleasure to invite you and young Mr. Murray to proceed to the table. I believe our dinner has arrived."

The conversation that evening soon turned to other topics, particularly my time in Scotland and Utrecht. Nevertheless, over the next few days my father and Drury would return time and again to discussing the need for pastors and teachers for the Sovereignty.

From my youthful perspective, they were like two old men chasing the wind. If the Dutch Reformed Church wasn't able to attract orthodox teachers for their schools in the Cape, how was the embryo church in the Sovereignty supposed to do so. And if there were countless vacant positions for pastors in the Cape, what was the likelihood of young candidates, including my friends, wanting to join me here. And was Drury really interested in these topics, or only trying to humor my father?

Oh me of little faith!

10

Four Inductions to Go

May 1849

As expected, my induction in Bloemfontein was poorly attended due to the light sprinkling of snow that had fallen the day before. We only stayed another day to discuss the purchase of a plot for the parsonage, before setting out for Winburg on Tuesday, a distance of four stages—each taking three hours, and covering between fifteen to eighteen miles per stage. Because of the lion problem in the Sovereignty, we were forced to leave after sunrise and pull in at a farmhouse well before sunset.

As Manie had returned home with his father after the induction service, I became the main driver of the Cape cart, with my father taking over now and again to give me a rest. Due to it being my twenty-first birthday on Wednesday, 9 May, I found the journey particularly forlorn without John and the rest of the family present to celebrate this milestone with me. In fact, my thoughts were constantly focused on them—wondering what they were saying about me while they packed John's boxes for his departure to Burghersdorp.

My thoughts then invariably turned to Willie who was on the high seas. I pictured him in the saloon pouring over a book of Latin exercises as the ship swayed back and forth. No doubt he was thinking of me as well.

All I could do was console myself with the thought that I'd be meeting up with Charles that evening in Winburg. Over the previous two weeks, he'd been teaching the catechism to the young people of that district on the Theron family farm. As I had anticipated, my father had only agreed to let Charles come for two weeks. The plan was that he would be at the village to greet us when we arrived. But when we got there, neither he nor the Theron family were there to welcome us. Our disappointment deepened when we heard that the invitations to my induction ceremony hadn't been sent out. All we could look forward to were two days of twiddling our thumbs.

As we settled in for the night at a farmhouse close to the village, my father shared the thought that we should pay a quick visit to the French missionaries Mr. Zoelen at Merumetzu, and Messrs Daumas and Cochet at Mekautling.

"We'll ride out there on horseback," he said, "and be back by Friday evening."

"How long will we be in the saddle?" I asked.

"All told, about fourteen hours for the round trip."

"Pa!"

"Andrew, they are deprived of Christian company and the little luxuries of life that we take for granted. Paying them a visit is the least we can do for them."

Despite the distance we had to cover, our visit proved to be a blessed time of fellowship and sharing. It also gave me pause for thought after experiencing their privations first hand. On our way back to Winburg, I couldn't help but repeat Psalm 16:6 over and over again: "*The lines are fallen unto me in pleasant places; yea, I have a godly heritage.*"

Because of the late distribution of the invitations, only the elders and deacons together with those presenting themselves for confirmation attended my induction. Fortunately, the return journey to Bloemfontein proved to be a happier experience with Charles present to take over the bulk of the driving.

In Bloemfontein, Manie joined us with the view to catching up with Charles and keeping me company on the return journey from Burghersdorp. On the way there, however, I still had to undergo a fourth induction at Smithfield. As with the others, this also turned out to be a non-event with only a handfull of families in attendance.

By contrast, John's induction in Burghersdorp proved to be a much anticipated event for the locals. The church was packed three days running. My father introduced John to his congregation on Saturday morning, with John following this up by preaching his inaugural sermon that afternoon. On Sunday morning, I administered communion, while in the evening *Dominee* Pears of Somerset East conducted a service for the English community. While this was happening, my father was conducting a service for the Coloreds in a separate building. Then, on Monday morning, the closing sermon was delivered by *Dominee* Taylor of Cradock.

With formalities over, I was able to spend a relaxing afternoon with John, Maria and my parents before departing for Bloemfontein on Tuesday morning.

As I hugged John goodbye, I was pleased to notice that he was back to being the brother of old I'd known in Scotland and Utrecht.

"I'm truly sorry I couldn't be present at one or more of your inductions, Andrew. Had they taken place a week or so after mine, I would have been there like a shot."

"Don't worry about it," I said.

"Nevertheless, I promise I'll make up for it by joining you in Bloemfontein in August to help you administer communion. If there's a large turnout, you'll need help, especially if the service takes place in the open air. It'll be a special time of sharing for both of us."

I smiled and patted him on the arm to acknowledge his new-found concern.

Not wanting to prolong our parting, I turned to kiss my mother and Maria goodbye. How different this leave-taking was to the last one. On that occasion, I was infused with excitement. Now I was facing the sobering reality of the Sovereignty.

II

Back in Lion Country

The fact that we'd stayed over in Burghersdorp on the Monday, put me in a quandary about reaching Bloemfontein by Thursday afternoon as planned. I'd originally aimed to cover two-and-a-half stages per day, thus completing the ten stage journey in four days. But I'd given in to the pleas of my mother to stay until Tuesday, and now I'd have to pay the price by arriving a day late in Bloemfontein.

Although my sermon for Sunday was prepared, I needed time to familiarize myself with the main points, time to spend in prayer, as well as time to recover from the journey.

As we set off, I turned to Manie who was driving the cart. "Do you think we'll be able to cover three stages per day instead of two-and-a-half?"

"Possibly, if we forego breakfast and leave at six. That's the only way we can make up time. We can't reduce the breaks between stages because the horses need to rest as well as feed. It's also essential that we turn off to the nearest farmhouse before four-thirty. After that the lions become active."

"I suppose there's no possibility of us turning off at five, is there?"

"None at all, *Dominee*. I promised my father we'd be turning off before four-thirty. "He warned me that you might want to continue until dusk. But it's far too dangerous."

"So when do you think we'll arrive in Bloemfontein?"

"About twelve on Friday. I'm sorry it won't be sooner, but that's the way it is."

As Manie was holding to his resolve, all I could do was accept his decision. After all, he knew the dangers of the veld far better than I did.

It was the third day of our journey, and my turn to drive the cart. At about four in the afternoon, we came across the first patches of snow on the track.

"This is going to slow us down," I said, "especially if the snow gets any deeper."

Manie looked anxious. He had his gun at the ready and was combing the veld for any sign of lions. "Hopefully we'll be nearing the turnoff soon. I must say, I don't like this section of the veld because there are far too many bushes near the track. That means we could easily be ambushed. So keep your hand on the whip."

We travelled in silence for several minutes. I kept my eyes glued to the track while Manie continued to scour the veld.

"Manie," I said, my voice quivering, "what are those objects up ahead? They're half covered with snow, so I can't make them out."

I slowed the cart, allowing Manie to stand up to get a better view. "Oe! I don't believe it," he said. "They're lion carcasses. I'm sure of it. Stop the cart so we can take a closer look. See . . . there are about four or five around here and a few more up ahead. And look over there. That's the carcass of old *vuilbaard* himself."

I looked in the direction to which Manie was pointing, and

could just make out the tangled mane of a male lion he'd referred to by the Dutch nickname: dirty beard.

"I wonder why they didn't cut off his head as a trophy?"

"Too difficult to carry if they were on horseback. There must have been several men to put down this number of lions—probably a small platoon of soldiers. It looks as if they were ambushed by this pride. Thank the Lord it wasn't us."

My heart was racing as I counted the carcasses. "There are at least eight or nine. What chance would we have stood?"

"None," said Manie.

He sat down, his breathing heavy. We exchanged knowing looks, then bowed our heads and offered up prayers of thanks.

We were barely on our way again, when a farmhouse in the distance came into view.

"How far do you think we are from Bloemfontein?" I asked.

"About a stage. Earlier on I thought it was more, but this is Deacon Griesel's farm, and he's definitely only a short stage from the village."

I was about to turn off onto the track leading to the farmhouse, when I thought better of it, and stopped the cart.

"Listen Manie, given that lions are territorial, what is the likelihood of encountering another pride between here and the village?"

"Nil, I should imagine."

"So there's no reason why we can't continue our journey. After all, there should be enough light, what with the full moon and the dusting of snow on the track."

Manie thought for a moment, then smiled. "*Ach*, why not, *Dominee*. But we'll take a break first. I'm dying for cup of tea."

Because it was slow going, we arrived in Bloemfontein at about twenty to eight that evening. At the sound of the cart being outspanned behind the house, Dr. Drury appeared with lamp in hand to greet us—or rather scold us.

"What on earth were you thinking—travelling in the dark? It's absolute folly, Mr. Murray. A hunting party of officers shot nine lions earlier this week along that track. Surely young Mr. Pretorius here warned you against travelling after four?"

"I assure you he tried—"

"Well he should have stuck to his guns. Now come inside out of the cold both of you and warm up beside the fire. There's still plenty of soup left over from dinner."

Manie, who had only a smattering of English, looked confused. "But I did have my gun at the ready," he whispered.

"It's an English saying. I'll explain later. What he means is that you shouldn't have given in to my request."

Manie flashed a wicked grin. "Don't worry, *Dominee*, I'll remember next time."

12

My Ministry Begins

June 1849

When I eventually surfaced the next morning, I found Mr. Stuart in the dining room. He was marking up two large blackboards that stood on easels alongside each other. As soon as he saw me, he placed the chalk on the easel ledge, dusted his hands, then extended a hand to greet me.

"A hearty good morning to you, Mr. Murray. I must apologize for not welcoming you yesterday evening, but I'd already retired for the night. Besides, I tend to avoid listening to Dr. Drury's little outbursts. But contrary to what you might think, Drury has your best interests at heart. He's with Major Warden at the moment."

As we shook hands, I immediately warmed to him. Although a magistrate, he seemed an affable fellow. His auburn hair, Scottish burr, and old tweeds reminded me of the typical lecturer at Aberdeen University. The only difference, perhaps, was his tall build and sunburnt features that signified an outdoor man. I judged him to be in his early fifties.

He pointed in the direction of the blackboards. "It's 1 June, you see, and time to mark up our schedules for the next two months. In my case, I'm hoping it'll be sweet blow all. Thankfully, it's too cold for people to get into trouble. You'll find June and July the best months for catching up on reading and work."

"I've already gathered that," I said. "I hope to spend July stocking up on sermons for the quarterly communion services that begin in August."

"Wise man. Just because we're out here in the bundoo doesn't mean that nothing happens. I vouch that come Spring you'll find it hectic."

"Hectic, Mr. Stuart?"

"Ah! Do I detect a healthy dose of skepticism? Just you wait and see. Now tell me young sir, when do you think you'll be available for a church meeting? On second thoughts, do you mind if I suggest a date? The reason is that it has to coincide with the availability of Major Warden and his clerk Mr. Allison."

"Please do, Mr. Stuart."

"What about Friday, 15 June? That gives you two full weeks to settle in."

He looked my way, waited for me to affirm the date, then recorded it in the square.

"And now, Mr. Murray, I'll leave you to enjoy your breakfast. Perhaps we'll be able to ride out together next week once you've purchased a horse. As an inveterate lover of nature, I try to ride out every day."

"That's very kind of you, sir."

"Not at all. It'll be a delight to have a companion. And before I forget, please convey my greetings to young Mr. Pretorius. I take it he's still asleep?"

"Afraid so."

"And another thing. The post between Smithfield and Burghersdorp will cease for a while because of skirmishes between the chiefs Moshesh and Sekonyela. So if you wish to send a letter to your brother, you'll have to avail yourself of other means. Fortunately, the Basuto only fight at night, so we weren't unduly concerned about your safety when passing that way. The danger of being killed by lions was another matter entirely."

He lowered his voice and adopted a conspiratorial tone. "A quick word of advice, Mr. Murray. The Lord in his mercy closed the mouths of those lions on your behalf. He now expects you to be sensible enough to stay out of harm's way. Promise me you'll always be back in Bloemfontein before sunset. As I've given the order that the post rider should not leave from Bloemfontein after four, I regard it as necessary for us to adhere to that order as well."

"I have every intention of doing just that, Mr. Stuart. Coming across those carcasses was a sobering experience."

"I had to ask, you see, because I was your age once. And sometimes I think I still am."

He threw back his head and laughed heartily. "You should see me ride into a heard of migrating antelope and keep pace with them on my trusty charger. Highly invigorating. You should try it sometime. Unlike a sortie with lions, this caper poses an acceptable risk[6]."

"Does Dr. Drury know?"

"Of course not. I'd never hear the end of it."

Sunday morning dawned bright and clear. Although I'd already preached numerous sermons by now, I realized that this one would be in a category of its own. It would be my first as an inducted minister of my own congregation.

On the way to the schoolroom, where the services were to be held, I passed by the fountain after which Bloemfontein was named. I noticed that it was covered by a thin layer of ice. Nevertheless, I knew that by mid-morning the ice would be gone and the fountain would be flowing freely. As I reflected upon this fact, I realized what an appropriate metaphor it was for the Christian life.

All God asks of us is that we should walk close to Him so that He can melt our hearts with His love. The water of life can then flow from our hearts to those around us.

With this thought in mind, I entered the schoolroom. After placing my Bible upon the makeshift lectern that would be my pulpit, I began to pray. I asked God to help me experience a soul-knowledge of the precious truths I was about to proclaim, and to enable my hearers to grasp the amazing wonder of Christ's love.

All too soon I was looking out on the faces of a hundred-or-so souls. But try as I might, I could not hold their attention. Some of the older children had left the building during the sermon, and had spent their time peering through the windows and waving to their parents. Mothers were coming and going with younger children, babies were crying, while some adults were even talking openly. The majority, I feared, hadn't heard a word of my sermon. When I pronounced the amen, everyone seemed relieved, including myself.

When I finally closed the door of the schoolroom behind me, I was still reeling from the shock of not being able to hold my congregation's attention. I was walking over to the outspan place where they'd assembled to enjoy a bite of lunch, when I passed the fountain once more. It immediately became clear what had gone wrong. I hadn't spent enough time drinking at the fountainhead of God's love. My strenuous preaching had therefore more to do with self-effort than being in the demonstration of the Holy Spirit's power.

It was with a heavy heart that I joined the Pretorius family beside their wagon. I hardly spoke a word as I shared their lunch. They had already started to pack up, when I caught sight of Karel Burger approaching us with a horse in tow.

"Accept his offer," whispered Pretorius. "I've examined the horse, and it's a good one. I think he wants to make amends for his rudeness."

My bruised spirit immediately lifted. I couldn't have wished for anything better at that moment than owning my own horse.

Burger was all smiles as he approached. "*Dominee*, look what I've got for you. He's going for £10."

I got up off my camp stool and made a show of looking him over.

"Are you sure you can part with him?" I asked.

"With a heavy heart, I fear. You see, he's my commando horse. But as I'm too old to be called up, I reasoned that you're the one in the Sovereignty who'll be able to benefit from him most. He's been grazing on my son's farm for the last nine months. But I'd prefer it if someone were able to ride him regularly."

He waited for me to complete my inspection, then said, "I'll throw in an old saddle for the price as well."

"It's a deal," I said. "I'll test him out tomorrow morning first thing."

Before we had even completed our transaction, several church members had started to crowd around to admire my new steed and congratulate me on my purchase. I noticed how Burger swelled with pride as a few onlookers went over to shake his hand and commend him for offering to sell the horse at a price well below its true worth.

"*Ach* man," I heard him say. "Someone had to present *Dominee* with a welcome gift."

A few days later, I was forced to go with cap in hand to Burger. The horse I'd bought from him had run away, and I needed his help to find it.

We were sitting at his kitchen table drinking coffee when I broke the news. *Mevrou* Burger was sitting opposite me, with Burger at the head of the table.

"I thought I'd better come and tell you, *Meneer Burger*, so that you can keep an eye out for him. The thing is, I didn't ride him this morning because it was raining, so I left him on the church plot, thinking that he'd be satisfied grazing there."

The expression with which he regarded me was one of disbelief mixed with amusement. He sighed briefly, then muttered something unintelligible under his breath before subjecting me to a reprimand that only stated the obvious.

"*Dominee* has to remember that horses are scarce in these parts and are therefore highly prized. It's essential that they are adequately looked after. All we can hope for now is that he ran home before the lions got him."

"Karel," said *Mevrou* Burger in a firm tone, "you have to remember that *Dominee* has spent most of his youth in Scotland and Holland studying books, not horses. He needs guidance about our way of doing things, just as we need guidance in interpreting Scripture."

I smiled at *Mevrou* Burger to acknowledge her empathy for my loss. She was a plump woman with kind eyes set in an attractive face that was enhanced by her snow-white hair. It was partially covered by a blue cap that hung like a doily over the back part of her head. She sat erect, her gnarled fingers intertwined and resting on the table. Her head was turned towards Burger, her eyes locked with his.

Burger was the first to drop his gaze. He turned to me and said, "Sarie is right. When the rain stops, we'll pay a visit to my son. Don't worry, we'll find him."

"Please don't put yourself out," I said. "I'm simply asking everyone I come across to keep an eye out for him."

"*Ach Dominee*, we'll do it gladly," *Mevrou* Burger said. "It's a good excuse to see what's happening on the farm. And along the way, we can also pay a visit to some of the neighbors."

She gave Burger a look that indicated she would brook no opposition. I was fast beginning to appreciate the strong character and determination of the average Boer *vrou*. At the same time, I dreaded to think what Burger would say behind my back.

Drury's response was little better. On entering the house, I caught sight of him writing up his notes at the dining room table. On hearing the news of my missing horse, he took off his wire spectacles with their long arms and teardrop ends, and laid them carefully on the table.

"Please sit down, Mr. Murray. I don't want to have to crook my neck. This happens to be an excellent opportunity to broach a few subjects with you."

"I dearly hope I haven't overlooked any matters that I should have seen to, Dr. Drury?"

"This is indeed the case, I'm afraid. It seems to have escaped your notice that both Mr. Stuart and I have designated servants to look after our horses. These servants fetch water from the well and heat it for ablution purposes. Their other tasks include running errands and chopping wood. So unless you don't mind losing numerous horses or fetching water from the well yourself, you need to hire a servant."

"Believe me, Dr. Drury. I had no idea I was supposed do that. In any case, I thought servants were in short supply here in the Sovereignty."

"We'll come to that in a moment. But tell me first. Doesn't your father employ a servant to take care of his horses?"

"Of course, but—"

"In that case, why hasn't it dawned on you that you might require one too? You need to learn to be more perceptive, Mr. Murray."

"Obviously so, Dr. Drury. But as I've only been back in Africa for six months and in Bloemfontein for six days, I'd appreciate the same guidance as you received when you first arrived here."

An uncomfortable silence followed during which Drury fiddled with the arms of his spectacles and sized me up anew. I knew I'd been rather brusque, so decided to repeat my request in a more mannerly fashion.

"I realize, to my regret, Dr. Drury, that I still have much to learn. To tell you the truth, I feel quite unequal to the task. So any advice would be much appreciated."

"I dare say it would, young fellow. But you need to understand that because you were born in the Colony and speak the lingo, there's the general perception that you know how things work around here. So please accept my apology for taking that for granted."

I nodded, feeling relieved that we were at last making headway. Nevertheless, I harbored no misconception regarding Drury's penchant for dishing out advice. He was sure to voice it at every perceived misdemeanor, and would probably also express it in relation to other matters that didn't concern him.

No sooner had this thought entered my mind, when he said, "Have you told Burger about this conundrum?"

"I felt I had to, Dr. Drury, because he's one of the few people who's able to identify the horse."

"Hmm, that's unfortunate. You see it's people like Burger who'll be quick to point out your immaturity and lack of judgment. And as soon as the Boer leaders get to hear of it, they are sure to take advantage of you, or worse still, write you off as ineffectual."

While Drury's insights were probably right, all they served to achieve was a dent to my self-esteem. Nevertheless, I knew it was to my advantage to know what he was thinking, because his views would undoubtedly mirror those of Major Warden's.

After being subjected to a further dose of advice about tipping his servant Ezra, we finally came full circle to the question of acquiring a servant for my horse.

"But are you sure I'll be able to hire such a servant, Dr. Drury? I've heard they're almost impossible to come by."

"For farmers, certainly. But as your status is equivalent to that of a paramount chief with oversight of 12,000 Boers in the Sovereignty, there shouldn't be any problem in obtaining a Rolong boy, especially if there's only one horse to look after."

I folded my arms, looked him squarely in the eye, then said with tongue in cheek: "A paramount chief, you say. But doesn't that cancel out your observations regarding my immaturity and lack of judgment?"

He returned my gaze with a skew smile. "Not at all, Mr. Murray. Although you'll be considered a paramount chief by the tribal chiefs in these parts, you still have to earn your stripes. Fortunately for you, the potential is there, otherwise I wouldn't be spending time offering advice. It's now a case of rising to the challenge."

"Or staying the course until I've learnt to jump the hurdles."

"Quite. So with your permission, I'll ask Major Warden to hire a servant on your behalf when he visits Winburg next week. I've heard that some of the chiefs are anxious for their sons to learn Dutch and European ways."

I was about to go, and had already risen from my seat, when Drury stopped me in my tracks. "I've been meaning to ask you, Mr. Murray. How did your sermon go last Sunday?"

I sat down again and looked him once more in the eye. What was the use of prevaricating, I thought. I'd tell it how it was. "I couldn't hold their attention, Dr. Drury."

"Well, my dear fellow, far be it from me to impose my views on how you should conduct church with your Dutch congregation, but a simple answer to this dilemma is to shorten and simplify your sermons. The Holy Spirit is able to achieve the same result in one hour as in two, you know."

"But my sermons are already short and simple."

"That may be so with the people of Graaff-Reinet in mind—certainly not the Sovereignty. Perhaps you should take a leaf out of Dr. Robertson's book. During the English service here, he announced a hymn just prior to the sermon and then again in the middle of the sermon."

"In the middle of the sermon?"

"Yes. And what a relief it was too. I was sitting on one of those damnable veld stools, and my legs had stiffened to such an extent that it was painful to rise, so a hymn in the middle was a godsend. That reminds me . . ."

Now what? Surely not more advice.

"I've just had a thought about the English service. I think it best to start as we mean to continue. If we wish to commence a Sunday School prior to the service, then it needs to start at a quarter past one sharp, so that the service can begin at half-past two, and end at four."

"Isn't that's rather short, Dr. Drury?"

"Not at all. Most of the English around here have never darkened the door of a church. So a service spanning one-and-a-half hours is more than adequate. Besides, Elder Pretorius, is keen to start an evening service for the Dutch in summer. He has suggested that it begin at half-past four and end just before six. This will enable farmers living close to the village to return home before sunset."

"So let me get this straight. You would like the bell rung just before half-past two for the English service next Sunday?"

"Just so, Mr. Murray. And in keeping with Elder Pretorius's suggestion, perhaps half-past four would be an optimum time to commence a Dutch service for the Coloreds on Saturdays— if that meets with your approval? It would be a crying shame to leave the Cape Corps out."

"Of course," were the only words I could muster.

At long last Drury had nothing more to say.

"Anything else, Dr. Drury?"

"Not for the moment, Mr. Murray. It's best to leave the rest for our official meeting on Friday-week."

I rose to go, my head in a whirl. The loss of my horse had become a secondary matter. I had sermons to prepare.

13
Learning the Ropes

The Dutch service on the following Sunday forced me to face my worst fears. Although the day dawned bright and sunny, the number of attendees had dropped from a hundred the previous week to only seventy. Neither did Burger put in an appearance. So I had no idea whether he had found my horse or not.

Then, to my chagrin, I found Elders Willem Pretorius and Jacobus van Zyl waiting outside the schoolroom after the service to discuss what should be done.

"The people need to get to know you personally, *Dominee*," said Pretorius. "It would be to your advantage if the deacons accompanied you on a visitation tour both to the north and south of here. Let's go back inside to discuss details."

Their suggestions made sense, but by the end of our discussions, a whole week in June had been allocated for a visitation tour between Bloemfontein and Winburg, and twelve days in July for a tour between Bloemfontein and Smithfield. Mr. Stuart's warning of my schedule filling quickly was fast becoming a reality.

On a brighter note, the English service had gone well—that is from a human point of view. Although Major Warden was away with the Cape Corps and a division of the Cape Riflemen, the turnout was excellent and numbered about seventy. I also received many-a-good comment that was supported by the discussions I overheard outside the schoolroom. I even received a pat on the back from Dr. Drury, who commended me for implementing his suggestions. But how was I to hold the attention of my Dutch congregation? That was the question uppermost in my mind.

My spirits lifted when Major Warden arrived back in Bloemfontein on Wednesday with a servant from the Rolong tribe. Shortly afterwards, Karel Burger came by with my horse. I'd also been working hard on my sermons during the week, and had spent much time in prayer. So by the time I walked into the dining room for the church meeting on Friday evening, all was right with the world.

Major Warden greeted me warmly, as did Mr. Allison, his clerk. Both looked rather dapper in their dark blue uniforms with their scarlet collars and cuffs and white, sash-like belts that stretched diagonally across their chests. Like Dr. Drury, they were wearing shell jackets with a cascade of gilt studs down the front. I couldn't help wondering how long it took them to fasten the hidden hooks and eyes each morning.

I noticed that Major Warden's uniform was distinguished from the others by the extra gold trim on his shoulder straps. They were adorned with a series of gold loops dangling across his upper arms. When on horseback, or walking outside, his peak cap, with a feather in the front, made him appear far taller than he was. But now that the cap lay on the sideboard, I realized that he was not only balding, but also short and stocky. Nevertheless, his aquiline nose and warm brown eyes afforded him an air of distinction.

Mr. Allison, by contrast, was tall and blond with freckles sparsely strewn across his upper cheeks. Although he looked to be in his mid-twenties, it was obvious, by the respect accorded him, that he was going places.

After the preliminary chit chat, we took our seats around the table. Mr. Stuart sat at the head accompanied by his trusty gavel. I sat next to Dr. Drury, with Major Warden sitting opposite me, and Mr. Allison opposite Dr. Drury.

"Before we begin," said Warden, "I think it necessary to report on my meeting with Moshesh."

"Please go ahead," Stuart said. "No doubt it affects us all. But perhaps you should fill Mr. Murray in first."

He faced me across the table and began to explain. "I dare say you've heard the name Moshesh bandied about before now, Mr. Murray. Well, he's the paramount chief of the Basuto, and has his headquarters at Thaba Bosiu in the Caledon Valley. Unfortunately, he won't agree to the boundary lines I've been trying to establish between him and Sekonyela, the chief of the Tlokwa tribe. Nor will he agree to the boundary separating the Basuto lands from that of the Dutch near Smithfield."

"Yes, I heard as much from Elder van Zyl on Sunday. I was due to conduct the quarterly communion services in Smithfield during August, but now they've requested that I go on a twelve-day visitation tour to that region in July."

"That's asking far too much of you at this stage." Drury said. "You've only been here two weeks. Why can't they wait until the Spring? Don't they realize that you need this time to prepare your sermons?"

"The tour is a good idea in principle," said Warden.

"That may be so," Stuart said. "But I doubt whether Mr. Murray knows what he's letting himself in for. I can't imagine having to sleep on uneven, clay floors in those pioneer homes. I hope you have a feather bedroll, or the like, Mr. Murray?"

"That he has," Drury said, with an air of satisfaction. "I spied two while his father was here."

I kept my eyes lowered and remained silent.

"Don't tell me you left yours in Burghersdorp?" said Drury.

"I nodded, feeling embarrassed that I had to own up to something as basic as forgetting my bedroll. It had been humiliating enough during my return trip from Burghersdorp. My forgetfulness had resulted in my hosts having to rearrange their families' sleeping arrangements on both nights during the journey. Manie, on the other hand, who'd had his bedroll at the ready, had been able to sleep on the floor in the parlor, as any self-respecting young male would have done.

When I looked up, I found Warden and Allison both wearing broad grins at my expense.

"I detect you're still dwelling in the heavenlies, Mr. Murray, Warden said. "Let me tell you, sir. There's nothing like forgetting your bedroll to bring you down to earth."

"You may use one of my mine," said Drury. "You'll have enough on your plate without having to deal with inadequate sleeping arrangements and lack of privacy. Have mercy on the poor fellow, Major Warden."

I could hear Mr. Stuart snigger as he tapped his gavel on the table. "I think those are sufficient observations from us. Please continue with your report, Major Warden."

"Now, where was I?"

Allison cleared his throat and said, "Before you proceed, Major Warden, I've just remembered something that might be of help to Mr. Murray." Looking directly at me, he said, "Mr. Adolph Coqui will be travelling to Graaff-Reinet in mid-July to pick up goods for his store in Harrismith. I'm sure he'll be open to collecting your bedroll if you grease his palm. I'll introduce you to him, if you like. He'll be in Bloemfontein to attend the first session of the Legislative Council in July. Although he's a Jew, he's well thought of by the Boers—even those across the Vaal. He's originally from Belgium, you see, and speaks Dutch fluently."

"That's excellent news, Mr. Allison. I'd be most obliged if you could introduce me. When in July does this council meet?"

"It starts on Tuesday the third, and continues for a week. You'll be expected to open it, by the way."

Noting my astonishment, Major Warden said, "I'm surprised your elders didn't inform you. During the church building committee meeting last month, Elder Van Zyl announced that Deacons Andries Erwee and Johan Griesel had been elected as representatives of their farming communities."

I leant back in my chair and chuckled. All was becoming clear.

"I think Mr. Murray has just experienced an epiphany," said Stuart. "But I'm sure we can wait until supper to hear about it. So please continue Major Warden."

"I'm afraid this question of boundaries might lead to war between Moshesh and us. According to the Wesleyan missionary Mr. Cameron, who's working amongst the Rolong people at Thaba Nchu, Moshesh has already amassed 15 000 fighting men and a further 1000 on horseback with the view to attacking Sekonyela. Cameron has also overheard rumors that an *impi* of Zulus is marching to join him. If this war eventuates, we'll be drawn into it as well. Unfortunately, I only had 130 men with me when I confronted Moshesh regarding this matter. I'm sure he's laughing behind my back—or so Cameron thinks."

"Oh, I wouldn't say that," Stuart said. "He's a wily old fox, and knows that you represent a great power."

"That may be so, Mr. Stuart, but it all depends upon the troops forthcoming from that power. And at the end of the day, that is what counts. All we can do now is pray that his dissatisfaction with my boundary line won't precipitate a war."

On that note, we bowed our heads in prayer. I'd heard much about the frontier wars in the Cape from my father while in Scotland and Utrecht. But they'd been of no consequence to my life then. Now the threat was in my own backyard—a different proposition altogether.

With Warden's report over, our church meeting got off to a good start. First on the agenda was the establishment of a Sunday School. It was decided that Mr. Stuart would take the English Bible Class and Dr. Drury the English children who couldn't read.

"Now about the Bushmen at Kafferfontein," Stuart said. "I rode over there today with Mr. Murray and invited them to our Sabbath School. Mr. Murray has agreed to teach them."

"Let's be practical here, Mr. Stuart," said Drury. "I've visited them on several occasions with *Meneer* Burger, and only one or two have a smattering of Dutch. The rest aren't able to understand a word. How on earth do you suppose Mr. Murray will be able to teach them?"

"The Lord is able to save to the uttermost, Dr. Drury. So why should we then despair?"

"Of course He's able, Mr. Stuart. But unless the Lord gives the gift of the Bushman tongue with the clicks to Mr. Murray, I don't see what headway he'll be able to make in proclaiming the Gospel to them. He's already spreading himself too thin. And now you're saddling him with a task—"

Stuart tapped the gavel on the table, interrupting Drury in

mid-sentence. "Your opinion on this matter can wait until later, Dr. Drury. Let's move on to the next item." He looked my way and in a business-like tone asked, "Could you tell us what your schedule will be over the next three months, Mr. Murray? We're particularly interested in recording the Sundays you won't be in Bloemfontein."

My large calendar for the year 1849 lay under my diary on the table. I whipped it out and examined the dates I'd circled.

"This coming Monday, which is 18 June, I'll be leaving for Fauresmith to conduct the quarterly communion services there. I hope to be back—God willing—on Saturday the twenty-third to conduct the Dutch service for the Cape Corps. Then on Tuesday the twenty-sixth, I'll be leaving on a visitation tour with Elder Willem Pretorius and Deacon Andries Erwee. Our first port of call will be the opening of Commandant Erasmus's new home. Then Deacon Erwee and I will travel north until we reach Winburg, where we'll be spending Sunday, 1 July. I hope to be back in Bloemfontein on Tuesday, 3 July in time for the opening of the Legislative Council on Wednesday. Then I'll be off again with Deacon Johan Griesel between Wednesday, the eleventh and Saturday, the twenty-first. That's about it, really."

I observed that Major Warden was wearing a puzzled expression. "I need to clarify something," he said. "You mentioned conducting the quarterly communion services at Fauresmith as well as at Smithfield. Does this mean that you have to conduct quarterly communion services at both these places on a regular basis?"

"Quite so, Major Warden. According to the Dutch Reformed system, I'm the official *consulent*, or acting minister, for these congregations. I'm therefore required to conduct quarterly communion services for all vacant congregations in the Sovereignty, including Winburg."

"You say services," said Drury. "How many do you have to give?"

"About five, Dr. Drury. At Fauresmith I'll be preaching once on Tuesday evening, three times on Wednesday, and then once on Thursday. Not only do these services include the preparation for communion and the communion service itself, but they also cover marriages, christenings and confirmations when applicable. But rest assured, I'll only be conducting four services here in Bloemfontein in order to leave Sunday afternoon free for the English service."

Drury looked flabbergasted, while the others exchanged glances.

"My dear Mr. Murray," Warden said. "There's no question of you conducting an English service while these quarterly services are on the go. As it is, I've no idea how you'll manage to keep on top of your workload. By the way, do you have any dates in mind for the Bloemfontein services in August?"

"Let me see. I've scheduled them to take place between Saturday, the eleventh and Monday the thirteenth. They will be preceded by catechism classes throughout the week. Thankfully, my brother John will be here to help me with the tables."

"Tables?" said Allison. "What on earth do you need tables for?"

"Well during the communion service itself, the communicants sit around trestle tables. The minister then administers the bread and wine followed by a homily and a hymn at each table in turn. It can be quite exhausting if he has a large congregation and the service is held out of doors."

"So how many are expected to attend?" Allison asked.

"Between two and three thousand, I'd imagine."

Mr. Stuart's cheeks ballooned as he blew out a long breath. "My goodness. That means an influx of hundreds of wagons every quarter. You'd better alert the storekeepers, Mr. Allison. I'll arrange for the convicts to prepare the outspan places."

Out of the corner of my eye, I noticed Dr. Drury stroking his chin.

"Before we leave this topic," he said, "I happen to notice that the communion services at Fauresmith will be held during the week. Tell me, Mr. Murray, will that be so for the other church centers as well?"

"Just so, Dr. Drury. It means I can be back in Bloemfontein for our regular services on Saturday and Sunday."

"But that's far too many services in one week—five in Fauresmith, then three in Bloemfontein. And in the summer months, it'll be four. In addition, there's all that travelling to be done. Your health will suffer, Mr. Murray. As you are already aware, you can't just switch off, or pray, or think of your sermons while travelling along our godforsaken tracks. You have to concentrate to avoid, rocks, potholes and ridges, not to speak of keeping an eye out for wild dogs and lions. Just because you have recovered swiftly from your return trip to Burghersdorp, doesn't mean this will happen in the future. You'll find that as you embark on more of these trips, it will take longer to recover. Ask Major Warden here. It's the accumulative effect of all the jolts on the body that's the cause of the exhaustion you're bound to feel."

"That's enough advice for now, Dr. Drury," Stuart said. "There are other matters to be discussed."

"They can wait, Mr. Stuart. This is far too important an issue to sweep under the carpet. Mr. Murray will become ill and have to give up the ministry altogether if this issue isn't addressed. And all of us here have to be aware of his workload so as not to impose extra duties on him, like teaching Scripture to Bushmen who don't understand a word of Dutch—as laudable as that initiative may appear. Now may I continue, Mr. Stuart?"

"Very well, Dr. Drury. But before you do, I'd just like to apologize to Mr. Murray for imposing extra work on him. But I'm still convinced that the Lord is able to save to the uttermost."

Out of the corner of my eye I observed Drury wiggling his pencil impatiently. I was about to speak words of reassurance to Mr. Stuart, when Drury spoke first.

"Now Mr. Murray, according to my calculations, you'll be travelling every second week and conducting up to nine services during the week of travel."

"Surely not every second week, Dr. Drury?"

"Well let's calculate it. There's your yearly leave of six weeks in December, not so?"

I nodded.

"Then there's the months of June and July when no quarterly services are held on account of it being too cold to camp out in wagons."

I nodded again.

"Well that's three-and-a-half months gone already, Mr. Murray. Is there any other fixed event that we need to take into consideration?"

I massaged my forehead and groaned. I noticed that Drury was waiting, his pen poised. I took a deep breath and blurted out: "The yearly Presbytery meeting in Graaff-Reinet that begins on 18 October."

"Graaff-Reinet!" chorused the others.

I looked over at Allison who appeared to be doing the calculations in his head. "If you subtract yet another month—give or take," he said, "you only have seven-and-a- half left in which to conduct your quarterly services."

"Let's be a little more generous," said Drury, "and make it eight."

He rounded his lips and observed me over his spectacles that were perched low on his nose. "That means, Mr. Murray, that you are only left with two months in every quarter to conduct a round of four communion services. And as I pointed out before, that equates to being on the road every other week."

"That's a ridiculous workload," Stuart said. "Surely there's something we can do?"

"I'll write to Sir Harry," said Drury. "I'll put in an urgent request for Dutch teachers and an extra Dutch minister. Do I have your unanimous support on this matter?"

We all said, "aye," and Mr. Stuart took up his gavel and tapped the table with a flourish.

If only it were as easy as that, I thought. What hope did the Sovereignty have of obtaining Dutch teachers and another minister when there was a dearth of both in the Cape Colony?

It wasn't so much the workload I was concerned about. It was the fact that I would have little time for sermon preparation, not to speak of prayer and reflection—the powerhouse of any ministry. Even more worrying was the fact that my elders and deacons expected me to minister to a spiritually-needy Sovereignty without the mainstay of God's power to do so.

I recalled Elder Van Zyl's words: "The two visitation tours with Deacons Erwee and Griesel will be quite leisurely, *Dominee*. We've ensured that you will be able to have a week's rest in between."

But from what Major Warden had just told me, Elder Van Zyl had known all along about the Legislative Council session in Bloemfontein and the hustle and bustle it would cause. What's more, I was certain that Pretorius had been aware of it as well.

My epiphany had come when I'd realized that Deacon Erwee might be using me to accompany *him* on his deputation tour to the farming constituents he was representing at the Legislative Council, instead of the other way around. It would also not surprise me if Commandant Erasmus was using the opening of his new home for the same purpose.

Another fact that had sprung to mind was that I'd have to offer both Erwee and Griesel a bed for the week while they were in Bloemfontein. This meant that I'd have to sleep on the clay floor. Not that I had any grounds to complain, mind you, except that I'd have to ask Dr. Drury for one of his bedrolls—a prospect I didn't relish. But sweeping these problem aside, it would be my time alone with the Lord that I would have to forfeit.

As I considered these facts, it appeared to me that my immediate challenge was to earn people's respect. Instead of being considered a naïve and bungling youth, whom others could push around to achieve their own ends, it was vital that I should be viewed as a spiritual leader worthy of respect. For surely this was a vital building block that had to be in place before I could ever hope to reach my people with the Gospel. And as an integral part of this challenge, I had to learn to say no.

14

An Encounter with Wolves

It was the Tuesday after my marathon preaching week of five sermons at Fauresmith and three at Bloemfontein. Yet, here I was on the road again. I was due to arrive at Willem Pretorius's farm by lunchtime in order to lead a service that afternoon. Then on the following day, we would travel to the opening of Commandant Erasmus's new home on a farm a few hours away. It would be there that I'd meet up with Deacon Andries Erwee, who'd accompany me on a visitation tour as far as Winburg.

On the way to Pretorius's farm, I forded a small stream with lush grass on its banks. As I didn't want to arrive too early for lunch—it being only about half-past ten—I decided to dismount to allow my horse, Scuttle, to graze. I chose a dry patch away from the damp of the long grass, and using my pack as a pillow, lay down to luxuriate in the peace of my surroundings.

I thought of the people of Fauresmith and their positive response to the building of a church. At my suggestion, they'd decided to ask Mr. Stuart to lay the foundation stone on Saturday, 1 September. I'd suggested Mr. Stuart because I couldn't envision travelling there with anyone else. The occasion would also present the perfect opportunity to deliver the next round of communion services for the third quarter.

My thoughts then turned to the community of Bushmen who'd dutifully arrived for their Sunday-school lesson as promised. I was stunned to find twenty-four adults, and as many children, gathered outside the schoolroom waiting for my arrival after lunch. I taught them a few basic elements of the Christian faith plus the first verse of the hymn: "*God Heeft De Wêreld Zo Bemind*" (God So Loved The World). To my surprise, they sang it heartily, managing to drown out the lessons being presented by Dr. Drury and Mr. Stuart in other corners of the hall.

Meeting up with Mr. Stuart later, I said, "I'm afraid I have no idea how much they were able to take in."

"Never fear, Mr. Murray. We need to constantly remind ourselves that the Lord is able to save to the uttermost."

While I lay there in the winter sun, I couldn't help smiling as I recalled Mr. Stuart's favorite phrase that he was forever repeating. My reverie, however, came to an abrupt halt when I became conscious that Scuttle's demeanor had changed. His head was upright, he was snorting wildly, and his eyes were wide with fear. I leapt to my feet in an effort to grab the reins, but I was too late. He was already galloping off at the speed of a bounding springbuck being pursued.

So what had disturbed him? I couldn't detect a thing—no snap of a twig or any movement in the bush. I should have knee-haltered him, I thought. How could I have been so trusting? And now I'd have to face the smirks and headshakes of Pretorius and Burger, not to speak of the others farmers I was about to serve. And as for Drury's response . . . it didn't bear contemplating.

I returned to my pack, and swung it over my shoulder. It was while I was adjusting its position that I caught a glimpse of something behind a bush nearby. I paused to see what it was.

There, as if out of thin air, emerged a pack of African Wolves—about eight in number[7].

Don't look them in the eye, I said to myself.

Pretend you haven't seen them.

Don't smile.

With these reminders, I turned and started to step it out.

Not too quick.

Keep it steady.

Show no fear.

Dear Lord, You, who can save to the uttermost, please save me now. Please close the mouths of these wolves as you did with the lions on Daniel's behalf, for You are the same God, yesterday, today and forever. Lord, have mercy!

The wolves were right behind me—the lead one trying to sniff at my boots, while the others yapped and gurgled, as if discussing whether to attack me or not. I knew they could bring me down in an instant, but something was holding them back. I also knew that their modus operandi when attacking a large buck was to wound the animal first and then to track it until it collapsed, thus making the kill easy. They would then eat their fill and regurgitate the meat for the pups and the other wolves on their return to the lair. The only difference in my case was that I wasn't wounded.

The further I strode, the more my confidence grew that the Lord would keep me safe from these wolves. I became conscious in my spirit that a miracle was taking place with each step. My frantic prayers for help turned into ones of thanksgiving and praise. I repeated every verse of the Dutch Psalter I could recall, and then began on the Scottish one.

After what seemed an eternity, a house on a low-lying plateau came into view. I couldn't help wondering how long it would take for someone to notice my arrival.

A light breeze was still wafting my way. This would mean that the teams of horses that had drawn the visiting wagons would have no idea that a pack of wolves was fast approaching. In any case, the aroma of cooking meat, which was now filling my nostrils, would camouflage their scent. I prayed that Pretorius would have had the good sense to yard them in his horse enclosure.

As I drew nearer, I noticed that the side of the house faced my way, while the front overlooked a picturesque little valley to my right. It appeared that one reached the top of the plateau via a broad track that ran parallel to the side of the house. The track ran from right to left along the entire length of the plateau, thus ensuring a gentle gradient for the heaviest of wagons. It ended at the rear of the house where the visiting wagons were now parked. Unfortunately, they obscured my view of the gathering beyond.

What now? I thought. Do I circumnavigate the plateau in the hope that someone will see me, or do I trudge up the track and call out to the people at the top? But the nearer I got, the more certain I became that the latter option was untenable. The laughter of the folk, plus the strains of the concertina I could hear playing, would drown out any cries for help. Besides, it would endanger the lives of everyone gathered there.

My only option was to trudge around the plateau. This would mean that when I reached the opposite side, the horses on the top, would now be downwind. They'd hopefully smell the wolves and raise the alarm via their panicked snorting. This, in turn, would send some of the men to reconnoiter the perimeter, where they'd become aware of my predicament and come to my aid—or so I pictured the scenario.

I was wondering how long this detour would take, when I noticed two boys, aged about nine or ten, running along the side of the house. They had evidently been sent as a lookout. They stopped at a good vantage point and scanned the track. It was clear from their frozen stance that they were dumbstruck by the scene that met their gaze. After a few moments, the one nudged the other and they bounded back to the picnic gathering.

Before long, the sound of voices and laughter died, and the concertina left off on a whining note. A few minutes later, I noticed people peering through the side windows. This was followed by a group of young men with rifles dashing along the plateau and then lying low behind the line of bushes there. Manie and his eldest brother, Petrus, were among them. It appeared that each was aiming to take a pot shot at one of the wolves as they came within range. The only problem was that the pack was following me in close formation. In addition, the breeze continued to blow my way in unpredictable little gusts, making it nigh on impossible for the men to fire without endangering my life.

I was fast approaching the ramp, when Pretorius strode into view and fired into the air. A volley of shots from those behind the bushes followed soon after. I glanced briefly over my shoulder and was relieved to discover that the wolves had long since sensed danger and were already making their getaway by zigzagging across the veld, each one widely dispersed from the other. Clever blighters, I thought.

Although I was thankful my encounter with them was over, I was pleased they would live to hunt another day. After all, God had chosen to use them in a miraculous way for my benefit. And as they hadn't touched me, why not spare their lives— not a view that would be shared by the farmers on the plateau, I feared.

As I stepped onto the track leading to the house, I could hear Pretorius chiding his sons and the other young men in a tone bristling with tension. It was almost an octave higher than normal.

"What were you waiting for?" he scolded. "Why didn't you shoot into the air? This wasn't the time for trophy collection. It was a time for immediate action. Those wolves should never be allowed to approach a farmhouse, let alone draw near to it. What would have happened if they'd turned on *Dominee* near the ramp? Do you think you would have been able to fire on them without hitting him? Use your commonsense, man!"

"You're right, Pa," said Petrus, trying to pacify him. "But it doesn't do to make a fuss about what didn't occur. So let's go and welcome *Dominee*. He's already halfway up the track."

I didn't hear Pretorius's reply because it was drowned out by the rest of the visitors who had started to gather at the top of the ramp. They cheered and clapped as I approached, while the children waved and bobbed excitedly up and down.

At the very front of the group stood Karel Burger—all smiles. He stretched out his hand to greet me, while using the other to pat my arm.

"You must be the apple of the Lord's eye," he said. "Fancy the Lord muzzling a pack of wolves to save your life. This is a miracle of biblical proportions. I just can't get over it! How long were you walking for?"

Before I could answer, Pretorius came striding up, still red in the face from his altercation with Petrus and the others. But his relief at my safe arrival was palpable.

"Welcome *Dominee*," he said. "Come and sit down. You must be exhausted. I can't believe what I saw out there. It can only be a miracle. Those wolves are some of the best hunters in Africa, you know."

Shortly afterwards, I was being fussed over like a prince of the realm. Everyone wanted to shake my hand or pat my back. As I sat there sipping tea, children would run up, stare at me to make sure I was indeed human, and then run away again. Older women would approach in tentative style to describe their anguish and heart palpitations while they'd witnessed the scene through one of the side windows.

At one level I'd become one with these farmers—a hero of the veld, with an unique story of survival to tell that could trump most of theirs. On another level, I was now regarded as their very own *Dominee* who had experienced God's special protection and favor. As such, I was someone worthy of esteem.

But as I bathed in the sunshine of my newfound status, I was unaware of the dangers of self-satisfaction and pride that lurked in the shadows. These would make themselves known soon enough. In the meantime, my elders and deacons would continue to use my inexperience to persuade me to do their bidding. Even as soon as the following day, they'd confront me with a scheme that had the potential to wear me out and drain me emotionally. But what could I say to men whose intentions were sound?

15
Ambushed

The official opening of Commandant Erasmus's home was over, and a hearty lunch of venison and vegetables was being served in the back garden. Seeing that I'd opened the proceedings with prayer and had already been introduced to the families, I felt I could now relax within the close-knit circle of the Pretorius family.

We had just started on our meal, when Commandant Erasmus strolled up flanked by Deacons Andries Erwee and Pieter Coetzer. He suggested that Willem Pretorius and I should join them for a short meeting over lunch. At the time, I thought this an excellent idea because I wanted to get to know these men a little better.

The younger of the two was Deacon Coetzer, who looked to be in his late thirties. He was tall and strapping with a full beard and curly crop of brown hair. He appeared to be a humble man of few words. I particularly admired the air of stillness and dignity about him. It seemed to cloak him in an aura of spirituality far beyond his years.

Andries Erwee, by contrast, looked to be in his early fifties. I guessed that he had declined the eldership because of his interest in politics. He was a distinguished looking man with gray-streaked hair and goatee to match. His excellent command of

Dutch together with his permanently-worn spectacles gave the impression that he was an educated man, or at least one who was well read.

This left Erasmus, a man somewhere in his forties who had lately been appointed to the position of Commandant by Major Warden. As such, he would be an official delegate to the Legislative Council that would be meeting in Bloemfontein the following week. His hair was a rusty color, as was his full beard. He struck me as an energetic and resolute man with a marked sense of humor. From what I could tell, he was not only popular, but also well respected by his neighbors.

We followed him into his new home that was built along the Dutch style. The entrance led into a large parlor that was divided into a sitting and dining room area. Erasmus immediately took charge and invited us to sit at one end of the twelve-seater table that filled the dining room. He placed himself at the head, with Pretorius on his right and Erwee on his left. I sat next to Pretorius, opposite Coetzer.

The seating arrangements reminded me of my meeting with Major Warden and Co. But I doubted whether there would be much chit-chat or wild tangents as during that meeting. In any case, I suspected that I had only been invited because of my social standing as a Minister of the Word.

"Welcome to my new abode," said Erasmus. "And a special welcome to you *Dominee*. I believe you would have been enjoying Paradise this time today if it weren't for the protection of our merciful God who knows how much we are in need of a pastor. It is therefore with humble and thankful hearts that we commence this meeting. You have the floor, *Meneer* Erwee."

I thought it an appropriate moment to tuck into my venison, being certain that the discussion topic about to get underway would have little bearing on my ministry.

"It has come to my attention," said Erwee, "that our people across the Vaal are up in arms about a rumor they've heard regarding the deputation tour that was led by Drs. Philip Faure and William Robertson. And it's because of the sensitive nature of this rumor that I've asked Commandant Erasmus to call this meeting."

"What rumor, *Meneer* Erwee?" I asked, with my mouth half full.

"I thought that remark would get your attention, *Dominee*. And so it should. This is a serious matter. You see, some of our Transvaal compatriots are threatening to break off ties with the Cape, and we simply cannot allow it."

"But why?" I asked. "What could Faure and Robertson have possibly done to deserve that response? By all accounts, their tour was a resounding success and a blessing to all who attended their services."

"It's not so much what they've done," Erwee said, "but who it was who commissioned them and paid for their tour."

To register my disquiet that this issue was even being raised, I pushed my plate away. How could they even think that Faure and Robertson's long and arduous tour could have had any other motive than to deliver the Word of God.

"So who on earth do the people in the Transvaal think commissioned them?"

"In a word: Sir Harry Smith."

"But Sir Harry does not have the authority to commission. Only the Synodical Committee on behalf of the Dutch Reformed Church. And by accusing Faure and Robertson of political motives, they are in fact undermining the integrity of the entire Synodical Committee."

"Precisely. And that's exactly what they're trying to do."

"But didn't the Boers across the Vaal welcome Faure and Robertson during their visitation tour?"

"They certainly did. But these allegations have only surfaced since their return. And before you sweep them aside as bogus, let's take a look at the evidence."

"I'd be pleased to," I said, thinking that the other three would express a similar keenness. But without exception, they were focused on their meal. They know all about this, I thought.

Erwee unfurled a letter, then slid it across the table for me to read.

"I received this letter from Dr. J. de Wet, an elder of the *Groote Kerk*. His suspicions about this matter were aroused even before the Faure-Robertson deputation arrived here. He says that he heard a rumor that Sir Harry Smith had instigated the deputation with the promise to reimburse all costs involved. He was also supposed to have expressed the wish that Drs. Faure and Robertson should promote social order and content among us."

"But none of these remarks are evidence," I said. "They're only hearsay."

"Not so hasty, *Dominee*. There's more. Dr. De Wet goes on to say that he conveyed this rumor to the Cape Presbytery. They, in turn, were anxious that the rumor should be put to rest. But when they asked the Synodical Committee to report on who would be paying for the deputation, the Committee refused to give a direct answer. Their reply simply said that they were solely accountable to the Synod for their reports and activities."

"Well, even if this rumor were true, *Meneer* Erwee. What of it? The Government pays the stipends of most of the ministers in the Colony, including my own. It also pays the salary of Commandant Erasmus here. And from what Dr. Robertson has told me, our Bloemfontein consistory invited Major Warden and Mr. Allison to be on the church building committee. Now, if that's not mixing matters of church and

state, I don't know what is. And furthermore, I persuaded
the consistory of Fauresmith to invite Mr. Stuart to lay the
church foundation stone there on 1 September. And as they
haven't made any arrangements to fetch me, I'll be travelling
there in Mr. Stuart's wagon—paid for by the Government, I
might add. So does this now make me a political agent of the
Government?"

A chorus of protests arose from the men. It was obvious
that they hadn't expected me to respond with such a vigorous
defense of the Faure-Robertson deputation. At the same time,
I was fairly certain that Sir Harry Smith had reimbursed the
costs involved. I knew he had done so for the first deputation
consisting of my father and P.K. Albertyn. But as their visit had
taken place prior to the Battle of Boomplaats, the question of
who had paid had simply not arisen.

"We want to assure you *Dominee*," said Erasmus, "that we
are not accusing you of being a lackey of the Government. Most
of the Boers in the Sovereignty—with notable exceptions, of
course—differ markedly in their views from our compatriots
across the Vaal. So please bear with *Meneer* Erwee a little longer."

Erwee looked directly at me and continued. "Unfortunately *Dominee*, the rumor that Faure and Robertson were mere
puppets of the Government has taken wings and has reached
influential leaders across the Vaal as well as in Holland."

"In Holland?"

"Yes Holland, *Dominee*. And there it has come to rest and
has hatched an egg."

"Speckled, striped or plain?" I said, trying to make light of
this featherbrained conspiracy.

Erwee's lips twitched, while both Erasmus and Coetzer tried
hard to compose themselves. Pretorius turned my way and gave

me a warning look. Erwee, meanwhile, composed himself and continued.

"*Meneer* Bührmann, a Hollander, who is also a member of the *Volksraad*, alerted me to an article he'd read in the Dutch monthly: *De Boeksaal der Geleerde Wêreld* (The Book Room of the Educated World). Fortunately, like you, he regards these allegations as ridiculous. But at the same time, he recognizes that they stem from the conspiracy theorists who are trying to sever all ties with our Synod in the Cape. We can't let that happen, *Dominee*. We have to nip this separatist movement in the bud."

"So what can we do?" I asked, still baffled by how far these separatists were willing to go to achieve their ends. Or was it simply the rumor-mongering of a peeved Dr. De Wet?

"Well, as one can expect," Erwee said, "there are a number of discerning folk in the Transvaal who are concerned that this rumor might spread. They are hoping you will be able to visit them in December to calm things down through the preaching of the Gospel."

I stared at Erwee for several moments, not believing what I'd just heard. I urged myself to keep calm and not to react to this unfair request based on a spurious rumor. I also needed to play for time to think the matter through.

"Could you repeat what you've just said, *Meneer* Erwee?"

"Certainly," he said. "We would like you to visit the Transvaal in December to help maintain the peace and to nip this separatist movement in the bud."

I leant back in my chair and looked him in the eye. "But *Meneer* Erwee, don't you realize that your objectives are mixed? You are in fact repeating similar motives to the ones Sir Harry Smith was supposed to have uttered. And like his, they do not focus on the Gospel alone. Don't you think you're being hypocritical?"

"Not really, because—"

"Of course our motives are mixed," interrupted Erasmus. "But they are good motives, worthy of your consideration. I'm of the view that Sir Harry Smith instigated the Faure-Robertson delegation as well as promising to defray the costs. And if that be true, it goes without saying that his motives were mixed. But what did Faure and Robertson do? They turned it to their advantage. It presented an opportunity for them to preach the Gospel to us, and they clasped it with both hands. And that is what we are asking you to do in the Transvaal. Our motives may be tinged with worldliness, but hopefully you'll be able to set that aside as you minister to those poor, neglected people."

He certainly knew how to argue a point. But I still couldn't see the justification for my going in December. Didn't they realize I was on vacation then?

I decided to play for more time by locating my hand-drawn calendar from the back of my Bible. It served as a handy diary while on the road. Each loose-leaf page covered two months, starting with June and July and ending with December and January. I shuffled the sheets until the December-January page came into view. I made a show of studying the six weeks of boxes I'd lovingly colored in with pencil.

"I'm afraid I'm on holiday then," I said, keeping my voice steady. "It was decided by Sir Harry Smith that I could claim my full six-weeks in order to recover from the extensive travelling I'm required to do."

"We are fully aware of that," Erwee said. "That's why we're asking you to go in December-January."

Didn't he hear what I'd said? So how could he ask this of me?

"Unfortunately," said Erasmus, "it's absolutely essential that you go during your vacation. There mustn't be the slightest hint that you've been commissioned by the Synod or by Sir

Harry Smith, for that matter. We'll convey the message to the people across the Vaal that you sympathize with their lack of pastoral care, and are keen to undertake a visitation tour to preach the Gospel to them."

"But I can't for the life of me see why they'd accept my ministrations when the suspicion still remains that Drs. Faure and Robertson were mere stooges of the Government."

"Ah," said Erasmus. "The difference is that you will not be inviting yourself. They are the ones who'll be inviting you and defraying the costs. You see, *Meneer* Erwee has worked out a fail-safe scheme for them to follow."

On cue, Erwee leant forward and slid an unfurled map of the Sovereignty and the Transvaal my way. He pointed to the Valsch-River region near the north-eastern border of the Sovereignty.

"The people of Potchefstroom—the nearest town across the Vaal from the Valsch River—will fetch you from there and take you back to Potchefstroom with them. They've already expressed the desire to invite you to preach there. Now, according to my scheme, if another district—let's call it B—wants you to conduct services there as well, then the Boers of that district will be responsible for fetching you from Potchefstroom in their ox-wagon. In a similar way, district C will need to fetch you from district B, and district D from C, and so forth. If the people of a district do not intimate that they would like you to visit them, they will simply miss out on hearing you preach."

"But how will we know which districts will invite me?"

"With the exception of Potchefstroom, we don't know at this stage. But as soon as we reach Winburg on Saturday, I'll send a message to the Valsch River people to let them know that you are willing to go to the Transvaal. They will inform Potchefstroom, who will then send out invitations to the various districts. We'll give them to the end of August to register their interest."

"But who will work out the schedule?"

I watched intrigued as Erwee and Pretorius eyed Erasmus. While I waited for him to speak, I realized that it was now a foregone conclusion that I'd be going to the Transvaal.

"As you can imagine, *Dominee*," said Erasmus, "a visitation tour of this type will have to be worked out in fine detail. The distances between church places will have to be calculated so as to establish the time it takes for an ox-wagon to travel from point A to point B. One has to remember that an ox-wagon can only cover two to three miles per hour in the Transvaal, depending upon the terrain, of course."

"Yes, but who will work out the schedule? And how much say will I have?"

"Rest assured, *Dominee*, we would never arrange such a visitation tour without you being present. A meeting will have to take place with the Transvaal delegation at the Valsch River in early September. It'll be at that meeting that all the visitation dates will be finalized. It can't be later. I'll make all the arrangements, and take you there in my wagon."

I shuffled the loose-leaf pages of my homemade calendar until the months of August-September appeared at the top. It was bad enough having my holiday taken away from me, now there was this proposal to visit the Valsch River as well.

Erasmus peered across at the calendar. "May I take a quick look at the month of September, *Dominee*?"

I slid the paper across to him.

"I see you'll be in Fauresmith from Saturday the first to Monday the third, then in Winburg from Tuesday the twenty-fifth to Thursday the twenty-seventh. The timing couldn't be more perfect. After you return from Fauresmith, we can visit the Valsch River via Winburg. It's only a day-or-so away. And while you're on the road, it will be advisable to travel east to Harrismith and then make a turn at the Wittebergen. On your return journey, you'll be able to conduct the planned communion services at Winburg."

"Surely this extended tour isn't really necessary?" said Pretorius. "It'll mean that *Dominee* will be away for the whole of September and most of October. When he arrives back from Winburg, he'll only have a week in Bloemfontein before he needs to depart for the Presbytery meetings in Graaff-Reinet."

"I'm afraid it's absolutely necessary, otherwise it wouldn't be fair on the people of the Wittebergen and Harrismith. How can *Dominee* visit all the other districts in the Sovereignty plus the Transvaal and leave them out? *Dominee* would never hear the end of it."

"Well, I suppose if it's a case of keeping the peace," said Pretorius.

"And another thing," Erasmus said. "Having met *Dominee*, I'm of the view that he will be able to cope far better than most with these visitation tours. After all, he's young, fit and active."

He looked my way and favored me with a broad smile. It was obvious that he was trying to humor me in the same fashion as he would a youth. I had to put a stop to this condescending behavior. If I didn't, I'd rue the day. I returned his smile with pursed lips and a penetrating stare that I hoped would convey my displeasure.

"Commandant Erasmus," I said. "Your assessment of me is based on the wrong criteria. They are all about externals and have nothing to do with the power that comes from above. Tell me, Commandant. Will you expect a commando to go out and fight without ammunition?"

I waited.

"You say nothing, because you think it an idiotic question. Yet that's exactly what you're expecting me, a poor foot soldier of the Lord, to do. I feel that I'm under spiritual attack by being compelled to go on these consecutive visitation tours. They simply won't allow me the necessary time for Bible study, sermon preparation and prayer. If our Lord needed to seek time for spiritual renewal, how much more do I need it. You don't seem to understand that it's only in God's presence that I am able to be spiritually anointed for the task. Without power from above, the work is in vain. And now, even the few days that were available for this purpose have been whisked from under me."

I looked down and waited for someone to speak. I focused on the June-July page of my calendar that happened to lay on top. I noted that it was 27 June—only four weeks into my ministry. And here I was knowing that I was going to be steadily stripped of my time with God through the decisions of church men who didn't understand the importance of spending time in His presence.

It seemed an age before Erwee broke the silence. "I'd like to be the first to confess the part I've played in organizing your visitation tours, especially the Griesel tour to the Smithfield district. I'm sure the others will agree that it wasn't absolutely necessary. The Lord forgive me for my lack of insight into your plight, *Dominee*."

I nodded, somewhat relieved that he, at least, had started to grasp my need to spend time with the Lord.

"But to maintain the peace," he continued, "I agree with Commandant Erasmus that the extended tour to the Wittebergen and Harrismith must go ahead. And as I have more time on my hands than he does, I will take you to meet the Transvaal delegation at the Valsch River myself. I suggest we leave straight after you arrive back from Fauresmith. This will allow us to take a slow trip with many rest stops before you need to be in Winburg on the twenty-fifth to conduct the communion services. I'll personally see to it that you have ample time for sermon preparation and prayer."

Pretorius laid a hand on my arm. "I'm sure our congregation will understand the demands being placed upon your time. Besides, they'll be able to attend church every Sunday in August."

"I'd also like to say a word," Pieter Coetzer said. "It will be my pleasure to accompany you on your tour through the Transvaal, *Dominee*. To be honest, I doubt whether there'll be much private time to spend with the Lord. But I'll be there to commune with the Father on your behalf when you're unable to. I also hope you'll feel at liberty to share your concerns with me. But most of all, it is my prayer that we can be friends."

I swallowed hard as I leant over the table to shake his hand. "I think the privilege will be all mine," I said.

Erasmus slid my makeshift calendar for August-September back to me. "I see you have circled 17 August rather vigorously. I couldn't help noticing that it says: 'English Church Meeting' in that block. I must say, I'd love to be a fly on the wall there."

I watched amused as Erwee and Pretorius exchanged glances. Erasmus, I realized, was stirring the pot.

"As there's nothing more to discuss," he said. "Let's spend some time in prayer. But before we do, just bear with me a moment while I order some tea and refreshments from the kitchen. I notice that *Dominee* has gone off his food. So perhaps I can entice him to scoff down some *melktert*."

As he passed by my chair, he grasped my shoulder in an action that conveyed understanding and friendship. Little did I realize then that my outspoken honesty would also result in a shift in my relationship with Pretorius and Erwee.

Almost immediately after lunch, the visiting families started to make tracks for home. I said my farewells to the Pretorius family, and followed Erwee to his cart. As planned, I'd be staying at his farm overnight in preparation for our short visitation tour as far as Winburg.

We were about to get into the cart, when Erasmus strolled up to say goodbye.

"It was a pleasure to meet you, *Dominee*," he said. "I look forward to renewing our acquaintance next week during the Legislative proceedings. I don't know if *Meneer* Erwee has told you, but he's been elected as the representative of the farming community in these parts. So don't let him use this visitation tour as a pretext to discuss his political views."

Although Erasmus had uttered the last statement in jest, I noticed that Erwee had taken the comment seriously. He stood erect and thrust out his chest. "I have no intention of talking politics to any of the families we visit. And as for informing *Dominee* about the Legislative Council, I'd planned to do so on the road."

"Pleased to hear it," Erasmus said. "But before you leave, could I urge you to make sure that *Dominee* is back in Bloemfontein by Tuesday 3 July, because he is due to open the Legislative proceedings in prayer on Wednesday."

Turning to me, he said, "I hope the consistory warned you about this, *Dominee*."

"I'm afraid not, Commandant Erasmus. But fortunately there were others who kindly informed me of this event together with the role I'd be expected to play."

Erasmus locked eyes with Erwee before turning to me again. "Unfortunately *Dominee*, all is not what it seems, even in church circles here in the Sovereignty."

He shook our hands, turned tail, and walked towards his new home.

I followed a rather subdued Erwee onto the cart, and took my seat on the driver's box beside him. I felt utterly alone and in need of a true friend—someone with whom I could share my deepest feelings and concerns. There was Mr. Stuart, of course, but I deemed it inappropriate to approach him with my problems at this stage. Oh, if only John were here!

16
John Lets Me Down

August 1849

August was the month that heralded the start of spring in the Sovereignty. By nine o'clock on a pleasant morning, the sun's rays would be warm enough to beckon one out of doors. August the seventeenth was just such a morning. Having moved into the parsonage a week earlier, I was determined to utilize the *stoep* to good effect. I had set up a folding table there for my Bible and sermon materials, and was now sitting back to relish the stillness.

This was a golden opportunity for concerted prayer. But before I'd even brought a single issue before the Lord, my thoughts were darting from one memory to another like a scampering meerkat through the veld. Oh, how I wished I could be like the father meerkat who stood guard and watched over his little ones!

The first memory that surfaced was my visit to the Smithfield district with Deacon Johan Griesel. One of the highlights of my trip was being taken by Commandant Snyman to the proposed town site. It was located on the farm Rietpoort in the lower Caledon valley.

When Snyman arrived at the farm I was staying at, he greeted me with a warm smile and firm handshake. I was conscious of his blue eyes scanning every crevice of my face, as if trying to find a tell-tale sign that would offer up the character information he was seeking. Judging from his graying hair and beard, I estimated that he would have been in his early fifties.

When we arrived at the place that was marked out for the village of Smithfield, I could tell from the fields filled with grazing cattle that this was a sought-after farming district. Wedged in between the lush pastures were paddocks where corn and other crops had recently grown. And in the distance, one could catch a glimpse of a number of African kraals dotting the landscape.

With a wave of his arm that took in the fields before him, Snyman began to recount some of the problems facing the district.

"This was all Moshesh's land," he said. "And what Major Warden has done is to annex swathes of it. He has then demanded that the thousands of Basuto, who were still farming on this side of his new boundary, should retreat to the other side."

"But that's ridiculous," I said. "What is his reasoning behind such an action?"

"That's not too hard to fathom. Firstly, he's obeying Sir Harry Smith's policy of expansion. Then there's the group we Boers like to call the British-Settler War Party who are egging him on. It is to their advantage, you see. They are all wealthy land speculators who wish to purchase the annexed land and then sell it later at a hefty profit. Unfortunately, there are also a few wealthy Boers amongst them."

"But how on earth is Warden able to justify his actions? Surely an outcry would go up from godly colonists, especially the missionaries?"

"Don't you believe it, *Dominee*. All he needs is a pretext. And a golden one has been handed to him on a platter. Magistrate Biddulph of Winburg, together with the English-speaking missionaries, are calling on him to break Moshesh's power. They want to ensure the independence of their African communities and their own little domains. But what we find disturbing is that Warden has chosen to ignore our objections as well as those of the missionaries to the Basuto—men like Eugène Casalis and Samuel Rolland. In a letter to Warden, a few of the British settlers have even referred to them as 'a cancer in the land.' I dare say it's because they're French Reformed and wish to halt Warden's expansionist policy."

This was confronting stuff that forced me to consider Warden in a new light. And as far as the missionaries were concerned, the last thing the Sovereignty needed was a disagreement between them.

We were walking towards the large plot set aside for the church building, when he broached the topic I myself was about to raise.

"I'm afraid we were forced to cancel the communion services next month, *Dominee*—not because there was any danger to the Boers of this region—but because of other factors. The thing is, soon after the original farm, Waterfall, was chosen for our proposed church place, we discovered that it did not have sufficient water, and was therefore unsuitable. So we asked Moshesh if he would give us permission to use Rietpoort for the purpose. We were naturally delighted when he granted it, especially when he added the words: 'in peace and with affection.'"

"So what did Warden say to that?"

"You may well ask. He went behind our backs and arranged for Frederick Rex to survey the site. We only heard of this when Magistrate Vowe of this district forbade us to go ahead with our plan to sell town plots. And as you know, it's been a century-old tradition for the church wardens to do that task. For how else is a congregation able to cover the cost of building a church and a parsonage?"

I looked at him stunned. "But what I don't understand is the reasoning behind such a decision. I'm sure Bloemfontein's magistrate, Mr. Stuart, would never agree to such an action."

"That may be so, but then Bloemfontein and Fauresmith have been awarded carrots for their compliance, whereas we have earned the stick."

For a moment there, I observed a defeated man. His shoulders had drooped, and he was staring into space. With a sigh he turned to me once more and continued his explanation.

"The reason why the church wardens have been forbidden to sell plots, is that we should not have approached Moshesh. According to Magistrate Vowe, the site falls this side of Warden's boundary line, and therefore belongs to the Government. As such, Vowe regards it as his right, and not ours, to sell the plots. He also warned that our church could only expect to receive £500 from the sales, with the rest going to the Government. If you consider that Burghersdorp was able to raise £6000 from the sale of their plots, £500 is a piddling amount."

"I'm really sorry to hear that. So what does the Smithfield congregation propose to do now?"

"As you know, we immediately cancelled the communion services in August to prevent an outbreak of discord amongst a large gathering of dissatisfied Boers. We also intend to boycott Vowe's sale of plots in November. At the moment, that's all we can do to signal our disapproval. But I tell you *Dominee*, if Major Warden wants us to fight Moshesh, none of the Boers around here will obey the call. And what is more, we are all of the view that he will lose."

❧

While sitting on the parsonage *stoep* and trying to make sense of it all, I realized there was nothing I could do except pray. I liked Major Warden, but couldn't understand his policy of aggressive displacement. Surely a fairer boundary line could have been drawn that would have satisfied all parties, including Moshesh? And why go out of one's way to antagonize the Smithfield Boers? On the one hand, Sir Harry Smith had tried to calm the situation by initiating a church deputation to our region. On the other, here was Warden acting counter to Smith's policy of appeasement. He was obviously no strategist.

Although I was coming to grips with both sides of the political divide, I knew that my standing with Warden was still too low to voice an opinion. In fact, it would not surprise me if it took a nosedive into negative territory at the meeting that evening. I cringed at the thought of his reaction to how I'd been brow-beaten into undertaking a month-long tour with Andries Erwee to the Wittebergen and Harrismith in September, and a further tour through the Transvaal during my vacation in December-January. Worse still, I knew I'd have to steel myself against the indignant outcries from Drury and Stuart. At least I'd be able to escape their post-meeting comments, now that I had moved into the parsonage.

Despite every effort to still my thoughts, they now came to dwell on the catechism lessons I'd been taking the week before. These lessons served as a stark reminder of the dire lack of Scriptural knowledge I'd detected amongst the fifteen young people who had wished to be confirmed. I was even tempted to abandon the lessons and to resume them at a later date, if it were not for the fact that my energy levels were buoyed by the thought of John's imminent arrival.

Late Friday afternoon, I had rushed back to the parsonage in anticipation that he and Elder Pelser would have arrived. But no one was there to greet me. I consoled myself with the thought that they'd be there the following day. But again, my hopes were dashed. When they hadn't appeared by Saturday afternoon, I knew they wouldn't be coming.

What could possibly have gone wrong? Had he forgotten? Surely he wouldn't have knowingly let me down?

My thoughts were still focused on this matter, when Pretorius's cart drew up. Interestingly enough, it was Manie who jumped out. He waved and pointed to a tiffin basket he was holding. He was smiling from ear to ear and was obviously in high spirits.

"*Môre Dominee*," he said, stepping onto the stoep. "I can't stay long because I'm on my way to visit my new girlfriend Marianna Venter. She lives on a farm close to Deacon Griesel's. I'm only here to deliver some *boerbeskuit* and *koeksisters* from Ma."

"How kind of her," I said. "By the way, there's a pot of coffee brewing in the kitchen. Why don't you grab a chair from the parlor and join me for a moment."

He nodded and disappeared inside. When he returned, neither of us could resist helping ourselves to freshly-baked *boerbeskuit*, which we then proceeded to dunk in our coffee. We were enjoying a companionable silence, when Manie said, "Have you heard from John yet?"

"No, but I'm sure he'll contact me whenever he's able to. He could be feeling unwell or suffering from influenza."

I was observing Manie closely, and noted a mischievous glint in his eye.

"Out with it Manie. What have you heard?"

"It has all to do with something Major Warden said."

"But what has that got to do with John?"

"A great deal, as I've discovered. You see, I've just been to the store to check whether Pa or any of our neighbors received post yesterday. And lo and behold, there was a letter for me from Charles in Burghersdorp. I won't show you the whole letter because he complains a lot about his studies and how fussy and strict John is."

"I can imagine."

"But he also says that if I see you I must tell you that John will be writing soon. He's waiting until after your meeting with Major Warden. It's this evening, isn't it?"

"Yes, but how on earth does John know that?"

"Ah well, by now you should know how things work around here, *Dominee.*"

Manie grinned, then slid his tongue back and forth over his teeth like a metronome. He had an intuitive sense of the theatrical, even though he'd never darkened the door of a theatre.

"John knows about your meeting because he heard about it from Elder Piet Pelser. And Pelser heard about it via a letter from Commandant Erasmus. Apparently, Erasmus saw the date circled on your calendar and asked you about it. Charles also said that Pelser was supposed to accompany John here."

Manie fished inside his jacket pocket, and extracted the letter. After shuffling through the pages he offered me two sheets.

"It's all there on those pages." he said.

"I don't think I should read them, Manie. It wouldn't be fair to Charles. Just tell me in your own words what it says."

"The main point is that Commandant Erasmus warned Elder Pelser not to come. The reason he gives is that Major Warden is furious with the Burghersdorp merchants for ignoring his instructions not to barter with Moshesh. By all accounts, they are purchasing Basuto grain with ammunition."

"Oh no," I groaned. "In Warden's eyes that would be tantamount to rebellion. What if they're captured?"

Manie looked up and shook his head. "They won't be, because Commandant Snyman of Smithfield is supposed to be turning their wagons back, but he isn't."

"I wonder if Warden knows that?"

Manie studied the scrawl on one of the sheets. "I think he does, because Charles says here that Commandant Snyman told Commandant Erasmus that he received a dressing down over the issue. But that's not all. During the confrontation, Warden let slip that he would be discussing the matter with John when he arrived here to help you with communion. Apparently, he wants John to read the riot act to the culprits from the pulpit."

Manie glanced my way to ascertain my response. I knew that such a discussion would have been a challenge for John, but it was unlikely to have put him off coming. Besides, he was good at disarming any combatant with his suave smile and reassuring response. This was especially so when the answer was clear-cut. He could have simply said that the pulpit was for the preaching of the Word. There must have been another reason for not coming—surely.

"You know, Manie, I can't believe that John would have been put off by such a comment. In fact, I think it was all bluff and bluster on Warden's part. Not even Sir Harry Smith would dare suggest the subject matter for the pulpit."

"I think you're right, *Dominee*. But old Pelser was certainly scared off. Charles says he refused to come. You'll also be pleased to hear that despite Pelser's decision, John was still planning to make the journey in a borrowed cart with Charles."

"So why didn't he?"

Manie grimaced. "You may not like what you're about to hear, but it seems that John received a sign that he should stay."

"A sign? What sought of a sign? That doesn't sound at all like John. He's far too reliant on rational thought than stirrings of the heart."

"Really? Well Charles begs to differ, *Dominee*."

I glanced at Manie and observed the smirk on his face. I thought I knew John through and through, but now I was beginning to doubt.

Manie began to speak in dramatic tones. "Two Sundays ago, John's friend Carel Ziervogel and his sister Maria-Anna appeared at church. When they told John they would be visiting friends in the district for several weeks, John told Charles that their coming was a sign that he should stay."

"And shirk his duty!"

The words were out before I had time to muster the wherewithal to hold them back.

"*Ach Dominee*, You have to realize that you are only a brother, while Maria-Anna is the love of his life. He'll expect you to understand that."

This time I nodded and smiled to make up for my previous faux pas—all the while trying to hide the fact that the words he'd just uttered had seared my heart. I was losing John at a time I needed him most. And who was there who could possibly take his place?

Once again feelings of dejection and loneliness threatened to overwhelm me. This time, however, I couldn't see any light at the end of the tunnel—only travel and toil. And if that were not bad enough, I still had this evening's meeting with Warden and Co. to get through.

❧

17
Doubting My Calling

When I eventually got around to unpacking *Mevrou* Pretorius's basket later that day, I realized there was a cake tin hidden below the sweetmeats. I lifted the lid to find a delicious-looking *melktert* that could have won first prize at any church bazaar. I was about to cut myself a slice, when I thought better of it. I would take it to the meeting that evening for afters. The mere thought of it sitting on the sideboard would help lift my punch-drunk spirit. For what else awaited me other than the combined censure of the others?

I arrived early, so as not to draw attention to the fact that I'd come bearing an edible gift. I knocked lightly on the door, then entered. I walked down the passage and into the large lounge-cum-dining room. Fortunately, both Drury and Stuart were still in their rooms, although they had doubtless seen or heard me arrive.

I walked through to the kitchen and busied myself lifting the *melktert* out of the cake tin and onto a large plate—a task far more difficult than I'd imagined. That done, I re-entered the dining room and placed the *tert* on the sideboard with the other tea things that had already been set out. I turned around, dusted my hands on my pants, and was about to proceed to the lounge, when I glanced at the two blackboards in the corner. The large squares indicating each day of the month had already been marked off for the months of September and October. And there, against my name, I saw a red chalk line that had been drawn through both months, with only the days between Friday, 28 September and Monday, 8 October left blank to indicate when I'd be back in Bloemfontein.

I stared at the blackboards in wonderment. I can't believe it, I thought. They already know about my extended tour to the Wittebergen and Harrismith. Perhaps this meeting won't be as emotionally draining as I'd anticipated.

With this knowledge under my belt, I ensconced myself in a comfortable chair in the lounge, and waited for the others to arrive.

The meeting began with Major Warden delivering his report on the latest tribal skirmishes and known deaths. He then looked across the table at me and sighed.

"I'm afraid, Mr. Murray, all is not well in Smithfield. I received a letter informing me that several Boers have been ordered across the Orange River by Moshesh."

I nodded, but remained silent. My time for offering comments had not yet come. But I couldn't help wondering whether Major Warden was aware that most of the Boers in the lower Caledon had received letters from Moshesh acknowledging their right to farm there. He must know, I thought, because Commandant Snyman would have definitely informed him of that fact. The others, of course, would have no idea.

"You must be at your wits end, Major Warden?" Stuart said.

"I'm afraid so. I still haven't made up my mind what to do about it."

"Just ignore it," said Drury. "I'm sure that's what those Boers will be doing. I vouch that nothing will come of it because Moshesh has enough problems with Sekonyela and the Korannas to deal with."

The next item on the agenda was my schedule. It seemed an age before Mr. Stuart got round to it. He folded his hands on the table and then gave me his full attention.

"Well now, Mr. Murray," he said. "*Meneer* Pretorius has already conveyed your schedule for September and October to us. He did so between communion services over the weekend. And like us, he's concerned that these latest tours you've agreed to undertake are likely to tell on you physically."

"Poppycock," said Drury. "As an elder, it's his duty to protect Mr. Murray from unrealistic demands. And what has he done? He's just sat idly by without coming to Mr. Murray's aid. I certainly gave him a piece of my mind. I can tell you that."

"I thank you for your concern, Dr. Drury, but I'm also partly to blame. After all, I was the one who agreed to these tour proposals."

"Proposals?" said Major Warden. "I think not, Mr. Murray. The operative word here is more likely 'demands.' Nonetheless, you are fast approaching the day when you'll know more about the people in the Sovereignty and across the Vaal than anyone else. So despite Dr. Drury's concerns, I, for one, expressed my relief to Willem Pretorius that you'd be undertaking the tour across the Vaal. The Lord knows, I've enough problems to deal with here than to worry about the situation there."

"But at what price to Mr. Murray?" Drury said, addressing Warden. "You, of all people, should understand his predicament, seeing that your own health has deteriorated from having to travel hither and thither to keep the peace."

Drury's words prompted me to examine Warden more close-ly. What I saw, made my heart go out to him. He looked weary and worn with dark circles under his eyes. I realized that we had more in common than I had initially thought.

"Well, if you have all expressed your opinions," Stuart said, "I'd like to close this segment with some added remarks to Mr. Murray."

Stuart regarded me with an earnest expression. "On the spiritual front, I believe you're presently under attack Mr. Murray. But I also believe that Satan has overplayed his hand. Even Willem Pretorius—counter to Dr. Drury's opinion— has acknowledged his folly and repented of it. So I would now advise that you make the most of the opportunities these tours afford."

"That I'll surely do, Mr. Stuart."

I breathed a sigh of relief. It was over. We could now move on to the next item. I was not wholly surprised to learn that it concerned the call of an Anglican minister to the English con-gregation. Who could blame them, especially with my frequent absences from the village?

"Before we move on, Mr. Murray, said Warden, "I would just like to express my disappointment that Rev. John Murray was unable to be present to help out with the Sunday morning communion service. I hope he isn't unwell?"

"I'm sure he's in excellent health, Major Warden. It was just that the elder who was supposed to convey him here decided not to come on account of the tribal skirmishes."

"A pity, especially for you, sir."

"Amen to that," Allison said. "I couldn't help noticing that the church wardens had set up no less than six communion tables. I also heard that you were already hoarse after delivering your homily at table four, and had to rely on the singing of hymns for the other two. I believe a sigh of relief went up—the service being so long and all."

He was baiting me, and I felt I owed it to myself and my position as a spiritual leader not to let him demean my efforts.

"More's the pity for those sighing souls, Mr. Allison. If the wind had been blowing, my throat might have given way far earlier, and the service might have been shorter still. But the Lord in his mercy knew that they needed extra time to repent and to consecrate their lives. Moreover, thanks to Dr. Drury here, who supplied me with some potent medicine, my throat was as right as rain for the evening service."

I could tell by his tight-lipped expression that he hadn't expected my tongue-in-cheek repartee. And being an intelligent young man who would be used to responding to witticisms, he had no intention of being outdone by me.

"I'm pleased to hear about the quick recovery of your throat, Mr. Murray, but I can't help commiserating with you over the failure of so many of your catechism students. You may not know this, but there was weeping and gnashing of teeth in the wagon camp."

"Oh dear," said Stuart. "How many did you fail, Mr. Murray?"

"Thirteen out of fifteen,"

"Goodness me! Why so many?" Drury asked.

"Well, some were rejected on account of their defective knowledge of the Heidelberg Catechism, others were quite open in stating that they had not received Christ as their Savior, and a third group did not even understand what believing in Christ meant."

"But surely they would have learnt this from your tuition?" Drury said. "You were teaching in the schoolhouse for a full five days, including some evenings. I used to see the lamplight flickering there until late."

"True, but I didn't teach them as a group, you see. I decided to spend four or five hours speaking to each in turn."

"Poor sods," said Allison, under his breath.

The others remained silent—a clear indication that they endorsed Allison's remark. So what had I done to deserve their disapproval? I noticed that Mr. Stuart was wearing a dumbfounded expression, while out of the corner of my eye I could see Drury shaking his head. Major Warden was staring at the table, while Mr. Allison was observing me with a cocked brow. Perhaps if I explained what I was about, they'd understand.

"The fact of the matter is, I wanted to discover their state of mind as well as their reasons for wanting to be confirmed."

"That's all very well," said Stuart. "But isn't it your role to teach them first before trying to ascertain these things? You have to remember that they have never been to school and are therefore semi-literate. They don't even speak standard Dutch, I'm told. So wouldn't it have been better if you'd spent time with them as a class before attempting personal work?"

"I agree with Mr. Stuart," said Drury. "It's also vital, Mr. Murray, that you learn to work smarter in order to conserve your energy, otherwise you won't finish the course."

I was once again back to being the bungling youth. All the feelings that had overwhelmed me earlier that day came rushing back. And added to them was the realization that my judgment and ability as a pastor was being seriously questioned—and that by a group of men I held in high esteem. To make matters worse, I noticed Allison stroking his chin in theatrical fashion.

"What I can't understand," he said, "is why those who hadn't received Christ didn't simply say that they had? I'm thinking particularly of those who had passed the catechism. They must be an exceptionally honest lot."

I shook my head. "They would never swear falsely to knowing Christ. I make sure of that."

"How so?" said Allison.

"Well, I lift my right hand and say, 'If you promise falsely to know Christ, this hand will witness against you at the day of Judgment.'"

Allison let out a low whistle.

"Mr. Allison, please," said Warden. "We don't need your theatrics."

"But didn't you hear what Mr. Murray just said?"

"Not now, Allison—please."

"He's just promoted himself in the afterlife to a position beside the Judgment Seat of Christ so that he can whisper in Christ's ear in order to testify against those poor, ignorant souls."

Mr. Stuart tapped his gavel loudly on the table and glowered at Allison.

"Mr. Murray is trying to do his best amongst semi-literate youths. That statement of his is purely an attempt to ensure that these young people take their commitment seriously. I'm sure the Lord will understand the sincerity of his heart in this matter. In the meantime, you do well to consider your own commitment and service. Do I detect a change of heart with regard to teaching our young people in the Sunday School? . . . No, I thought not. So let him who is without sin caste the first stone."

Allison lowered his eyes under Stuart's glare. A painful silence followed during which his stiff-lipped expression began to soften. When he looked across the table at me again, I noted a faint smile hovering at the edges of his lips.

"My sincerest apologies, Mr. Murray. It's my Methodist enthusiasm getting the better of me. Or rather—as Mr. Stuart has just pointed out—my lack of it."

He leant across the table and offered me his hand. I grasped it in mine, feeling ashamed that my bruised pride had given rise to the verbal brinkmanship between us. I should have taken his comment about my lengthy homilies on the chin, and left it at that. Instead, I'd reacted with a student-like retort that had let God down as well as myself.

It goes without saying that I found it difficult to focus on the rest of the meeting. All I wanted to do was slink off home to lick my wounds. Even the thought of a slice of *melktert* had lost its appeal. But despite my descent into the pit of despond, I knew I had to stay for supper. I also knew I had to mend my relationship with Allison by letting him know that I'd be giving his comments due consideration. With that accomplished, I could then put this undignified episode behind me.

After a decent interval of chit-chat over supper, I excused myself and made my way home. Try as I might, I could not shake off the thoughts of failure and incompetence churning around in my mind.

In the past, this group of men had rendered the important service of being a counterbalance to the demands of my consistory. And despite my inexperience with regards to a few practical matters, I had always been conscious that they held me in high esteem. I also knew they would never take advantage of me, were on my side, and fretted over my health. But oh, the expressions on their faces this evening—the looks that said I was hard and demanding, that I lacked organizational ability and insight, that I considered myself a high-handed judge instead of a loving shepherd. Oh, those looks were too much to bear. What must they think of me now? Why couldn't I be steady and level-headed like John?

I strode into the parsonage and collapsed into a lounge chair. I didn't bother to stoke the dying embers in the hearth or adjust the lamp light that I'd turned down before leaving the house. These were minor concerns compared with the thoughts assailing me.

Did I really receive a call to the ministry? I was only sixteen when I'd made that decision. And in hindsight, I wasn't even saved yet. It was not until a few months into my theological course in Utrecht that I'd received God's pardon and was born again. So was this the reason why I didn't have power for service and why the Holy Spirit didn't accompany my preaching? Was it really the case that I wasn't called, or did the problem lay at my door? And if so, how could I rectify it?

For the umpteenth time, my thoughts went back to the sermons I'd heard by William Burns as a lad in Scotland. On the face of it, his speech had been measured and slow, and his sermons without charm or natural eloquence. Yet, his words had been full of weight and power because he carried about him an aura of the divine presence of God.

Then there was Uncle William. How was it that he could convert over a thousand Muslims within a short span of three years? And how was Helperus Ritzema van Lier able to take the *Groote Kerk* by storm with his powerful preaching when only twenty-two?

As I sat there thinking on these matters, I knew that the truth pointed to one glaring fact: I was simply unaccustomed to wrestling with God in prayer, even when the opportunity was there—like this morning.

I was jolted into the present moment by a faint knock at the front door. It opened slowly, and Mr. Stuart tiptoed inside, closing it silently behind him. Through the dim light, I caught sight of *Mevrou* Pretorius's cake tin under his arm.

"Mr. Murray?" he called in a low voice. "Are you still up?"

"I'm in here, Mr. Stuart."

"Goodness, dear fellow. Why haven't you stoked the fire? It's freezing in here. By the way, I've brought back your cake tin."

He placed it on the dining room table, then eyed me through the gloom.

"Do you mind if I join you?"

I scrambled to my feet. "Please forgive my bad manners, Mr. Stuart. Make yourself comfortable while I see to the fire."

He walked over to an armchair and carefully lowered himself into the sagging seat.

"I've some wonderful news to share with you," he said. "We—that is Dr. Drury and I—didn't want to mention it before the others. I'm delighted to report that Sir Harry Smith has agreed to Dr. Drury's request for an extra Dutch pastor and two Dutch teachers for the Sovereignty. What do you think of that?"

I'd just placed a log on the fire, and was busily stoking the crackling embers. I decided to remain silent, rather than voice a reply in cheerful tones I didn't feel. As far as I was concerned, the news sounded like pie in the sky.

"Did you hear what I said, Mr. Murray?"

Satisfied that the fire was burning brightly, I returned to my seat and plonked myself down.

"Yes, I heard you, Mr. Stuart. But I'm afraid I can't see how this scheme can possibly come to pass."

"Why ever not?"

"In the first place, there are numerous pastoral vacancies in the Colony. And as for Dutch teachers . . . well, besides the few in and around Cape Town, this breed of men are almost extinct in the rest of the Colony. And when such a person does happen to land on our shores, he is either snapped up by schools in the Cape Winelands, or by church councils in large inland towns like Swellendam. Do you realize, Mr. Stuart, that not even Graaff-Reinet has a Dutch teacher at present. And as far as an English one for the free school is concerned, the school council hasn't been able to appoint a suitable one for over a year now."

"Ah, but you underestimate Dr. Drury's influence upon Sir Harry. Did you know that Sir Harry named the first fort in Bloemfontein *Fort Drury*? Now who has ever heard of a fort being named after a doctor, especially one with a rank of non-commissioned sergeant? It's unheard of."

"I dearly hope you are right, Mr. Stuart. But I can't see how an extra Dutch pastor will be appointed if the English community are able to persuade Sir Harry to appoint an English one. It will be either one or the other."

Mr. Stuart tapped the side of his nose with his forefinger. "You're quite right, Mr. Murray. But I can assure you, it will be the Dutch appointment that will prevail."

More conniving, I thought, and right under Major Warden's nose.

I remained silent, hoping that Mr. Stuart would take the hint and leave. But he appeared to be searching for something in his pocket. He finally extracted a flimsy sheet of note paper that had been neatly folded in half.

"Thank goodness," he said. "I thought for a moment that I'd left it at home. I'm afraid the message has been hastily scribbled, but as you will see, it's been written by Dr. Drury and countersigned by Major Warden."

I unfolded the sheet and tilted it towards the light so as to read the spiky strokes more easily. I looked up and laughed.

"I can't make out a word, Mr. Stuart. Please enlighten me."

"It's a doctor's certificate stating that you are to rest up in Graaff-Reinet for two weeks during your stay there in October."

"Now that is good news," I said. "Tell Dr. Drury that my spirits have lifted already."

Mr. Stuart patted my leg, then got up to go. "Remember that you're a son of the Most High, Mr. Murray."

I was ushering him to the door, when he stopped half way. "I've just remembered," he said. "I have further glad tidings to share with you. One of your flock has found your horse Scuttle. He lives rather far from Bloemfontein, but is nevertheless hoping to present him to you on Sunday. It was supposed to be a surprise, but matters being what they are . . ."

"What wonderful news! It's like icing on the cake."

"Would you like me to place a cherry on top as well?"

I couldn't help smiling at his boyish enthusiasm and readiness to cheer me up. "I'd be delighted," I said.

"It's a word from the Lord taken from Psalm 37:4: '*Delight thyself also in the Lord; and He shall give thee the desires of thine heart.*' It's one of my favorites."

I met his compassionate gaze and nodded. "It's a word in season. Thank you."

I shut the door behind him and leant against it for a moment. Yes, Mr. Stuart, I thought. You have placed your finger on the crux of my problem. I need to spend more time delighting myself in the Lord. But that's exactly what I find so hard to do.

❧

18

Home Truths Learnt at Graaff-Reinet

October 1849

The first thought that passed through my mind when Willem Pretorius and I drove through the wagon gate of the Graaff-Reinet parsonage was "home again at last." For me, the parsonage in Bloemfontein was still only a house, and one that was both impersonal and hauntingly empty. How could it ever compare with this?

There was Amos at the gate giving his traditional salute. And before we'd even begun to outspan the horses, I could hear the squeals of joy coming from the younger siblings as they came tripping down the steps of the *stoep* to greet me. Four-year-old Georgie was running ahead, with Charles trying to catch up with him. Maria was bringing up the rear while calling after Georgie to slow down and to be careful of the horses.

It was exactly how I'd remembered it. Nothing much had changed during the five months of my absence. But oh, what a change those months had wrought in me. I had left here a bumptious youth ready to make my mark on the world—or at least

Bloemfontein—but was now returning as a young pastor achingly conscious of my shortcomings and lack of spiritual power.

Georgie came flying into my arms. He giggled uproariously as I swung him into the air. I then proceeded to hug and kiss each of the others in turn, mentioning them by name and making a fuss of their age, how they'd grown, or how pretty they'd become—all except Charles, of course, whom I was careful to treat as an adult. The first was Kitty aged eight, then Isabella—ten, James—twelve, Jemima—thirteen, Maria—eighteen, and last of all Charles—sixteen.

"So when did you and John arrive?" I asked Charles, while giving him a hug.

"Yesterday afternoon about this time. I'm afraid John's visiting the Ziervogels. And as he won't be able to accept their lunch and dinner invitations while the Presbytery is sitting, he'll be staying over for dinner this evening."

"Oh well, I'll catch up with him later tonight."

"I wouldn't count on it. You'll probably be in bed when he arrives back."

I hid my disappointment by turning my attention to the younger members of the family who'd been waiting patiently for me to finish my conversation with Charles. They were now bobbing up and down with excitement.

"We have a big surprise for you," chorused Kitty and Isabella. "Come and see."

"I have to first help *Meneer* Pretorius and Amos outspan the horses. Then, I have to tidy up in the washroom before greeting Ma and Pa."

"Don't worry about the horses," said Charles. "I'll help with them."

I looked at Maria for a clue as to what to do.

"You can wash and change later," she said. "I'll ask cook to fill the jug in your room with warm water."

"Are you sure?" I said.

For an answer, she gave me a sheepish grin. This must be some surprise, I thought.

The younger girls now started to propel me forward. We were soon climbing the steps, entering the house, and then making our way towards the dining room.

"Now close your eyes tight and don't peep until I say so," said Kitty.

She held my hand and led me in the direction of my mother's sewing corner, while the others maneuvered me this way and that from behind to avoid the furniture.

"You may open your eyes now," she said.

There, only a few paces away, sat my lovely mother beside a crib that had been decorated with pink ribbons and homemade paper roses. When the girls saw my mouth drop open, they clapped their hands and whooped for joy.

"It's a girl," cooed Kitty. "She's only a week old."

I walked over to the crib and peered inside at the sleeping baby. "She's gorgeous Ma. Have you chosen a name for her yet?"

"The girls have settled on 'Helen.' What do you think?"

"Sounds good to me."

There were smiles all round as I bent down to kiss my mother.

"*Ach,* my *liefling,*" she said, "it's such a joy to have you home again."

"Believe me, Ma, it's a blessing pressed down, shaken together and running over for me to be here with all of you."

❦

The next morning while at breakfast, my father put his head around the dining room door and requested that I meet him in his office as soon as I had finished. Because of accumulated tiredness from the journey and the four services I'd conducted in conjunction with communion at Smithfield on the way, I'd risen late. Fortunately, this never proved a problem for visitors or adult members of the family because breakfast was always a self-serve buffet that we were free to partake of as early or as late as required—within limits, of course.

I was particularly looking forward to my time alone with my father. Although I'd written much about my experiences in letters, there was nothing that could take the place of a face-to-face discussion with the one person I could confide in with total abandonment. At times during my lowest ebb in the Sovereignty, I had imagined myself sitting in his study, pouring out my inmost thoughts, while he listened intently and offered words of wisdom spoken with compassion. It was this type of an exchange that I was hoping for from this visit.

"Come in my boy and close the door behind you," said my father in answer to my knock on his open study door. "Please sit down."

He'd been writing, but now lay his pen down. He stood up and went to stand behind his chair where he proceeded to do a few stretches, followed by a vigorous massage of his left knee. My heart slumped because I knew that if his knee was playing up, he'd start to pace, just like he did on Sunday evenings after household devotions. It was then that the family would gather for private prayer. While we knelt at the dining room sofa or at a chair, my father would walk up and down, leading us in a hymn, or quoting Scripture between calling out the topics and people to be prayed for. And if he were to resort to pacing now, it wouldn't bode well for the tête-à-tête I was counting on.

"Sorry about this, Andrew, but I've been sitting too long."

"That's fine, Pa. Take your time."

"Before I hear from you, my boy, there are a few issues I would like to raise first."

I nodded, sensing by his serious expression that what he had to say might not be to my liking.

"Firstly, what on earth were you thinking by agreeing to visit the Transvaal during your vacation? That's a time for rest and spiritual renewal. You should never have agreed to it."

"I explained the reasons in my letters, Pa. I felt that Commandant Erasmus and Andries Erwee's arguments were compelling. Surely we don't want the Transvaal to break off relationships with the Cape church over the spurious issue of whether Drs. Robertson and Faure were political pawns of Sir Harry Smith? And if I go during my vacation, and they see to the transportation, it is more than likely that the whole issue will fade into the background. In any case, it will lessen the scope for such accusations."

"Yes, I know all that, Andrew. But not during your vacation and not without the agreement of the Presbytery.

"But surely it's my holiday and my decision as to how I'd like to spend it?"

"For a holiday, yes, but not for an extensive preaching tour. I've no idea what the Synodical Committee will say to this independent action. It's unheard of for members of a consistory to send out their pastor on such a mission without the official endorsement of the Presbytery. What happened to your knowledge of church law, Andrew?"

"But Pa, if the Presbytery sends me out, it may raise the suspicions of the separatists again."

My father let out a deep sigh and shook his head. "Andrew, where are your brains? Don't you realize that by pretending to visit them on your own accord, you are actually feeding their separatist ambitions? For the Transvaal to retain their link with the Cape church, they need to acknowledge that you are one of its pastors, and that you have been sent out by the Graaff-Reinet Presbytery. Our ultimate aim is for them to be incorporated into the Cape Synod. Do you now understand what you are supposed to be about?"

"I do, Pa."

"Well, I hope so, because from now onwards you are always to make your request to me or to Dr. Abraham Faure before setting out on any preaching tour beyond the borders of the Sovereignty."

I watched as he began to pace, stopping now and again to work his left leg.

"What can you tell me about the Transvaal, Pa?"

Another sigh.

They're a divided lot who are always squabbling amongst themselves. There are those like the Hollander Bührmann who think it's time to form a stable government. Others again want to maintain the status quo, and show no inclination to submit to any government. Then there are large numbers who prefer to follow chieftain-type leaders like Commandant-Generals Andries Pretorius and Hendrik Potgieter. Needless to say, there's an equally large group who regard these leaders as only having a military function. And to make matters worse, there's a major rift between Andries Pretorius and Hendrik Potgieter."

"Speaking of Pretorius, Pa, he's invited me to stay at his farm overnight. I can just imagine what Major Warden would say to that, especially after Pretorius and his commando ousted him from Bloemfontein."

"You'll have to be careful, Andrew. The fewer persons who know about this visit the better. You have to remember that after the Battle of Boomplaats, the British declared Andries Pretorius an outlaw, and placed a price of £2000 on his head."

My father pulled out his chair and sat down. At last, I thought. We can now have a decent discussion without the pacing.

"Tell me Pa. Are there any elders in the Transvaal with the status and clout of elder Willem Pretorius?"

"Oh yes. I can recall one in particular. His name is Frederik Wolmarans. And believe me, nothing church-wise happens without his consent. My only question mark concerning him is that he ties baptism with salvation too closely, and therefore feeds the superstitious inclinations of the people. It appears to be a strategy on his part to encourage couples to present their children for baptism. Nevertheless, my advice to you is not to argue the point with him. Instead, preach the Gospel clearly so that the Spirit can work in the hearts of your hearers."

He paused, then started to shuffle some papers on his desk.

"That reminds me. I believe someone else closer to home also feeds the superstitions of our young people."

He found what he was looking for and placed it with a thump on top of the other papers. He then tapped it several times with his finger.

"This is a letter from Dr. Drury who has asked me to discuss some issues with you."

I groaned inwardly and let my gaze drop to the carpet. I was certain that Drury would have told my father about the hours I'd spent with each confirmation candidate in turn. This would have been accompanied by a warning that I was over exerting myself. No doubt, he'd also mentioned Mr. Allison's query over the theological accuracy of my raised hand as a witness at the

Last Judgment. But all this had happened in August, and now it was mid-October. I couldn't believe that it was about to be raked over again.

"I can see you know exactly what I'm referring to," said my father. "And while I understand the reason for warning your confirmation candidates against swearing falsely, you have to be careful not to fall into the trap of feeding their superstitions. You have to remember that your catechists are no longer under the law, but under the New Covenant of grace. I'm afraid to say that the Lord can turn your hand against you for striving to accomplish Kingdom work in your own strength. No one is able to earn it, and you're certainly not able to drill it into them."

"I don't think that's a fair assessment of what I was trying to do, Pa. I just thought personal work would be more effective."

"For four to five hours at a stretch, and without giving them breathing space to spend time alone with God? My goodness, Andrew. Those poor candidates! You probably scared them witless. That's not what Christ has called you to do. What on earth did you learn at Utrecht?"

"Not much. All the lecturers were liberals. I told you so in my letters. That's why I wanted to further my studies in Halle."

"Well, let me enlighten you."

He shifted back his chair, stood up with ease and started to pace, seemingly oblivious to his wonky knee.

"In my experience," he said, "swearing falsely to being a follower of Christ is not the overriding issue that worries our young people. They are far more likely to think they are not a Christian, even when they have given their lives to Christ. Think back to when you were a young lad in Aberdeen and went to hear William Burns preach. You experienced a touch from the Lord then, didn't you?"

"Yes, but—"

"Didn't you give your heart to Christ then?"

"I did, Pa. But it wasn't like my born-again experience in Utrecht."

"Hmm! Be that as it may, Andrew, I now want you to think back to John's response. Remember how anxious he was that God had bypassed him because he hadn't *felt* anything. His angst was so great that it compelled him to write to William Burns. Do you remember that?"

I nodded.

"Let's move on. Did you think you were a Christian when you were confirmed?"

"I did."

"And what did you base it on?"

"My commitment to live for Christ, I suppose."

"So don't you see what is happening here? You are basing the date of your rebirth on the profound spiritual experience you had in Utrecht. But it's obvious that the Holy Spirit had been drawing you and working in you from your youth. When it's all boiled down, Andrew, we don't always know the exact date of our regeneration, only the date of our surrender."

"That may be so, Pa. But you have to admit that for many people these dates are known to coincide."

"Undoubtedly, my boy. But the point I am trying to make is that there will always be young people like John who are never blessed with a profound experience, and will therefore doubt whether they are a Christian. There will also be those like Maria who receive touches from the Lord every other week. Mind you, when she was about fourteen, she also went through a stage of angst and doubt. Then, besides these, there will always be the tares. But it's not your task to identify them or weed them out. That will be done at the great harvest at the end of the age."

"So what would you suggest I emphasize when instructing my catechists, Pa?"

"You have to teach them to walk by faith and not by sight. You need to help them understand that Jesus will accept them just as they are; that He invites them to come; that they are to rest on the promise in John 6:37: '*Him that cometh to me I will in no wise cast out.*' Preach that promise as if it's a large superscript above the door of the Kingdom. When they are once inside, they'll come to understand the first part of that verse: '*All that the Father giveth me shall come to me.*'"

"Well said, Pa. But to tell you the truth, I covered most of that with my catechists."

"I'm pleased to hear it my boy. But if I discern your problem aright, it's that you are trying to teach in your own strength. You have to realize that you can do *nothing*. You have to cease striving and hand it over to Christ to convict the lost and to open their spiritual eyes. When you're in the Transvaal, you'll find that you will only have six to ten minutes to evaluate forty to eighty candidates at one time."

My mouth fell open as I took in this statement. "Surely not."

"The procedure is quite straight forward, Andrew. As I mentioned before, it's not your task to separate the wheat from the tares. All that's expected of you is to pass those who can read the Scriptures with ease, can explain the way of salvation, have indicated that they want to follow Jesus, and can answer one or two questions you may pose. If a candidate is not able to answer one or more of the above to your satisfaction, you simply fail them. In other words, you send them back to study the Word, because it's there that Jesus will communicate himself and His grace to them."

My father was about to add another comment, when something caught his eye in the street outside. I followed his gaze down Parsonage Street and spied a Cape cart coming our way.

"It's John Pears from Somerset East," he said. "He told me he'd be arriving early. He mentioned something about wanting to visit a friend."

"I should have got up earlier this morning," I said, knowing that my father would go out to greet Pears when he arrived.

"Not at all, Andrew. You needed that sleep. In any case, there'll be plenty of opportunities for us to continue this discussion after the close of the Presbytery meetings. In the meantime, I have a pleasant piece of news to convey to you before Pears arrives."

He sat down and beamed at me across the desk.

"John told me that you were still asleep when he left, so he's asked me to convey this news to you: He'll be announcing his engagement to Maria-Anna this evening. He wanted you to be one of the first to know."

Although this news wasn't entirely unexpected, it still came as a shock. John should have told me himself, I thought, especially after all we'd shared and been through together. He could have told me last night when he came in late.

I put a brave face on it, smiled and said, "That's wonderful news, Pa. When do they expect to get married?"

"On 5 January."

"But I'll be in the Transvaal then."

"Just so, Andrew. But life goes on. The date was set with the expectation that you'd be home for your vacation. And as it was set by Maria-Anna, John has no intention of changing it."

I felt crushed by this news, but was doing my best to hide it. Nevertheless, I was under no illusion that my father was conscious of that fact.

Again he beamed across the desk at me. "I have a special request to make of you, Andrew. Would you be so kind as to baptize your little sister Helen at the baptismal service on Monday?"

"It will be my pleasure, Pa," I said, knowing full well that this was his way of trying to ease my pain.

19
Thrilling News

December 1849

It was Monday, 3 December, and the day before my departure for the Transvaal. I was in the throes of packing, when I received an impromptu visit from Dr. Drury and Mr. Stuart. I was half expecting them to lecture me on "sparing myself," although—heaven knows—I didn't need any warnings on that score these days. But no, it appeared that their visit was motivated by something else entirely.

"Please sit down, gentlemen," I said, pointing to my hand-me-down arm chairs.

"That won't be necessary," said Stuart. "This won't take a minute. We've come because Dr. Drury has some important news to convey to you. All his exertions on your behalf have paid off, I might add."

I noticed Drury's broad smile and uncharacteristic high spirits—a spectacle I seldom witnessed.

"Well now, Mr. Murray," said Drury. "I've just received some news that surprised even me. According to Sir Harry, a Dutch Reformed pastor as well as two Dutch teachers have recently landed in Cape Town. Now what do you think of that, dear sir?"

I kept my smile subdued, although I felt exhilarated by the news. I also knew that the Sovereignty's gain would be the Cape's loss. I couldn't help wondering for which congregations these three had originally been earmarked. But as Sir Harry Smith would be paying their salaries, there was naught the Synodical Committee or anyone else could do about it.

"Ah, Dr. Drury," I said, "the key question is: are they bound for the Sovereignty?"

"From what Sir Harry has to say, they are. There's a *Dominee* Dirk van Velden, who will be pastor of Winburg, a *Meneer* Van der Meer, who will be appointed to Bloemfontein as its schoolmaster, and a *Meneer* Groenendaal, who will be appointed to Fauresmith in a similar capacity."

"Well I never! You even know their names. How on earth did you manage to pull this coup off? All those vacant pastorates in the Cape will be green with envy."

He tapped the side of his nose by way of reply, and after a theatrical pause said, "Mark my words, Mr. Murray, you'll be entering a new chapter in ministry on your return. And I'm sure you'll be your own man by then as well. Now take care and spare yourself whenever you can. You're already looking tired."

Mr. Stuart winked and offered me his hand. When I grasped it, he covered it with his free one. "God's speed, my dear fellow, and may the Lord protect you on the journey. We'll be praying for you every step of the way."

"Thank you Mr. Stuart," I said. "It's really kind of you to go out of your way to pay me this visit."

I turned to Drury and favored him with a heart-felt smile. Dear old Aloe, I thought. True to his nick name, he's as prickly as can be on the surface, yet oozing with goodness beneath.

"Be assured, Dr. Drury," I said, "your words of warning will be ringing in my ears. At the same time, the amazing news you've just conveyed will help bolster my energy every time it starts to flag."

He sighed, then grasped my hand firmly in his. "May that be so, Mr. Murray. May that be so."

20

Over the Vaal to Potchefstroom

Deacon Pieter Coetzer and I set off early next morning for the Transvaal. As it was summer, and the days were long, we made good time to the Valsch River, which we reached on Friday morning. On arriving there, we transferred our belongings from his Cape cart to an ox-wagon, which then transported us across the Vaal River to Potchefstroom. We arrived there in the late afternoon of the same day. Contrary to expectations, we were welcomed with the greatest friendliness, although we heard later that Landdrost Lombard had been in two minds to let us come for fear of British influence.

Our welcome reception was short-lived because of the church service that was scheduled for that evening. I'm afraid to say, my sermon didn't go well. For one thing I was tired. For another, I couldn't hold their attention. Later that evening, when Coetzer and I were alone in our tent, I broached the subject with him.

"What am I doing wrong, *Meneer* Coetzer? Many in the congregation were chatting amongst themselves, while some at the back were even walking around while I was preaching."

"Don't concern yourself too much about that, *Dominee*. You must remember that they've been separated from the means of grace for some time now."

"But it can't just be that. . . ."

I studied him for a moment across the glow of lamplight and between flicking away every flying insect and beetle imaginable. He had cut his brown hair short and had cropped his beard for the journey. This had given him the appearance of a man far younger than his late-thirties. His newfound youthful looks had helped break down the age-barrier between us, to the extent that we'd been able to develop a firm friendship within the space of a few days. I'd also come to appreciate his insightful comments and close walk with the Lord. I therefore trusted him to tell me the truth concerning my present predicament.

"So what do you advise, *Meneer* Coetzer," I said at length."

"Let me first turn down the lamp before we discuss this further, otherwise we'll be eaten alive. We can always read our Bibles at daybreak, because if we read them now, they'll be ruined by the insects."

We lay in silence for some time. The tent still teamed with beetles that were hitting against the canvas and then dropping dazed to the ground. But it was the high-pitched whine of the mosquitoes overhead that was most annoying of all. Their sting, it seemed, could even be felt through the sheet I was forced to cover myself with. This was my first camping experience in summer, and a vastly different kettle-of-fish from my cool, airy bedroom in the Graaff-Reinet parsonage.

At last Coetzer began to speak in his slow, thoughtful style. "You know, *Dominee*, the best sermon I ever heard you preach was to the Hottentots of the Cape Corps one Saturday evening. I was passing through Bloemfontein after a trip to visit a friend, and decided to stay for the service. When I entered the schoolroom, you were going over your sermon. To my surprise, I only observed one sheet of paper on the lectern. It contained three or four main headings with a few points beneath each. You spoke so simply and earnestly that I couldn't help wishing you would preach like that to us. That's the type of preaching they need here—simple and from the heart."

I heard him roll over.

"*Nag Dominee*," he said, in a muffled voice. "There'll be plenty of opportunities to hone your preaching skills on this trip."

I lay awake considering what he had just said. It was obvious that my overarching problem was raising its head again.

Please Lord, I prayed, *deliver me from the need to make an impression, and from always wanting to strive in my own strength. Help me to be like Brainerd who speaks of desiring nothing but Your glory.*"

The service next morning went far better than expected. Fortunately, there was no time to savor the moment because I was faced with the onerous task of testing numerous candidates for church membership before the evening service.

I was sitting in a large family tent with Elder Wolmarans on my right and Elder Van Stander on my left. All three of us were dressed in waistcoats and shirt sleeves on account of the heat. But that is where the similarity between us ended. They were dignified silver-heads, who sported full beards, while I looked little older than the catechists I was about to test. Being painfully conscious of this fact, I was determined to show leadership in the testing process. I needed to be my own man, as Drury had suggested. And there was no better time to start than now.

Directly in front of us was a small trestle table on which we could lay our Bibles and the papers that would be presented to us by the candidates. On each would be written their personal details, with enough space for my signature and an indication of whether they'd been accepted for membership or not.

I'd come well prepared with numerous sets of questions that I was now reviewing with the elders. The church wardens, meanwhile, were sitting at a similar trestle table under a tree nearby. They were busily transcribing the personal details of a long queue of candidates. In the meantime, those young people who had already registered were clustered in small groups wherever there was sufficient shade. The study fest—as I liked to call it—had begun. Over the next few hours, they'd be poring over the Word and asking each other questions until it was their turn to appear before us.

Both Wolmarans and Van Stander seemed impressed with my preparation. All that remained for me to do now was to convey a few ground rules.

"We need to agree on the spot whether a candidate is through or not," I said. "The papers of those we pass, I'll hand to you, *Meneer* Wolmarans. While those we fail, I'll pass on to you, *Meneer* Van Stander."

We were now ready, and so apparently were the wardens. One opened the flap of the tent and eyed us with a grin.

"There are sixty-five candidates, gentlemen," he said. "And may I remind you that you have until seven-thirty to examine them. I'm sure *Dominee* would like at least half-an-hour to prepare for the service this evening, which will begin at eight. You'll be able to adjourn for a quick break and a bite to eat between four and four-thirty. As it's just on one o'clock now, you have six hours to complete this task, giving you around eight minutes for each candidate."

He waited for our chuckles and groans to subside before closing the flap.

"I wonder how the Lord will tackle the Last Judgment in the hereafter?" ventured Wolmarans.

"Believe me," I said, "it'll be beyond our wildest imagination."

Just then the flap opened and our first candidate entered the tent.

We had only processed a handful of catechists, when we encountered our first borderline case. She was a pretty blond of about seventeen, who, judging from the smiles she gave Wolmarans and Van Stander, knew them well.

After she had left the tent, Wolmarans said, "*Ach*, let's pass her *Dominee*. She's planning to marry a most worthy young man this weekend. Besides, I'm sure he'll do his best to lead her correctly in spiritual matters."

I knew I needed to handle this situation with the greatest care. I also had to appear evenhanded.

"What do you think *Meneer* Van Stander?" I asked.

"In my opinion the final decision should be yours, *Dominee*, because both *Meneer* Wolmarans and I are friends of the family."

After a moment's reflection I said, "Well gentlemen, in this particular case, and all other borderline cases, I think we should follow my father's advice to fail them. He deems it an excellent opportunity to send all doubtful candidates back to study God's Word."

I turned to Wolmarans and looked him in the eye. "And in the case of this young lady, *Meneer* Wolmarans, I think she would benefit from some tuition by that God-fearing fiancé of hers. It'll probably do wonders for their relationship."

I didn't wait for a reply, but handed the sheet with her details to Van Stander, who slipped it under his Bible, then folded his hands on top.

"A sensible solution," he said.

"*Ja-Nee, Dominee*, spluttered Wolmarans, "seeing you put it like that. . . ."

We had barely completed this exchange, when one of the wardens opened the tent flap. "Ready *Dominee*?" he asked.

I nodded.

As I smiled at the next candidate who entered the tent, it suddenly dawned on me that saying "no" hadn't hurt at all. And best of all, Wolmarans had accepted my decision with equanimity. As far as I was concerned, I had just turned the corner and become my own man. And I had every intention of keeping it that way.

It was just before eight when we completed our testing of the candidates and presented the wardens with the papers of the thirty-two we'd passed and the thirty-three we'd failed. The wardens were now left with the onerous task of conveying the results and preparing the certificates in time for the confirmation service on Monday evening.

As matters turned out, I was given a half-an-hour to look over my sermon after all. We simply decided that the bell for church would be rung a half-an-hour later.

"*Ach Dominee*," said one warden, "we are all campers here, so it doesn't really matter when the service begins." He studied me thoughtfully, then winked. "But I need to give you fair warning that we are also farmers who are used to going to bed early. So you might find yourself in competition with snores from the congregation if you preach too long."

"Believe me, *Meneer*," I said, winking back, "it will be the shortest sermon I've ever delivered."

I fell into bed that night with the thought that this hectic schedule was going to be the norm at each church place throughout my tour. There'd be no time for preparation, no time for Bible study, and little time for private prayer.

I counted my blessings that there'd be only two services the following day, with a whole afternoon at my disposal—fancy that! But as for Monday, another marathon lay ahead. The morning would be spent meeting the couples who were to be married, or have their marriages solemnized, followed in the afternoon by their weddings. Then in the evening, I'd have to conduct a lengthy confirmation service. At least the wardens had had the sense to postpone the baptismal service until my homeward-bound stop. The reason they gave was that it would mean two extra days in Potchefstroom. As they explained, the first would be spent interviewing parents, followed by the lengthy process of preparing baptismal certificates on their part.

"I'm afraid we didn't factor in these extra two days," they said. "And because the rest of your schedule is so tight, it is far better that the baptismal service be conducted at the end of your tour when you arrive back in Potchefstroom."

I sighed as I realized what lay ahead. No wonder the Synod had always sent out a delegation of two pastors. When I eventually fell asleep, I dreamt of a never-ending line of crying babies waiting to be baptized.

21

The Jerusalem Pilgrims

We left early on Tuesday morning for the Zwartrug-gens north-west of Potchefstroom. The journey, I was told, would take three days to the next church place on the border of the Marico District. As there were only intermittent tracks—and rough ones at that—Pieter Coetzer and I were given horses to ride in order to help relieve the monotony of sitting for hours in an ox-wagon having to endure its jolt and rolls as it rumbled over stones and bushes.

The landdrost, a *Meneer* Lombard, accompanied us on horseback for the first *schoft* of the journey. The reason he gave for wanting to do so was to discuss the state of the country with us. The idea was to ride ahead of the wagon for a few miles, dismount, then find ourselves some comfortable rocks to sit on. This would give him the necessary time to speak with us before the wagon caught up.

From my brief dealings with Lombard, he struck me as being a fastidious man, both in relation to his personal grooming as well as to upholding the law. Yet I found him open to reason and willing to change his mind once presented with the facts. What I admired most about him was his taste in light-tan suits that matched his hair and hazel eyes. Had I not been a *predikant*, where dress requirements favored grays and blacks, I might have followed him in his choice of color and riding attire. Very serviceable, I thought.

I was still casting an admiring eye over his getup that morning, when he started to speak.

"I feel I need to warn you both about the unsettled state of the Marico District. Do you plan to conduct a service there, *Dominee?*"

"Not to my knowledge, *Meneer* Lombard. We were careful to only arrange services in districts to which I'd been invited."

"But do you intend to travel through that district on your way to other parts?"

"I'm fairly certain we're not. From my understanding, the church place to which we're headed is only on the border of the Marico District."

"Good, because I'm sad to say, I doubt whether they'd let you through."

This statement didn't exactly come as a surprise to me, as both Coetzer and I had been led to expect some opposition from certain quarters. But what Lombard had to say next, accentuated just how tenacious this opposition could be.

"You see, *Dominee*, they consider the King of England to be one of the horns of the beast in the Book of Revelation. And as you are a pastor whose stipend is paid by the Cape Government, they regard you as being in the employ of the Antichrist. I tried to reason with them, of course, but as they pointed out, my knowledge of such matters is almost non-existent."

"So who on earth is teaching them this nonsense?"

"I'm afraid to say, it's Commandant-General Johan Enslin, who claims to be a prophet."

I glanced over at Coetzer, who shrugged his shoulders to indicate that this was news to him.

"So when did he become a Commandant-General?" I asked.

"It happened in May, around the same time as we established the *Volksraad*—our new people's council. It came into being because Commandant-General Andries Pretorius thought it time that the various Boer factions beyond the Vaal should unite to form a combined front against the English. And in order to achieve this end, the delegates divided the *Overvaal* into four districts, each with its own Commandant-General. Johan Enslin became Commandant-General of the Marico District in the west, Willem Joubert of Lijdenburg in the east, Hendrik Potgieter of Zoutpansberg in the north, and Andries Pretorius of Potchefstroom and Rustenburg in the southern and central areas."

"Very interesting, I said. But please tell me more about Enslin. Do you think his assertion about the English nation is politically motivated?"

Lombard shook his head. "Not to my mind it isn't. Having spoken to him personally, I'm certain it's based upon the prophesies in the Book of Revelation."

"I assure you, *Meneer* Lombard, there is no mention of the English nation in that book or anywhere else in the Bible, for that matter."

"Well, I beg to differ, *Dominee*."

Lombard cocked his head to one side and regarded me with amusement. He appeared to be enjoying the fact I was becoming hot under the collar. When he spoke again, it was in a commanding tone.

"It's written in the margin of the old Dutch Bible. I read it with my own eyes."

"You mean the old *Statenbijbel* of 1637—the one issued by the States-General?"

"*Ja*, that's probably the one. When I visited Enslin, he showed me the marginal note that listed the ten kings who were supposed to represent the horns of the beast. And the King of England was definitely one of them."

"Was Holland mentioned?"

"Of course not, *Dominee*."

I glanced across at Coetzer who was eyeing me with a quizzical expression. To be candid, I was just as nonplussed as he was. Surely the translators hadn't recorded their own speculations. They should have realized that their theories could have unforeseen consequences on future generations. I would definitely have to look into this.

"I'm afraid I don't possess a *Statenbijbel*, *Meneer* Lombard. So I can't comment at this stage. But I'll definitely try to visit a follower of Enslin who owns one. I'll then report back to you on my return journey."

"Thank you, *Dominee*. But I think I already know what your findings will be."

His response took me by surprise. If he knew the outcome beforehand, why take the trouble to ride out here at the break of day to inform me of all this? There was obviously something of greater import that he wanted to discuss.

As I observed him more closely, I noticed a frown on his brow.

"You look worried, *Meneer* Lombard. How can I help?"

"I'm afraid there's another matter I need to raise regarding Enslin. Others I've spoken to have simply swept it aside as too ludicrous to consider. But in my opinion, there's a distinct possibility that it could eventuate and lead to devastating consequences. And as it's of a religious nature, I feel duty-bound to share it with you."

He paused, seemingly fearful of uttering the words. When he did, he pronounced them with emphasis.

"Enslin and his followers are determined to trek to Jerusalem."

The concept was so irrational that I burst out laughing. It was only when I noted Coetzer's daggered looks, and observed Lombard kicking a few pebbles while he waited for my laughter to subside that I was jolted into silence.

"I apologize, *Meneer* Lombard, but I couldn't help myself."

"I understand, because that was my initial response as well."

"But don't they realize how far they'll need to travel?" I asked.

"Unfortunately, Enslin thinks they've reached North Africa because, while on a hunting trip, he noticed a pointed hill that looked like a pyramid. Shortly afterwards, he came across an Arab-looking tribe supposedly on Arabian horses. So he concluded that this tribe must be the sons of Ishmael, and that Palestine must be close by."

"But didn't you explain that he was still in Southern Africa?"

"I attempted to, but Enslin has no understanding of cartographical scale. The more I tried to explain, the more worked up he became. He then countered my arguments by pointing to the fact that his party had come across a north-flowing stream that he declared was obviously the source of the Nile. They've even christened it *Nylstroom*, would you believe. I tried to neutralize this argument by telling him that this stream was the source of the mighty Limpopo River that flows east into the Indian Ocean. I also added that on its way it passes just north of the Zoutpansberg District where Commandant-General Hendrik Potgieter lives."

"Did he believe you?"

"No. He just got more upset and stuck doggedly to his guns. I got the impression that he thought I was making it up."

I reflected on this last statement a moment, then said, "But if they trek north, or even north-east, they'll probably die of disease."

"Exactly. But unfortunately, I'd reached the end of my tether by then. So in order to get through to him, I pretended to believe his arguments so that I could focus on the dangers of the journey from a biblical angle. *May the Lord forgive me.*"

Lombard seemed deeply aggrieved that he'd been forced to resort to such a strategy, although to my mind, it seemed quite sensible, given the circumstances.

"But for all we know, *Meneer* Lombard, the biblical angle might be the only one he's prepared to consider. And it might be the only one he's prepared to use to finally abort this idea of trekking to Jerusalem."

"I dearly hope so, *Dominee*, otherwise I'm afraid his party might die."

"So what did you say?"

"I told him that he'd have to cross the desert and pass through the Red Sea like Moses. I also explained that he'd have to face Arab tribesmen as well as unknown diseases."

"So how did he respond to that?"

"It beggars belief."

I watched Lombard shake his head and begin to laugh—the tears rolling down his cheeks. I waited for him to wipe them away, before I prompted him to continue.

"I take it that Enslin's answer must have been comical, to say the least?"

"Quite ridiculous, really. He said that Aunt Grieta had prepared a remedy for the tsetse fly, and that he knew that the Arabs couldn't shoot as well as his party could. As for passing through the Red Sea, well, the Lord would provide a miracle, just as He had done for Moses."

"He's not pulling your leg, is he?"

"No *Dominee*. He's deadly serious, and perfectly sane, although some might beg to differ."

Lombard rose and dusted himself off. "I feel absolutely helpless to prevent this impending disaster. That is why I felt compelled to share my observations with you. Hopefully, while you are near their district, you might be able to visit one of his followers. If the light dawns, and he accepts your explanations, he will tell others. I believe that's the only way to abort this trek."

I turned to Coetzer to ascertain his response. He smiled and gave a definite nod.

"We'll try our best, *Meneer* Lombard."

"*Ach*, you have no idea what a blessing it is to hear you say that. I've been having graphic nightmares of Enslin and his party dying of thirst or perishing from some tropical disease."

"It's obviously time for you to hand this matter over to the Lord," I said. "May He grant you peace."

Lombard nodded and gripped my hand as he bade me journeying mercies.

"I'll be praying that the person you visit will see sense. After all, you're an educated man, *Dominee*, and your arguments should carry weight. But I doubt whether you'll ever be able to persuade any of Enslin's followers that the King of England—albeit that she's now a queen—is *not* one of the horns of the beast." He shot me a mischievous grin. "That's an open and shut case, I'm afraid. And a separate issue entirely."

Lombard was still chuckling as he mounted his horse. I couldn't help noticing that he exuded the air of a satisfied man who'd achieved his objective. He'll sleep well tonight, I thought.

True to our promise, we made arrangements to visit one of Enslin's followers on the border of the Marico District. After conducting the usual clutch of services over several days, we departed the district early on Wednesday morning and headed for Commandant Gert Kruger's farm. On our way there, we dropped by the home of the Enslin follower in question.

On entering the small parlor, I noticed the huge *Statenbijbel* on the mantelpiece above the fireplace. Even while studying theology at Utrecht, I'd never bothered to take one off the shelf in the theological library on account of its weight. But now I was as eager to do so as my host was to show off his prize possession.

He took the Bible down with care and laid it on the table. He then proceeded to show me his lengthy family tree at the front. At my request, he then turned to the back section. It contained the Belgic Confession, the Heidelberg Catechism with its compendium, as well as the psalter and liturgy of the Dutch Reformed Church. To my disappointment, the translators hadn't included the Canons of the Synod of Dordrecht that had been written in 1619.

Having congratulated him on maintaining his Bible in peak condition, I posed a question that I knew would elicit the views of Enslin and his faction.

"*Meneer*," I said, "I observe that you are a religious man. So why didn't you come to church and have your children baptized?"

"You see, *Dominee*, it's like this: England is one of the horns of the beast as described in the Book of Revelation. And those, like you, who receive their pay from her coffers are made partakers of her sins. So you must come out from her employ before we'll come to church."

"But where does it mention England in the Bible?"

"Right here. Let me show you, *Dominee*."

He turned to the Book of Revelation 17:12, and read: "*And the ten horns which thou sawest are ten kings which have received no kingdom as yet; but received power as kings one hour with the beast.*"

"Now look carefully at what it says in the margin alongside that verse. Can you read it aloud, *Dominee*, so that we can all hear."

I began to read: "And these ten kings have been long reckoned and described in this manner: the King in Naples, the King in Portugal, the King in Spain, the King in France, the King in England, the King in Denmark, the King in Sweden, the King in Poland, the King in Hungary, the King in Bavaria."

He tapped the place in the margin where it said England. "See for yourself, *Dominee*. It says there the King in England. You will also notice that Holland isn't mentioned. So her people are the true believers. And as we Afrikaners are linked to her through our ancestors, it stands to reason that we are also God's chosen people."

I tried to explain that the marginal note was pure speculation on the part of the translators. But to his mind, the marginal notes had just as much canonical status as the text itself. And when I tried to tell him that *Nylstroom* was not the source of the Nile, but a stream in Southern Africa, he shook his head adamantly.

"That's not so, *Dominee*. Let me show you."

He paged to the map of Africa at the back of the Bible and pointed to the Nile River.

"As you can see, there is only one Nile River in Africa, and it's up there near the Red Sea."

When I left him, I was deeply upset that I hadn't been able to make any headway with my explanations. I turned to Coetzer before mounting my horse and said, "Now that I have some notion of their prophetic interpretations, I'd like to visit the Enslin faction on my next tour to the Transvaal."

"What 'next tour' *Dominee*? You must be careful not to mention a second tour within earshot of the Transvalers—or *Overvalers,* as they call themselves—because they'll hold you to the vaguest promise. Elder Willem Pretorius told me about the Presbytery's consternation that this tour was planned without their permission. So I have strict instructions to warn you against hatching any plans for a second tour. I also regard it as my role to protect you from unrealistic demands and persuasive invitations."

I did not answer until I'd mounted my horse. I liked Coetzer, and appreciated the important role he was playing on this tour, but as for bowing to every demand of the consistory . . . those days were over.

"You can relax, *Meneer* Coetzer," I said in light-hearted fashion. "If I make any promises to return, I'll do so with the proviso that the Presbytery and the Synodical Committee will have to endorse the invitation as well as the duration of my visit."

Coetzer sat motionless in his saddle for a moment before breaking into a broad smile and doffing his hat in appreciation of my plan. "Well thought-out *Dominee*. A burden has just been lifted from my shoulders. I'll know exactly what to answer when I'm approached with a request for you to visit the Transvaal again."

"That might never happen, *Meneer* Coetzer."

"True. But if I were a betting man, you'd lose hands down."

"But what about the people's responses when they hear that the Presbytery and the Synodical Committee will have to endorse the tour?"

"*Ach*, you know what . . . they won't even bat an eyelid. You have to realize that the views of the average Afrikaner are apt to blow this way and that depending upon which direction offers the most benefits or meets the required need. From where I'm sitting, it looks as if the wind will be blowing in your direction. Just you wait and see."

22

A Letter from Hendrik Potgieter

Christmas 1849

After spending the night at Gert Kruger's farm at Hekpoort, we set out in his wagon for the next church place in the Rustenburg District. After crossing the Magaliesberg Mountains, we travelled through some beautifully wooded areas with fine streams. Further along the route, I was surprised to note many well-established farms with orchards of peaches, figs and apples. I even noticed a few vines as well as orange trees laden with fruit.

Gert Kruger, or *Oom* Gert, as I felt obliged to call him, had been a close friend of my father's before trekking north. As a result of this familiarity, he couldn't resist offering a commentary on the stalwart character of the Afrikaners of that region plus their desire to build a church and call a pastor. These comments, however, were only a prelude to what was really on his mind.

At our rest stop, he proceeded to bemoan the fact that my father had reneged on his promise to send either John or myself to that region.

"Please remind your father of the promise he made while at Potchefstroom last year. And now that you say that Winburg will be getting *Dominee* Dirk van Velden, there is no reason why you can't come here. The field is ripe for harvest, and many are longing for the Word."

"But I've only been in Bloemfontein six months *Oom* Gert. I can't just up and leave."

"*Ja*, but what about that group of young students from the Cape who are now studying for the ministry in Utrecht? You told me yesterday that your friend Jan Neethling will be arriving home soon. So why can't you come here and let him go to Bloemfontein?"

I glanced across at Coetzer who wasn't looking too happy with that suggestion.

"*Ach, Oom* Gert," I said. "You must remember that Jan would have to agree to this plan in the first place, as would the Presbytery. You also have to realize that even before he lands, he'll be receiving calls from vacant pastorates in the Cape."

Oom Gert opened his mouth to reply, but observing Coetzer's disapproval, thought better of it.

"I'll say no more on this topic for the time-being," he said. "But tell your father that a promise is a promise. Either you or your brother should have been appointed as pastor here."

The church place to which we were headed was located on Caspar Kruger's farm. When we arrived there on Friday morning, *Oom* Gert instructed his driver to drop us off at the farmhouse.

"The two of you will be staying here as Caspar's guests," he said, "while Hettie and I will be camping next to our sons and grandchildren. I can't wait to see them all again."

He turned his back on the house to survey the multicolored landscape in the distance.

"Isn't the farm situated in a beautiful area?" he said. "Just look at that view."

My eyes were drawn to the chain of distant hills that folded one within the other—some green, others gold, a few brown. Directly below the rise on which the farmhouse stood, I could see a lightly wooded area that stretched a short distance to a winding river beyond. In the center of this area, was an open field that had been cleared of trees and veld debris. At the one end was a large tree with overhanging branches that I surmised would serve as a canopy for my home-made pulpit.

This thought had barely crossed my mind, when I noticed several teams of oxen drawing wagons into the clearing. Their arrival was accompanied by the cracking of whips, and a good deal of coaxing from their drivers. It was the necessary prelude to putting a covering over the sanctuary by stretching buckskins across from one wagon to the other.

Besides the hustle and bustle in the clearing, I was surprised to note that the campsite was already packed with numerous wagons that were strategically parked under shade trees. And as with most church camps, it was noisy and bustling with activity. Particularly noticeable was the cacophony of crying babies and the high-pitched squeals of excited children. Many families who'd arrived early were either greeting newcomers, sitting in groups, or helping newcomers outspan their horses or oxen.

"It's a wonderful site for families," commented *Oom* Gert. One of its major attractions is the safe swimming area for the children close by. I'm only sorry it won't be so relaxing for you, *Dominee*. Nevertheless, Caspar hopes that his home will serve as a haven away from the pastoral demands of the camp. Come,

I'll introduce you to his wife. From the looks of things, Caspar is busy preparing the sanctuary."

Oom Gert's comment, that it wouldn't be a relaxing time for me, was the understatement of the year. The next three days proved to be my busiest ever. My first service was due to take place that very evening, followed by two preparation services the next day. And sandwiched in between was my talk to the parents of over eighty infants who were due to be baptized that same afternoon. This had forced me to dispense with the usual interview process in favor of a general address. Fortunately, the certificates had already been prepared by the wardens and endorsed by the elders prior to my arrival.

By Sunday evening, I was well and truly exhausted. On arriving back at the farmhouse, I fell into bed early so as to feel fresh for the dawn service the next morning and the testing of eighty catechists that would follow directly afterwards. This meant a grueling Monday with few planned breaks and a late confirmation service at its close.

It was already mid-afternoon on Monday, and the elders and I had only managed to test two-thirds of the candidates. We were in dire need of a concentration booster, when the unexpected arrival of an ox-wagon peaked our curiosity, and did the trick. In the distance we could hear the cracking of a whip, followed, a short time later, by sustained applause and whoops of joy.

Who on earth, I thought, would be arriving on Christmas eve after all the services were over?

Fortunately, the elders and I didn't have long to wait to find out. For as soon as the catechist we'd been testing had left the tent, one of the Wardens stuck his head around the flap and said, "You wouldn't believe who's just arrived, gentlemen. It's a two-man delegation from Hendrik Potgieter in the Zoutpansberg. They've just delivered a letter to Commandant-General Andries Pretorius. And you know what that means."

I had a vague idea what he was referring to, but wasn't about to ask. So despite the excited voices we could hear outside our tent, we plodded on, determined to keep to our schedule until our tea break at four. Needless to say, we adjourned promptly when that hour arrived.

The elders and I had just begun to discuss the arrival of the deputation over tea, when Pieter Coetzer entered the tent.

"I'm sorry to interrupt, gentlemen, but I've come with a request for *Dominee* to accompany me to the farmhouse to meet the deputation from the Zoutpansberg.

"Can't it wait, *Meneer* Coetzer?" I asked. "You have to understand that we don't have a minute to spare. We still have twenty candidates to get through before seven o'clock. So I'd be much obliged if you could explain my situation to them."

"I already have, *Dominee*, but they are adamant they want to speak to you. They've travelled fourteen *schoften* over four days, so it would appear rude if you didn't meet with them over afternoon refreshments."

"*Ja-Nee, Dominee*, you must go," said the elders. "This is the breakthrough we've all been waiting for. We can always begin the evening's service a little later."

"And don't forget, it's Christmas tomorrow," said Coetzer. "So it's much better meeting them this afternoon than tomorrow morning. After all, you deserve to enjoy a break from church affairs at Christmas."

As Coetzer's statement resonated with me, I put down my cup, grabbed my hat, nodded to the elders, then indicated to Coetzer that we should go.

We strode as fast as we could through the camp to avoid being waylaid. When we reached the pathway leading to the farmhouse, I said to Coetzer, "Do you know anything about this breakthrough that the elders were referring to?"

"As a matter of fact, the talk around camp has focused on nothing else. But to understand the breakthrough, you need to know the events that led up to it. From the reports I've heard, Hendrik Potgieter and his delegates walked out of the second *Volksraad* meeting at the Olifants River in March. And worse still, they didn't even attend the third meeting at Derdepoort in May."

"So what triggered that response?"

"Apparently, it was at Olifants River that it was decided that the *Volksraad* would be the highest authority in the land, and that everyone, including the leaders of the four main factions, would be expected to yield to its authority."

"Ah! So Potgieter wanted to remain a law unto himself, did he?"

"I dare say that's true. But he also wanted the Zoutpansberg District to remain independent. According to camp talk, his party no longer farms like the rest of the Boers, but are now elephant hunters and ivory traders, with some raiding of African villages on the side. He has also forged close trading ties with the Portuguese in Delagoa Bay. So he regards the Zoutpansberg District as different from the others."

"My Goodness! Ivory trading you say? Well that *is* a major change in direction."

"*Ja*, so much so, that many of his people aren't happy about it. From what I understand, when he moved from the farming district of Ohrigstad to the Zoutpansberg to set up his trading posts there, a large, disenchanted faction remained behind. But because of the outbreak of Delagoa-Bay fever in Ohrigstad, they've since establish a new settlement with Lijdenburg as its center. It's now considered a district in its own right with Willem Joubert as its leader."

"I see. So the fourth district consists of this breakaway faction?"

"So I believe. And they've been hard at work at trying to rein Potgieter in ever since."

Coetzer and I had been so absorbed in the surreal world of Transvaal politics that we hadn't noticed that we were fast approaching the fenced off area surrounding the farmhouse garden. As both of us needed to catch our breath, I suggested we shelter under a nearby tree so that he could complete his story. It was essential that I learn the reason for Potgieter's change of heart before meeting his delegation.

"Now the story becomes really interesting," continued Coetzer. "You see, the *Volksraad* decided that they were not going to let Potgieter get away with his independent policy. So they thought up a plan to bring him to heel. They broke off all ties with him, and even bade him join the Portuguese—with tongue in cheek, of course."

"How clever."

"Just so. But be that as it may, the campers still think it a miracle that he gave in so quickly. In fact, the general view is that our arrival across the Vaal served as the necessary tipping point."

I was about to ask another question, when we heard voices coming from the front entrance. Coetzer, who was a tall man, stood on tiptoe and craned his neck over some high-growing bushes to see.

"It's Andries Pretorius," he said. "Our timing is perfect, *Dominee*. When he walks to the gate, we'll head there as well. Perhaps he'll give you a word of advice."

Pretorius was grinning from ear to ear when he offered me his hand. He was wearing a tanned-colored waistcoat over a cream shirt that had seen better days. It was unbuttoned at the top to reveal some graying chest hairs that matched his graying goatee. He looked no different from any other farmer at camp—what with his broad-brimmed hat and leathery, sunburnt face.

"Oh happy day," he said. "Our people over the Vaal are all one at last."

He extracted a folded envelope from his pocket and fluttered it in the air in a gesture of victory.

"The Zoutpansberg delegation has just presented me with this letter from Hendrik Potgieter. And thank the Lord, *Dominee*, Potgieter says that all the issues that have come between us have now vanished."

I wanted to congratulate him on this breakthrough, but I couldn't get a word in edgeways. He simply rushed on with barely a pause.

"I think they have a letter for you too," he said. "But just a word of advice. Listen and say nothing. These are God-fearing men who have paid a heavy price to get here. And reading between the lines, it's clear that there's been a revolt in the Zoutpansberg ranks that has forced Potgieter's hand to re-establish relations with us. It's also obvious that his decision was made at the last moment. His letter to me is dated Thursday, 20 December. That's why these men had to travel on a Sunday to reach us before we break camp."

He paused a moment while searching my face. I could tell that he was in two minds whether to express what was on his heart. Fortunately, he considered me worthy of his honest opinion.

"Just another word of advice," he said. "We are all anti-English in these parts. But the Zoutpansbergers are even more so. They're also suspicious of the Cape Synod and all her pastors. But at the same time, they also wish to hear the preaching of the Word. So you might find that their arguments don't always accord with reality. Don't try to put the record straight, *Dominee*. We'll do that in the *Volksraad*. What these men need now is a word of encouragement."

He tapped my arm in a playful manner, and said, "I look forward to your visit on Wednesday. We'll talk then."

He nodded to Coetzer, then strode with a bounce in his step towards the camp.

I didn't know what to expect from my interview with the Potgieter delegation. Fortunately, my host, Caspar Kruger, and his neighbor, Frans Schutte, were present to introduce us. The first action on the part of the delegation was to present me with a letter from Potgieter. But before I had time to open it, they had already launched into a heartfelt plea for me to return to the Zoutpansberg with them.

It was only after I'd described my detailed itinerary that they finally understood that their pleas were in vain. And with this realization came their tears. To my embarrassment, they just sat there in silence, with tears streaming down their cheeks. It was a heart-wrenching site to watch. And to make matters worse, the eyes of the other men were brimming over as well. I didn't know where to look, or what to say.

With my own eyes averted, I decided it was time to open Potgieter's letter. To my relief, he conveyed a realistic grasp of my situation. He also intimated that he understood that I might not be able to accompany his men on their return journey.

"*Please appoint a time when you or some other minister can come to us,*" the letter read.

His request struck home.

I'll just have to return next year, I thought. There's no two-ways about it. It will give me the opportunity to visit the Enslin faction as well as the Zoutpansbergers. I'll plan a much longer tour with more frequent free days in between. I'll also ask the Synodical Committee for permission to let *Dominee* Van Velden accompany me. And as for Pa, I know he'll never allow me to come during my vacation in December. So it'll have to be during September/October. And as for my consistory, they'll just have to make the necessary sacrifice. After all, they'd expected me to give up my vacation to go on this preaching tour.

I cleared my throat and smiled at the dispirited men before me.

"Gentlemen," I said, "Please convey my greetings to Commandant-General Potgieter, and tell him that I'll try my best to visit the Zoutpansberg District in September/October next year. It will depend on the agreement of the Graaff-Reinet Presbytery and the Synodical Committee, of course. But I'm hopeful they'll support my application. If not, perhaps someone else can come in my stead. I'll write all this in a letter to Potgieter tomorrow, and deliver it to you before you leave."

To my surprise, the men didn't bat an eyelid at the mention of the Presbytery or the Synodical Committee. Instead, they expressed their appreciation by rising silently from their seats to shake my hand. To my relief, Coetzer nodded in agreement, while Kruger and Schutte looked positively perky.

"It's out of our hands now," I said to Coetzer as we strode back to camp. "It will depend entirely on the Synodical Committee."

"But what about the Governor Sir Harry Smith?"

"Him too, I suppose. But I can't see him putting a spoke in the wheel."

"Don't you believe it, *Dominee*. You never know which way the wind will blow with him."

23
A Visit to Andries Pretorius

We left Rustenburg early on Wednesday morning, and travelled in a south-easterly direction to Andries Pretorius's farm. As numerous wagons of the Pretorius clan were headed that way, I found myself riding next to one wagon then another, sometimes speaking with one or other rider, but mostly keeping to myself and reflecting on the camp that had just been.

Time and again, my thoughts returned to Christmas Day, when one person after another had approached me with a testimony of how the Lord had touched them through my messages. Some even pleaded with me for hours to accept a call. Amongst these were Caspar Kruger and his neighbor Frans Schutte. Both declared that they were so thirsty for the Word that they'd decided to accompany Coetzer and myself on the rest of the tour.

I was so moved by these unexpected responses, that I began to plan a course of action. I'd even jotted my thoughts down in a letter to my father. The relevant paragraph read:

Suppose another minister, say Jan Neethling, should refuse to come here, but be willing to take Bloemfontein, what would you think of my coming here? Perhaps you will say, "Foolish boy!" But the way in which some of the people have pleaded with me, really moves my heart. Many are also in a fit state for receiving the seed of the Word. May the Lord in His mercy help them.

I was still mulling over my experiences at camp, when we reached Pretorius's farm. His brothers Piet and Bart had made sure that everything was in readiness for our arrival. Coetzer and I also learnt that they would be the ones conveying us to our next church place the following day. To our relief, we heard that it was on Daniel Erasmus's farm, only a short *schoft* away. This meant that I'd be able to spend the following morning with the Pretorius family—an opportunity I was looking forward to very much. After all, Commandant-General Andries Pretorius was the celebrated hero of the Battle of Blood River, and who would not deem it a privilege to converse with him?

After breakfast the following morning, Pretorius suggested we ride on horseback to survey the beauty of the countryside. In reality, I knew that he wanted to speak with me alone.

As we excused ourselves from the breakfast table, I was conscious that we were leaving a deeply disappointed group of men behind, particularly Coetzer. He'd been present at all my meetings, and was therefore on the verge of rising to follow us, when an almost imperceptible hand gesture from Pretorius indicated that he should stay. This gesture alone gave me an insight into the type of authority that a leader of Pretorius's stature could exert.

We rode a considerable way until we came to a small hillock. After dismounting, we scrambled to the top to take in the vista of the Magaliesberg Mountains in the distance.

"This is my favorite lookout," he said. "And as you can tell from the roughly hewed bench I've placed here, I come to this spot fairly often. Let's sit a moment and take in the view."

While doing so, I took the opportunity to observe Pretorius through the corner of my eye. He had once again donned farm clothes that I knew he'd exchange for a double-breasted suit to wear to the service that evening. But despite his casual attire, it was plain from his confident bearing that I was in the presence of a leader.

It was not long before he broached the topic that was on his mind.

"As you are aware, *Dominee*, I didn't take communion at either Potchefstroom or Rustenburg. But I feel ready to do so this Sunday. I'm very mindful of the fact that as a leader it's important for me to observe what the Bible teaches about forgiveness and reconciliation. And believe me, I hear enough about it from Elder Wolmarans. Nevertheless, I feel I now have a clear conscience. And because of this, I would appreciate your blessing on this decision."

"It's not for me to say, *Meneer* Pretorius. You will have to search your own heart to see if you are not living in enmity with anyone. If your conscience is clear on that score, then you are most welcome to sit at the Lord's table."

He lent back on the bench, and stretched out his legs, crossing them at the ankles. "As you know, Hendrik Potgieter and I are now reconciled. And as for my fury over the British takeover of the Sovereignty, well, that has long since abated. In any case, our *Volksraad* is now the government here. The only action left for me to do now is to seek reconciliation with that terror of a Hollander Bührmann. While I feel I've done so in my heart, I haven't had the opportunity to visit him personally because he lives in Lijdenburg. Unfortunately, he's a difficult customer, so in the past our political discussions have tended to become acrimonious."

I needed a moment to think this through. I leant forward on the bench, my forearms on my knees. I hated the predicament in which he was placing me. From what he had implied, it appeared that Elder Wolmarans had warned him against taking communion. But because Wolmarans would not be present at the service on Sunday, he was now hoping that I, as a pastor, would grant him absolution. But that I couldn't do. And if I were to be honest with myself, his attitude was far from forgiving. In fact, he seemed to be placing the blame squarely on Bührmann's shoulders. I decided that I owed it to the Lord to point this out.

"I'm afraid I couldn't help noticing a hint of bitterness in your voice, *Meneer* Pretorius. Are you sure you've forgiven Bührmann in your heart?"

"*Ach Dominee*, I've asked that question of myself many-a-time. I know I shouldn't take his political views personally, but I do. According to him, there is no place for elitist warlords like Potgieter and myself in a farming community. He also argues that the trek is over and that we should be moving towards a representative government where the *Volksraad* members are elected and not appointed by leaders. But that's all very well. What he fails to understand is that we have to crawl before we can walk. And because he's an educated teacher from Amsterdam, he's inclined to be high and mighty and lord it over others."

My mouth must have dropped open while witnessing Pretorius's indignation, because he burst out laughing.

"Don't worry, *Dominee*. I recognize the symptoms of unforgiveness. I'll have to ask the Lord for special assistance in helping me reach an understanding with this Hollander."

"But doesn't he acknowledge the great strides you've made in establishing the *Volksraad?*"

"Perhaps so, but he wants us to take it further. In any case, the *Volksraad* didn't come about because of him. I was stimulated to set the ball rolling by something Dr. William Robertson said while he was here in January. And let me tell you, he's a crafty one."

It was my turn to laugh now. "Don't I know it," I said.

"*Ja,* and he knows how to spar with words and thrust the sword in when you least expect it. He's also a brilliant tactician, and unlike Bührmann, as cool and collected as can come. But at least he made me see sense."

Pretorius lent sideways to extract a tobacco pouch and pipe from his trouser pocket. I knew from watching other pipe smokers that the rigmarole of filling and lighting a pipe would be part of the theatrical backdrop to his story. After doing just that, and taking a few puffs, he launched straight in.

"So there I was sitting at the dining table with Dr. Philip Faure on my right, and Dr. William Robertson on my left. I had just dismissed the family after devotions, when Faure broached the subject of the Battle of Boomplaats. He asked me what I thought I was doing by taking on a superior British force in a major engagement. I tell you *Dominee,* I was seething inside, but outwardly very respectful. For after all, Dr. Faure is the moderator of the Synod."

"So what did you reply?"

"*Ach,* I put forward the usual complaints about the English not leaving us alone, while at the same time giving the African tribes leeway to rule themselves. I also commented that Gideon, in the Book of Judges, had won the battle against the Midianites with only three hundred men. Well, you should have seen the expression on their faces."

He chuckled while peering into the distance. I could tell by this well-chosen pause that he had a penchant for storytelling. He certainly had me hooked.

"So I take it that they didn't appreciate your answer, *Meneer* Pretorius."

"Not at all. Dr. Faure became quite animated and told me some home truths. 'But you lost,' he said. 'And why is that so? Because your outlook on life is based on the Old Covenant. Let me remind you,' he said, 'that we are now in the New Covenant where Christ calls upon Christians to live in peace and harmony with one another and to respect the Government. And as long as there's no unity amongst you Afrikaners across the Vaal, nor any laws, nor any governing body to make them, the Cape Government will continue to regard you as citizens of the Cape. That is how it is, and that is how it works in civilized societies.'"

"Ah, I see now why you felt the need to establish a *Volksraad*."

"True, but I only saw the light when Dr. Robertson followed this up with some very unwelcome news. You see, he told me that Hendrik Potgieter had held formal discussions with Sir Harry Smith's private secretary Richard Southey. Apparently, they'd met on the Mooi River near Potchefstroom only three months after the Battle of Boomplaats. As I had just arrived back from the Sovereignty myself, I had no idea that such a meeting had taken place. In fact, I only heard about it through Dr. Robertson."

"Just as well you did, otherwise you may never have heard about it."

"Exactly. It seems that Potgieter went to a lot of trouble to hush it up. You have to understand that we were fierce rivals at the time."

At this point Pretorius took another puff. When he finally took the pipe out of his mouth, he started to gesticulate with its stem like an orchestra conductor with a baton.

"According to Dr. Robertson, Potgieter agreed to accept the British takeover of the Sovereignty and not to intervene in Sovereignty affairs. In exchange, Richard Southey assured him that the Cape Government would leave the Afrikaners of the *Overvaal* alone to manage their own affairs. Nevertheless, Southey stipulated that the Cape Government would retain the right to veto the appointment of any official who did not meet with its approval. And it goes without saying, that Potgieter interpreted that to mean me. So he had no difficulty agreeing to that demeaning requirement. But I have to be honest here, *Dominee*. Potgieter, at that time, regarded himself as a one-man *Volksraad,* and therefore had no intention of appointing anyone else."

"While that may be true, *Meneer* Pretorius, it was still rather arrogant of Richard Southey to suggest what he did. You must have been furious with Potgieter?"

"I was. My consternation soared so high that I had to steel myself to keep it in check. But then Dr. Robertson took my focus off Potgieter and planted it squarely on Southey. He told me it was important to read between the lines. What, for instance, was Southey really saying when he mentioned the appointment of officials? After discussing the issue with Dr. Robertson, it became clear that what the Cape Government desired was a state on the border of the Sovereignty that could maintain law and order through a central governing body." He flashed me a smile then continued, "Well, that body has now come into being. It's our *Volksraad.* And for us, it's the acknowledged government of the *Overvaal.* But I tell you this, *Dominee,* we have no intention of becoming an outlying province of the Cape. Our aim is to remain independent. And in order to do so, we plan to keep the peace, and thus the British at bay."

It was now my turn to read between the lines. It was obvious that Pretorius wanted me to tell Major Warden that all was at peace in the Transvaal. I looked his way and smiled to indicate that I understood.

"You must be very proud of this achievement." I said.

"*Ach Dominee*, we still have a long way to go. As you know, the Cape Government still considers me an outlaw with a bounty of £2000 on my head. So my next step is to seek a pardon. In the meantime, I'll keep a low profile, and when I feel the time is right, I'll test the waters. So please don't hesitate to contact me if you think there's a change in government policy that could help my cause. I need someone close to the English camp to interpret events and detect a shift in the wind."

I was waiting for him to suggest something of the kind, but although I felt an urge to be of help, I didn't want to raise his hopes.

"I'll gladly be of assistance, *Meneer* Pretorius. But be warned, I still have a number of stripes to earn before Major Warden will share confidences with me or take my views into account."

"*Ach*, you know what, *Dominee*, pastors don't need stripes. They're in a category of their own. And from observation, some are able to wield as much power in their sphere of influence as any ruler, especially if they have their ear to the ground and respond to situations without fear or favor. And given the extent of your pastorate, your influence is as great as that of a bishop, even an archbishop, perhaps."

I guffawed loudly at his exaggerated remark. "Flattery will get you nowhere, *Meneer* Pretorius. Remember, I'm supposed to respond without fear or favor."

He winked and chortled back. "I'm serious," he said. "Major Warden will be aware of the influence you wield, and so will Sir Harry Smith. Let me give you an example. Take Elder Wolmarans, for instance. Because he's an elder, he holds no formal position on the *Volksraad*. Yet, after completing our deliberations at Derdepoort in May, there we all were, listening obediently while he delivered a sermon on Hezekiah and admonished us to follow in God's path. And I'm pleased to say, it didn't fall on deaf ears."

He returned his pipe in its pouch and got up to go. "Just one more thing, *Dominee*. When you get to Lijdenburg, tell Bührmann that I've wiped the slate clean. He'll know what I mean."

"I'll do so with pleasure," I said, relieved that he had taken the first step towards reconciliation.

24

The Scourge of Malaria

January 1850

My day at Pretorius's farm was one of the most relaxing I'd been able to spend on tour. This was no doubt due to my relief that I was now making headway with my sermons, and that the Lord was touching the lives of my hearers. Nevertheless, I was achingly conscious that I was being forced to preach with little preparation. I therefore decided that the only option open to me was to try and live each moment in God's presence, despite the lively company of men around me. I reasoned that by doing so, God would make up for my want of regular study.

This intentional decision became my mainstay during the weeks ahead, for without warning, I fell ill with a severe fever on Sunday afternoon. And although I was too unwell to preach that evening, I was forced to drag myself into the pulpit on Monday morning to confirm a group of young people. And if that didn't sap my energy enough, I then discovered that I needed to ride on horseback for several hours to catch up with the wagon that had gone ahead earlier that morning.

"We're really sorry that we had to send the wagon on ahead," said Caspar Kruger. "But it was the only option if you are to reach Lijdenburg by Friday afternoon."

The following day turned out to be the worst on tour. Despite it being New Year's day, we found ourselves having to travel for eleven-and-a-half hours across lion-infested country until we reached the safety of a farmhouse. To make matters worse, Coetzer also came down with a fever along the way. And because he was now unable to fulfil his role as main organizer and general dogs-body, I was only too thankful that Kruger and Schutte were there to step into his shoes. At each rest place, they saw to the horses and helped outspan the oxen, leaving Coetzer and myself free to stretch out on the grass.

When we finally reached Lijdenburg on Friday afternoon, both Coetzer and I were still ill. Thankfully, the Lord strengthened me sufficiently to be able to conduct the usual set of services, including a baptismal one for seventy-five infants. But I'm afraid to say, I was hardly *compos mentis*. It was more a case of going through the motions.

My poor state of health also prevented me from speaking face-to-face with individual members of the congregation, including the Hollander Bührmann. But lo and behold, there he was, riding next to the wagon when it pulled out of Lijdenburg on Tuesday morning. He told me later that he had decided to travel back to Potchefstroom with us to be present at the *Volksraad* meeting that was set for Monday, 21 January. En route, I was able to discuss an assortment of topics with him, including his self-appointed role as peacekeeper between the factions.

Having enjoyed a much needed rest on Sunday at Rustenburg, we finally reached Potchefstroom on Thursday afternoon. By this time I was feeling much better, whereas Coetzer's health had deteriorated.

"You'll be able to sleep without any interruptions in the

family tent they are sure to provide for us," I told Coetzer. "I'm sure you'll recover quickly once you've had sufficient rest."

Unfortunately, I failed to detect the seriousness of his condition. It was probably because I, myself, was on the road to recovery, and therefore took it for granted that the rest he'd be enjoying over the coming days would likewise do the trick for him. But to my regret, as soon as I saw the hundreds of wagons parked at the campsite, my concerns immediately switched to the task of preaching and pastoring that lay ahead. And although Bührmann had intimated that the *Volksraad* would be sitting on Monday, I had no idea that the turnout would be so great.

I had just made our beds and had helped Coetzer onto his, when a bumptious Wolmarans darkened the entrance to our tent. So as not to disturb Coetzer, I stepped outside to greet him. I noticed that he was already in elder mode, having donned his double-breasted black suit. And because I was still unkempt from our long journey, I was only too conscious of the air of authority his formal attire and polished demeanor lent him. Nor could I help admiring his neatly trimmed gray hair that was suavely parted just a smidgen off center.

"I'm so pleased I've been able to catch you before you settle down to an afternoon nap," he said. "I've just come to inform you that I've managed to postpone the sitting of the *Volksraad* until Tuesday. As there are over 400 wagons here, I couldn't help thinking what a wonderful opportunity it would be to extend the services to Monday."

I responded with a wan smile because Monday was scheduled to be my rest day in preparation for the services I'd need to take at the Rhenoster River in the Sovereignty. It was clear that Wolmarans knew nothing of my illness, nor that I was still in recovery mode.

"Your preaching schedule will be as follows," he said. "There'll be the usual service tomorrow evening, with two on both Saturday and Sunday, as well as on Monday."

"Two on Monday?" I said, my voice rising sharply to indicate my alarm that my rest day was being ripped from under me. "But there's usually only one thanksgiving service on Monday, *Meneer* Wolmarans."

"I'm aware of that, *Dominee,* and know that you are tired, but these are special circumstances. You see, a great deal of contention and enmity often prevails at our *Volksraad* meetings. So I was hoping you would address this situation by preaching on God's love for us and His expectation that we should mirror His love in return—something along those lines."

I observed the challenging look in his eye and the tone of authority in his voice. Pretorius was right, I thought. Wolmarans wielded a type of power that stemmed from his desire for the Afrikaner to follow the Lord. And few men would be able to gainsay him, especially when they knew that he had the best interests of the people at heart.

I did not answer straight away because I was too busy wracking my brain to recall sermons that I had already preached on love.

"Just hand it over to the Lord," he prompted. "He will provide the energy and insight you need."

"I'm certain He will, *Meneer* Wolmarans. But the problem I'm facing is that I have little time to prepare the special sermons you've requested."

"*Ach,* you don't have to write them out, *Dominee.* Just choose an appropriate text for each sermon, write a few headings, and then preach from the heart like you did at Rustenburg. The people there are still speaking about it. So what do you say?"

He made it sound so easy. But he seemed to forget that most of my so-called spare time would be dedicated to revising my other five sermons.

"Very well," I said. "Just as long as you understand that these sermons will be off the cuff as you suggested."

"Excellent. Now one more thing, *Dominee*. I would like to hold a short church meeting after the Monday evening service. It is essential that we start building churches in these parts. And while all the leaders are here, it will be an excellent opportunity to pass a special resolution to set the ball in motion."

"Good idea, *Meneer* Wolmarans. But surely you don't need me to be present?"

"I'm afraid I do. You see, your presence here is the pretext I've given for organizing this meeting in the first place."

I heaved a sigh to let him know that I considered this extra meeting an imposition. I was about to acquiesce, when Coetzer appeared in the doorway of the tent, his face flushed, his breathing coming in gasps.

"*Meneer* Wolmarans," he said, "you are not being fair to *Dominee*. He's still recovering from a fever. And asking him to preach an extra sermon on Monday evening followed by a meeting afterwards is far too much for one pastor to bear. You have to realize that he still has to take services at both the Rhenoster and Valsch Rivers on our way home."

I exchanged a knowing look with Wolmarans, who was now the epitome of concern for Coetzer. "Please, *Meneer* Coetzer, you're not well and need to rest. Come lie down."

He ushered Coetzer back inside the tent, then held onto his arm as Coetzer lowered himself onto the bed.

"I promise to look after *Dominee*. And at the first signs of hoarseness or fever, I'll order him to take a break. As for the meeting on Monday evening, it'll only be a short one, I assure you."

"Short?" said Coetzer. "Since when has a church meeting ever been short?"

The weekend rolled passed with the speed of a flood-driven wave coming down the Orange River after torrential rain. And contrary to all expectations, I found myself being swept along without feeling unduly wearied or suffering chest pains from the effort of making myself heard.

"It's a miracle," said Coetzer, when I entered our tent on Monday evening, still buoyed by the positive feedback I'd received from my sermons on love. "I don't know how you do it?"

"It's not me, *Meneer* Coetzer. I've been sustained by the Lord due to all the prayers being offered up on my behalf, especially yours."

"That's the least I could do for you in my condition. But even so, I feel that we shouldn't have organized services at the Rhenoster and Valsch Rivers this week. What on earth were we thinking?"

"We weren't to know. Anyway, how are you feeling this evening?"

"I must be honest with you, *Dominee*. It's no good hiding it. My whole body is wracked with pain, especially my back. I've tried sitting, walking around, as well as standing for a short time while listening to you preach, but nothing seems to help."

"I'm really sorry to hear that," I said, not knowing what else to say.

Coetzer continued to patter on. "I've no idea how I'm going to cope with the sways and jolts of the ox-wagon when we cross the Vaal. I suppose the Valsch-River people who've come to fetch us didn't think to bring extra horses for us to ride?"

"I'm afraid not, *Meneer* Coetzer."

I wanted to give him my full attention, but felt I needed to rush in order to change as well as pack our things in readiness for an early morning start while it was still twilight. And the last thing I wanted to inflict on Coetzer was a swarm of insects that would undoubtedly materialize if I lit a lamp.

After having completed the said chores in record time, I flopped on my bedroll, fully dressed in the travel clothes I intended to wear the next day. My relief at having packed our things before nightfall was short lived, however, because now I had to break some unpalatable news to Coetzer.

"You were right about the church meeting," I said. "It has since been arranged that a *Volksraad*-style meeting will take place around a campfire tonight at ten, when everyone else is in bed. The agenda will focus solely on the building of churches, both here and in Rustenburg. So I hope you don't mind if we skip our prayer time, because I'd really like to get an hour's shut-eye before the meeting."

"*Ach* shame," I heard Coetzer say as I rolled over. "It will go until well past midnight, you know. I'm just so sorry that I've been too ill to protect you from this type of demand. But one thing is sure. I won't be waking you up if you oversleep."

I chuckled in appreciation of the sentiment. "I'm afraid *Meneer* Wolmarans must have guessed as much, because he has offered to wake me when he passes by."

ॐ

25

Storm Clouds Gather

By the time the church meeting drew to a close, it was two o'clock in the morning. The last item on the agenda was to inform me that the church leaders had decided to send me an official letter of call. They also intimated that they would be petitioning the Synod to release me from Bloemfontein.

As we were all tired, I did not want to prolong the meeting a minute longer than necessary. With this in mind, I simply thanked them for the confidence they'd placed in me, and promised to prayerfully consider the call. In reality, I was thrilled by the news. All I had to do now was to persuade my father that serving in the Transvaal was the right move for me, and that the Lord was calling me to it.

Unfortunately, all the unwarranted flattery that had accompanied these statements had led to a surge of pride. And if I'd learnt anything at Utrecht, it was that pride was *the* major stumbling block to spiritual growth. As I shook each leader by the hand, I couldn't help thinking what little spiritual progress I'd made by taking for myself the glory that belonged to God alone. Surely I had reason to praise the Lord for His loving kindness and to weep in the dust for my own wickedness.

May You pardon and renew me Lord, I silently prayed. But the feelings of pride still persisted.

❧

Meanwhile, Wolmarans had been standing a little to one side. I now turned to bid him goodbye, but he intimated that we should walk together. We followed the others along the well-trodden path that stretched from the river bank to the campsite, the moon lighting our way. I waited for him to speak, but he appeared preoccupied—even a little nervous—and decidedly unlike his authoritative self.

"Is anything the matter, *Meneer* Wolmarans?" I asked.

"*Ach, Dominee,* I've been putting off this moment since this afternoon. But the time has now come for me to tell you."

As he didn't follow this statement up immediately, I said, "Come now, *Meneer* Wolmarans. It can't be that bad."

"Perhaps you need to hear what I have to say first." After a short pause he began to explain. "Early this afternoon, Jan Kok from a nearby farm arrived at camp insisting to speak to you. And because I knew you were preparing your sermon, I didn't have the heart to disturb you."

"What on earth did he want?"

"According to him, his young wife, who gave birth to a fine son on Saturday evening, has got it into her head that unless the baby is baptized, he won't go to heaven if he dies."

"Is the child ill?"

"Not to my knowledge."

"But didn't you tell him that baptism doesn't confer rebirth but only incorporates the child into the visible church?"

"I certainly did. And I'm sure he understands that fact. But he told me that he couldn't persuade his young wife that that was so."

"Well, she must get her ideas from somewhere?"

"They have been passed down from mother to daughter, *Dominee*. And then there's the Belgic Confession at the back of the *Statenbijbel* that clearly links baptism with rebirth, while the Heidelberg Confession can be interpreted either way. And as these poor, destitute people have not had a pastor to teach them otherwise, what can you expect?"

Heeding my father's warning, I had no intention of discussing the history of baptism in the Reformed Church with him at that hour of the morning. I also had no intention of giving in to any request he might make for me to baptize this child. It simply wasn't necessary. The Kok family could wait until September when I returned to Potchefstroom. Nevertheless, I wanted Wolmarans to stop dithering and make the request so that I could refuse it. I was exhausted and wanted to get to bed.

"So what would you suggest, *Meneer* Wolmarans?"

"If we left on horseback just ahead of the wagon at six, you'll have time to baptize the child before joining the wagon. The turnoff to the Koks' farm is on the same road as you will take to reach the Vaal crossing."

"Hmm, sounds feasible. But how far is the farmhouse from the road?"

Wolmarans stopped in his tracks to consider this question. "Just over an hour, I'm afraid."

I made a quick calculation and realized that if I gave in to his request, it would put my schedule out by at least two hours. I was thankful that he'd made no move to walk on because I didn't want anyone to overhear our conversation.

"Before we discuss this further, *Meneer* Wolmarans, I need to make you aware of my schedule. I would like to arrive at Daniel Cronje's farm by mid-afternoon so that I can have a few hours uninterrupted sleep. I'm in dire need of it. I also owe it to the Rhenoster-River people. You will recall that I gave up my rest day to preach two additional sermons to the Potchefstroom congregation, not to speak of the church meeting I attended tonight. So to be fair, I've completed my ministry here. With this in mind, I've no intention of asking the wagon to wait a few hours while I baptize this child. You will just have to visit the Kok family and explain that their son can be baptized on my return in September."

To my surprise, Wolmarans didn't react to my statement. Instead, he appeared to be peering at the moon. What on earth was he about?

"Not so hasty, *Dominee*. I have an idea. I fully understand that you would like several hours unbroken sleep when you arrive at Daniel Cronje's. But what puzzles me is why Coetzer needs to accompany you there. Cronje's farm is situated east of the Rhenoster River, which means that you'll have to cross it when you travel west on your way to the Valsch. And let me tell you, it's a terrible track. In fact, hardly one exists. I doubt whether Coetzer will be able to cope with that journey."

I nodded in appreciation of his analysis, and was now all ears to hear what he was about to suggest.

"Just take a minute to hear me out, *Dominee*. Let the wagon take Coetzer along the main wagon track to the Valsch-River crossing. It will be a quick ride that will only take until mid-afternoon. Meanwhile, you can easily cross the Vaal on horseback near the Rhenoster-River crossing, and be at Daniel Cronje's place by lunchtime. That will enable you to get four to five hours unbroken sleep."

"But what about the baptism at Jan Kok's place?"

"I'm just coming to that. Look, there's almost a full moon tonight, so it's bright enough to travel by its light. If we leave here around four o'clock, we can be at the Koks' farm at quarter past five at the latest. We can enjoy breakfast with them, baptize the child, and be back at the turnoff by eight, in time to meet the wagon."

"Four o'clock, you say. But that only gives me two hours sleep."

"*Ja*, but if you kept to *your* schedule and travelled with the wagon without going to the Koks, you would only reach Daniel Cronje's place by mid-to-late afternoon, giving you less time to rest."

"That's true," I said hesitantly.

"Just work it out. If I lent you a good horse, you'd be at Cronje's farm several hours earlier than you originally planned, enabling you to enjoy the uninterrupted sleep you crave. I'll ask my son Dirk to accompany you so that he can bring my horse back once you arrive at the Valsch River. What do you say to my plan now, *Dominee?*"

What could I say? I was well and truly trapped. I looked up at the moon, and had to admit that his plan was feasible.

"It makes sense, *Meneer* Wolmarans, even if I have to say so reluctantly. And I'm sure Coetzer will bless you for it. But I'm not so sure about your son Dirk."

"*Ach*, he will just have to do what I say. He's about your age, so if you can get up at four, so can he. Believe me, *Dominee*, my sons get it far too easy."

We both chuckled, knowing that this statement was far from the truth.

"Just one more thing, *Meneer* Wolmarans. Could you wake me just before four?"

"No problem. I doubt whether I'll sleep tonight in any case. Just punishment for my sins, I fear."

"What on earth is the time?" asked Coetzer, as I crept into the tent."

"About two. And just before you explode or say anything negative, I have good news for you. The wagon will be taking you directly to the Valsch River via the main wagon track. Fortunately for us, Wolmarans has just offered to lend me a horse so that I can ride directly to Daniel Cronje's place. This means I can arrive there early in order to catch up on my sleep. So what do you think about that?"

I heard him sigh with relief, then whisper: "*Bless the Lord O my soul, for You have answered my prayers.*"

I'm afraid I didn't have the heart to mention that I would be conducting a baptism along the way. In any case, I reasoned that he'd discover that fact soon enough in the morning.

We left for Jan Kok's at four on the dot. But about twenty minutes into our ride, there was a loud thunderclap followed by a cloudburst. While it only lasted about five minutes, we got thoroughly drenched. Sensibly, Wolmarans insisted that we shed out clothes and let them dry on horseback while we continued on our way. Just as well it was dark, because I imagine we looked like the male versions of Lady Godiva. And although we joked about it at the time, the result of having to don damp clothing just before arriving at the Koks' place had devastating consequences for me a few days later.

26

Staring Death in the Face

February 1850

It was on Monday morning, just after delivering my last sermon at the Valsch River on 28 January, that I felt a fever coming on. And before the close of the day, it had begun to rage. The kindly farmers at the Valsch River were adamant that my high temperature was the return of the same fever I'd contracted while at Rustenburg.

"All the symptoms point to Delagoa-Bay fever," they said. "And it's not unknown for it to return again and again."

But I was unconvinced, assuring myself that it was more likely to be a bout of influenza. I was therefore hoping that some freshly squeezed orange juice together with spending the rest of the day in bed would lead to a cure. But first, I wanted to check on Coetzer.

Unlike Potchefstroom, where we'd been lent a family tent, there was no such luxury at the Valsch River camp. Coetzer had been allocated an ox-wagon, while I, on arrival, had insisted on sleeping beneath it in order to be within calling distance if he needed me during the night.

After speaking with some of the farmers after the church service, I wandered over to the wagon and peered inside.

Coetzer's eyes were closed, and his breathing heavy. I noticed that his face was flushed and damp with perspiration. He was obviously very ill. Yet, when I called his name, he opened his eyes and smiled.

"I won't climb in, *Meneer* Coetzer because I think I'm about to come down with influenza. But thankfully, I have the rest of the day to sleep it off."

"You must be so relieved that your tour is over, *Dominee*. And what a blessing it's turned out to be! God has certainly used you to bring a powerful word to all who have been privileged to hear you proclaim the Gospel. To be honest, you are a vastly different preacher from the one who set out with me two months ago."

"And from my point of view, *Meneer* Coetzer, I'm convinced that the hours you spent before the throne of grace achieved far more for the Kingdom than your original role as organizer could ever have done."

He nodded. "Strange as it may seem, I agree. It appears that the Lord has used my affliction to teach me how to pray."

"Nevertheless, I'd like to see you well again. So I propose that we leave for Bloemfontein as soon as possible so that Dr. Drury can examine you. If we leave at daybreak, we can be home by Saturday."

Coetzer didn't reply, but looked over my shoulder into the distance. "Home," he whispered. "I never thought that word could sound so sweet."

And that was the last thought I ever heard him express.

I must have been delirious for most of the night because I imagined one hand after another being placed on my forehead while prayers were being whispered into my ear. Then I fancied

I was again on tour, one moment preaching to the crowds, the next, being chased by lions. Between these flights of fancy, I was conscious of being forced to sip numerous drinks— some sweet, others foul. Then oblivion, as my fever began to subside and I fell asleep.

I was awakened the following morning by a cacophony of voices and footfalls coming from inside the wagon above my head. By my side knelt a farmer who appeared to have been dabbing my face with a damp cloth. As soon as he realized that I was awake and conscious enough of my surroundings to speak, he offered me a drink. He was about to support my shoulders with one arm, when I indicated that I was able to lean on an elbow to accept the mug he offered.

"I'm afraid you *do* have Delagoa-Bay fever, *Dominee*. We are therefore going to rush you to Winburg in *Meneer* Coetzer's cart. I noticed that the seats are upholstered and fold down to make a comfortable bed. So you will be able to lie down for most of the way."

"Why can't I just rest here, *Meneer*?"

No, you need special attention. *Mevrow* Theron in Winburg keeps some veld medicine handy for this disease. Even the doctor in Bloemfontein has used her bush remedies."

"Dr. Drury?"

"That's the one. Two of our young farmers have already left to let *Mevrou* Theron know. We want to make sure that a tent will be ready for you at the church place when you arrive."

"But what about *Meneer* Coetzer? He needs to get to Bloemfontein as soon as possible to see Dr. Drury."

"You don't have to worry about him for the moment because he's enjoying a wonderful banquet."

I handed the drink back to him and fell back on my bed. As I couldn't detect any movement above my head, I took it for granted that others had helped Coetzer out of the wagon.

"*Ach*, I'm so pleased to hear that he's up and about and enjoying a decent-sized breakfast."

The farmer let out a long sigh, then began to dab the perspiration off his forehead.

"*Ja*, he's now in heaven, *Dominee*, and like I said, enjoying a wonderful banquet."

"In heaven? *Ach* no! What are you telling me *Meneer*. I need to see him."

I sat bolt upright, and, sick as I was, threw off the layers of bedding that had been covering me. Although the morning was warm, I found myself shivering uncontrollably.

"Where are my clothes?" I said, frantically looking around for my shirt and pants that I'd laid out next to my bedroll in readiness for the journey back to Bloemfontein.

He gently pushed me down on my bedroll again and covered me with a sheet and several blankets. "They're being washed along with some of your other items. And as for *Meneer* Coetzer, he's with the Lord now, so we can do nothing more for him. Just lie still until the men have finished digging his grave. We'll then take you there so that you can say a prayer and a few words before we bury him."

"But what about his family?"

"*Ja*, it's very sad that they can't be here, but he has to be buried this morning. It's too hot to let him lie in the open."

"I'll need to wear my Sunday shirt and suit," I said with emphasis.

"Of course, *Dominee*. We've already located them. They're right here. When the grave is ready and the neighbors have arrived, we'll help you wash and dress. I think it best if I leave you now to mourn in peace."

He crawled backwards until he was clear of the wagon. As

soon as he was upright, he nodded a goodbye, before limping stiffly away.

Once he was gone, I lay there, trying to imagine Coetzer's reception in heaven. It brought a smile to my face and helped me accept his going. I then traced our journey together and marveled at his faithfulness in prayer, even when laid low with illness. He had seen the tour through to the bitter end and had completed the task. Good and faithful servant, I thought. Then my tears began to flow and my sobs came hard upon each other.

To avoid travelling home in the heat of the day, most of the farmers had stayed at the campsite after the service on Monday. They'd planned to leave at daybreak that morning, but with the news of Coetzer's death, had stayed for the funeral. They were now wending their way to the gravesite on foot, while I was being conveyed there in Coetzer's cart. As I passed by, I was thankful that most would be present at this event.

"Now remember, *Dominee*," said the farmer who was driving the cart, "all that is required of you is a prayer and a few words of blessing. By the looks of you, it will be a strain even to say that. So instead of a sermon, we'll sing *Meneer* Coetzer into heaven. Once you have said your piece, you can lie down in the cart and listen to the wonderful words of the psalms. I'm sure you'll agree that a sermon could never compete with that."

He was right. It certainly couldn't. So I was more than content to lay back in the cart in the knowledge that their raised voices in song was a fitting farewell to Coetzer.

Although the funeral had taken place mid-morning, we only left for Winburg after lunch in order to ensure that my washing was thoroughly dry. On arriving there on Thursday afternoon, I was bundled into the prepared tent. Surrounding it were several other wagons. They were occupied by older couples who had volunteered to take turns to keep a watchful eye over me. It took just over three days of constant nursing, hand feeding, and downing of bush medicine before my fever finally subsided.

Early on Monday morning, I awoke to find *Meneer* Theron sitting on a veld stool by my side.

"Welcome to the land of the living, *Dominee*. You have no idea what a relief it was when your fever finally broke last night. You see, for a moment there, we thought you might not pull through. But the Lord showed you mercy. We now need to get you back to Bloemfontein as soon as possible so that Dr. Drury can examine you."

I groaned at the thought of what Drury might say. He had been the furthest from my mind while in the Transvaal. But now the prospect of his negative assessment cast a pall over my return to Bloemfontein.

As planned, we left Winburg early the next morning and arrived in Bloemfontein just after midday on Wednesday, 6 February.

How can I ever forget that day! Barely fifteen minutes after arriving home, Drury let himself into the parsonage and entered my bedroom. Because of the heat, I was lying with legs akimbo on the top sheet. He drew up a chair beside the bed and studied me for a moment.

"Thank you for coming over, Dr. Drury. It seems that the Valsch-River people, as well as the Therons of Winburg, are of the opinion that I've contracted Delagoa-Bay fever."

"You mean malaria?"

"I have no idea what the correct terminology is. All I know is that they think I contracted the disease while at Rustenburg, and that it returned while I was at the Valsch River. But I doubt that very much. I'm sure it was just influenza."

"Really? What makes you think that?"

"Well, I was forever in some kind of draught—one minute being overheated from preaching, the next in a tent under a tree, or sitting in a through-breeze in a farmhouse parlor."

Drury let out a snort to let me know that he deemed my suggestion ridiculous. He then lifted my shirt and began to pummel my stomach and upper body.

"What about Deacon Coetzer?" he asked.

"Well, he came down with the same symptoms as I did in Rustenburg. But then after his fever had subsided, he complained bitterly of aches and pains throughout his body, especially his back. My personal opinion is that he died of something else."

"Could be," said Drury. "But the question is: where were you before you travelled to Rustenburg?"

I thought for a moment. "Hmm, I see what you are trying to say. It was on the border of the Marico District."

"And do you know if there's been any outbreaks of malaria there?"

"I'm not sure. It's possible, I suppose."

Throughout the rest of the examination, he didn't say a word. I tried to read his face for clues of what he might be thinking, but his expression remained serious throughout.

At last he placed his instruments in his bag. I waited with baited breath for him to pronounce his prognosis, but instead, he just sat there in silence. I knew then that I must be in a bad way.

"I need a second opinion," he said. "I'll be back shortly."

"A second opinion? Who around here is able to give that, Dr. Drury?"

"Ah, you haven't heard then. A Dr. Fraser will be taking over from me in a day or two. He's a perfect gentleman and a first class doctor."

"So what on earth is he doing out here if he's that good?—present company excluded, of course. I know you came to study bush medicine."

His lips twitched into a half smile. "To tell you the truth, I asked the same question myself. Apparently it's been a boyhood dream of his to do some big-game hunting[8]. I wasn't sure how this would sit with Mr. Stuart's appreciation of the wild, but it appears that Dr. Fraser's charm and good humor has overcome all difficulties on that score. They're already firm friends, and I dare say you will warm to him too. He's a Scot, of course."

"So where are you off to next, Dr. Drury?"

"To England, Mr. Murray. To home, sweet home. I'm getting out while the going is good. I fear that this administration has made too many mistakes to last much longer."

He closed his bag and got up to go. "I won't be long."

Barely fifteen minutes had passed before he walked through the door with Dr. Fraser in tow. The latter was much younger than I had anticipated—somewhere in his mid-to-late forties. This indicated that he probably had access to a private income, especially if he anticipated going on expensive hunting safaris in his spare time. Although clean-shaven—like most of the British in these parts—he nevertheless sported sideburns and a moustache, both of which were fashionably flecked with gray. To complete his lord-of-the-manor look, he wore a green, velvet waistcoat over a cream ruffled shirt. While these clothes would have been considered run-of-the-mill ware in Scotland, out here, they lent a genteel look to his kindly face.

After a formal introduction, followed by several minutes of questioning, Dr. Fraser began his examination. Dr. Drury, meanwhile, looked on while standing a few paces to one side.

After what seemed an age, Fraser stood upright and shook his head. "I'm very sorry to have to tell you this, Mr. Murray, but I doubt whether you'll ever be able to preach again."

"But that's ridiculous," I said, looking from one to the other. "Dr. Drury, please tell Dr. Fraser that his prognosis isn't true. It can't be!"

"I'm afraid it is, dear chap. So listen to what he has to say."

"You see," said Fraser, "the problem isn't so much that you contracted malaria, it's that you contracted it at a time when your system was already at a low ebb due to constant travel and overwork. The result has been a complete physical breakdown that I doubt will ever be totally repaired."

I could feel my eyes welling with tears. Surely God wouldn't let this happen to me. I knew my spiritual walk with Him wasn't up to scratch, but then it wasn't all my fault. It was all those demands I had to fulfill. And I certainly couldn't help contracting Delagoa-Bay fever, or malaria, or whatever they liked to call it. God would just have to heal me.

My thoughts were still whirling around when Fraser said in a gentle voice, "I'll let you be for the time being, Mr. Murray. I'm sure Dr. Drury will want to discuss matters further with you. He'll also want to say his farewells."

When he had left, Drury drew up a chair again and regarded me with an earnest expression. "Decision time," he said. "This is your opportunity to resign from the ministry here in Bloemfontein. After that, who knows? If you recover sufficiently, you may be able to be appointed to a less demanding pastorate."

"But I want to stay here, Dr. Drury. I've promised to go to the Transvaal again in September. And strange as it may seem, when Fraser announced that terrible judgment on my ministry, my call to be here became crystal clear. God will just have to heal me because I'm not going home."

"I see," he said, looking thoughtful. "Of course the Lord is able to heal you. There's no doubt about that. I've observed several instances of unexpected healing during my time as a doctor. But in your case, what's the use of the Lord healing you if you're going to abuse His mercy by continuing to overwork?"

"I won't, I assure you. But I still have to go to the Transvaal. I promised, you see."

Drury shook his head. "My dear Mr. Murray, it's no good telling me that. You have to make your promises to the Lord."

"But it does say in Matthew 18:19 '*that if two of you shall agree on earth as touching anything that they shall ask, it shall be done for them of my Father which is in heaven.*' And as my request for healing is directly associated with my ministry, I'm sure thousands will be interceding on my behalf. All I ask from you now is that you agree to my decision to stay put."

He bent low from the waist and clasped his hands together. Although his eyes were open, I knew he was communing with God. After a short interval, he sat upright and favored me with a wry smile.

"Alright, Mr. Murray. But I'll set the parameters."

I nodded, although I suspected that they'd be stringent.

"You are to suspend all ministry duties for six weeks so that you are able to enjoy a complete rest. You will not preach, ride a horse, or be conveyed in a cart."

"But surely I'll be able to ride out with Mr. Stuart to give my horse some exercise?"

"Absolutely not. I'm sure *Meneer* Burger will only be too pleased to look after him for you. The main reason for this bar is to prevent your congregation from thinking that you are well enough to visit them. I assure you, your healing will be curtailed unless you agree to my rules. What is it to be: home or Bloemfontein?"

"Bloemfontein, Dr. Drury."

"Well then, if you are feeling better by mid-March, you may resume your preaching duties here in Bloemfontein. But there is to be no travelling until the second quarter starts in April. That's when your ministry may begin in earnest. But this will depend on whether the Lord sees fit to hasten your recovery, of course."

"What about my proposed tour to the Transvaal? Does our agreement cover that?"

Drury folded his arms while thinking this question through.

"I'll tell you what. . . . I'll suggest to elder Pretorius that it would be a good idea if he took you home to Graaff-Reinet in July. You can discuss this issue with your father then. I'm sure he'll stop you from going if he thinks you aren't up to it. Agreed?"

"Agreed."

As I considered the ramifications of my lengthy recuperation, I realized that it was not going to be a walk in the park. I'd been such an active person, that I couldn't imagine myself staying put for long. Then there was the specter of endless streams of visitors.

"Do you perceive a problem, Mr. Murray? You look concerned."

"It's going to be exhausting, Dr. Drury."

"What is?"

"Having to make endless cups of coffee for all the visitors

I'm bound to be receiving. You have no idea what the Afrikaners are like on that score—illness or no."

"I have a fair idea, believe me. But I think I have the answer to that problem."

I knew that Drury hated entertaining, so I thought he might propose a ban on the number of visitors I could receive. If so, it just wouldn't work.

"I'll have to accept visitors, Dr. Drury—like it or not."

"Certainly, my good fellow. But what you need to do is to curtail their stay and bypass the necessity of having to brew coffee."

"Exactly. But how on earth do I do that?"

"By spending time every day in the vestry. Let me explain. While you were away, the roof was erected over that section of the church. It's also furnished and ready to be used. As a parting gift to your congregation, I've donated my chaise longue as well as my dining-room table and chairs. You'll be able to rest on the chaise when you need to, and write your letters and sermons on the table when you feel up to it. As the roof is high and vaulted, it will also help you escape from the summer heat."

"And presumably from having to make endless cups of coffee" I added.

"Undoubtedly."

He became serious again and studied me for a moment. "The time has come for you to make your promises to the Lord, Mr. Murray. Are you ready to do so?"

By way of answer, I drew myself upright and swung my legs slowly off the bed. I clasped my hands between my knees and bowed my head. There in my bedroom, on Wednesday, 6 February, I promised the Lord to adhere faithfully to the parameters Drury had set. I followed this up by announcing a blessing on Drury, and he on me.

"You know, Mr. Murray," he said, as he rose to go, "just remember what the Lord has already done for you. He has seen fit to close the mouths of that pride of lions and that pack of African wolves. It seems to me that He has great plans for you. But now you need to release your faith so that He can heal you."

He walked to the door, then turned again to face me. "One last thing," he said. "I've already boarded up my house, so I'm staying with Dr. Fraser over the next few days. If you require my services, please don't hesitate to ask Mr. Stuart to contact me or to point out Dr. Frazer's home. And that reminds me. Mr. Stuart is presently your guest because he has nowhere else to stay. I hope you don't mind?"

"Not at all. In fact, it will prove most helpful."

"I thought as much. Nevertheless, from his point of view there was a slight problem in coming here."

"Really?"

"Nothing to concern yourself about, dear chap. It's all been taken care of."

He flashed a wink in my direction, then said, "Mr. Stuart told me that he couldn't possibly cope with those sagging lounge chairs in your parlor. So I exchanged my sitting room suite for yours. Mine is now in your parlor, while yours is now in my sitting room in readiness for the arrival of *Meneer* Van der Meer, the new teacher. It gives me great satisfaction to know that you and Mr. Stuart will be lounging in my suite, rather than some stranger."

Before I could thank him for his generosity, he was gone.

27

Becoming My Own Man

February-June 1850

During my six-week recuperation period, I learnt a great deal about the goings-on in the Sovereignty. I had set up shop in the vestry, and had found this arrangement so convenient that it had become my custom to spend several hours there a day. When I was not resting on the chaise or speaking to visitors, I'd be going for short walks, writing letters, or preparing sermons.

As expected, one of my first visitors was Willem Pretorius. After expressing concern about my health, he then let fly over the political situation in the Sovereignty.

"I need to warn you, *Dominee*," he said. "You'll be receiving a stream of visitors from Winburg shortly. And they won't be coming to inquire after your health. They'll be here to ask for your help."

"Help? What for?"

"Just listen to this. I still can't get over it. *Dominee* Dirk van Velden has been appointed to Harrismith instead of Winburg, as previously promised."

"What!" I almost shouted. "What unprincipled robbery!"

I'd been relaxing on my chaise, but was now so upset by this news that I sat up and swung my feet to the ground, my breath coming in gasps.

"I can hardly believe what you're telling me, *Meneer* Pretorius. Fancy debasing the office of a servant of God to make a political point. I can't comprehend the thinking behind this decision. There are barely thirty souls in the Harrismith area, whereas in Winburg there are three thousand who are hungering after the Gospel. Enough! Tell the Winburg people that I'll be writing to Cape Town forthwith."

The information about Van Velden had upset me to such a degree that I was forced to lie back on the chaise again. But I could tell that Pretorius had more news to convey.

"Things haven't been running smoothly in Smithfield either," he said. "In fact, the people there have been on a knife's edge for some time now. Just after you left for the Transvaal, about sixty-or-so Boers held a meeting in the lower Caledon valley. The outcome was that they decided to support the Basuto chief Moshesh rather than the British over the boundary issue. They also declared that they wanted nothing more to do with the Sovereignty administration. According to my friend Hans Smit, who was an observer at this meeting, about half of them decided that they would no longer be paying their taxes."

"But that's tantamount to rebellion."

"*Ja*, but what do you expect if Major Warden doesn't listen to us Boers?"

While Pretorius prattled on about the stupidity of the Government, I couldn't help thinking back to the statement Drury had made about getting out while the going was good. It was obvious that even he could see the mistakes Sir Harry Smith and Major Warden were making. What was more, their carrot-and-stick mentality was not only petty, but getting them nowhere.

At last Pretorius stopped speaking to clear a frog in his throat.

"You know, *Meneer* Pretorius," I said, "the defiant action of those Boers has probably a lot to do with the fact that Magistrate Vowe refused to let the church wardens sell the town plots."

"True. But despite the Boer boycott, I believe Vowe sold forty in the end."

"Well, I'll just have to discuss the matter with him when I visit Smithfield again in April."

"I doubt whether that will do any good."

"I'm not so sure, *Meneer* Pretorius. The last thing Sir Harry Smith needs is a Boer revolt, especially with Moshesh on the war path. And it appears to me that both Sir Harry and Vowe have made bad errors of judgment—very bad in fact. They seem to have missed the point that Major Warden might need to call upon the commandants to form a Boer commando."

"They won't obey that call. I can tell you that right now."

"So that's exactly what I'll claim in my letter to Sir Harry. I'll also argue that if he doesn't want a rebellion on his hands in Winburg, he'll need to overturn his decision to send Dirk van Velden to Harrismith."

"What about Magistrate Vowe?"

"I'm sure the commando argument will resonate with him as well. But because he's on our doorstep, I'll help him save face. I'll offer to conduct an English service whenever I visit Smithfield in exchange for allowing the church wardens to sell the town plots. What do you think of that?"

He regarded me with concern. "You're obviously learning quickly, *Dominee*. But don't take on extra work until you're well. Drury told me about your promise to the Lord, and asked me to help you keep it."

"Did he mention the need for me to go home to Graaff-Reinet in July?"

Pretorius eyed me with a glint in his eye. "Let's just say that I agreed to take you, and leave it at that."

"So he was that forceful, was he?"

"Forceful enough for me to want to take his place in acting as the guardian of your health."

"Heaven forbid, *Meneer* Pretorius. You'll never be able to match Dr. Drury for prickliness. As it is, I'll be hearing his warnings reverberating in my ears for ever and a day."

Pretorius chuckled, then stood up to go. "I wouldn't be too sure about that, *Dominee*. I can put my mind to anything, you know, especially if it's for your own good."

Surely he's not serious, I thought. But then I observed a quiver of a smile as he exited the vestry. It was obvious that he wanted to keep me guessing.

By the time Willem Pretorius and I set out for Graaff-Reinet in July, I was nearly myself again. My positive mood was aided by the fact that Sir Harry Smith had heeded my advice to reappoint Dirk van Velden to Winburg. And to bolster my confidence even more, Magistrate Vowe had agreed to let the church wardens take over the selling of the Smithfield plots in exchange for my conducting English services there[9].

When I had broached the subject with him in April, a wave of relief had swept over his face.

"I dare say that your offer to preach is a good compromise that will be acceptable to the English community in these parts. I had no idea what a kafuffle my selling the town plots would cause."

"It's a century-old tradition, Mr. Vowe, and one to which the Boers tenaciously cling. In a new town that has yet to be established, the church is always built first. And if sufficient funds have been collected, a high steeple is added, like the one in Graaff-Reinet. It can be seen for miles around, and is an important symbol that declares the town to be the Lord's."

"Yes, I understand all that. But I wasn't trying to put a stop to the building of the church. I'm all for it. I even promised the Boers that I'd donate sufficient funds for both their church and a parsonage. What I didn't expect was that I'd have a rebellion on my hands."

"It's a biblical principle, you see."

"Well, it's the first I've heard of it. It might be a Dutch Reformed tradition, but a biblical principle—I doubt it."

"It goes back to Ezra 4:3 where Zerubbabel tells the non-Israelite men living in the vicinity of Jerusalem that it would only be the Israelites who would be building the House of the Lord. And the principle is also there in the Book of Nehemiah. The exiles who had returned to Judah from Babylon had put off rebuilding the walls of Jerusalem. Instead, they had built their homes, ploughed their fields, and got on with everyday life."

Vowe held up his hand for me to stop. "Fine, I get your drift. The Boers around here obviously think they are the new Israelites. So in their eyes, the Lord's house has to be built first, and the church officials need to be the ones to raise the money to do it. Is that the gist of it?"

"Precisely so. You see the church wardens at Fauresmith have been selling their town plots—with Mr. Stuart's blessing, I might add. And a few years ago, the church wardens at Burghersdorp did the same. So the Boers around here think they've been hard done by."

"Mr. Stuart warned me not to go ahead with the sale of the plots. But then he's a Scot, and understands these matters better than I do. But the question remains, Mr. Murray: Will the Boers allow the English to worship in their church?"

"They'd welcome it—as long as I'm the preacher, or someone else from the Reformed Church."

Vowe snorted. "I thought as much. But with that said, you can tell the church wardens that they can have the full amount I've managed to collect. I'll also give them permission to sell the rest of the plots."

"Thank you, sir. They'll be most relieved to hear it."

"And while we're on the topic of preaching, I'd suggest that it wouldn't go amiss if your first sermon to the English community would be on Nehemiah and the building of the walls of Jerusalem."

He let off a roaring guffaw, while I chortled along to keep him company.

As he ushered me to the door with smiles and pleasantries, I couldn't help recalling William Robertson's predictions only a year before. At the time, I had smirked at his claim that I could undertake a reconciliation role at my young age. But here I was, having done just that.

Almost overnight, these victories had helped to raise my profile amongst the English, and garner further esteem for myself amongst the Boers. The general consensus within my church council was that I was now experienced enough to set my own agenda. And set it I would. After all, I had turned twenty-two on 9 May, and was therefore ready to embark on a new chapter in ministry with myself at the reins.

Epilogue
Clairvaux, Wellington

May 1915

The sun had dipped for a time behind the clouds while Dr. Murray had told his story, but had burst forth again as if on cue towards the end.

"I think we should stop at this point, Johan. It's always good to conclude on a high note, don't you think?"

I sat with pencil poised. "I agree, Dr. Murray. But may I ask a quick question first?"

"By all means."

"What was the number one thing you learnt during your first year in ministry?"

He turned his head awkwardly in my direction, prompting me to shift my chair around to face him once more.

"Never to disobey church law, Johan. That is what I learnt."

I chuckled, thinking it was one of his wry jokes. But no, his jaw was firmly set and his expression deadly earnest.

"I should never have been sent out beyond the borders of the Cape to fend for myself at the tender age of twenty-one. It was utter madness. What were my father and William Robertson thinking?"

"Probably, that you were bold and tenacious enough to make

a success of it—as you most certainly did. They were therefore right on that score."

"But that's a worldly assessment, Johan. From a spiritual perspective, the reality was quite different. I knew they had twisted Sir Harry's arm to let me go to the Sovereignty. So when the going got tough, I doubted that I should have been there. And by the time Willem Pretorius and I set out for Graaff-Reinet in July 1850, I was facing the spiritual dangers associated with self and pride."

"Is that why you focus so much on those aspects in your books, Dr. Murray?"

A mirthful chuckle lit up his face. "I'm pleased you noticed, Johan. I just hope you took heed."

I answered with a wan smile and moved on quickly. "From where I sit, Dr. Murray, you appear to have surmounted the difficulties and challenges that came your way. It seems that you were now on the high road to achieving your goals."

"Johan, where is your spiritual insight? I was about to set foot on the low road of self-satisfaction, self-aggrandizement, self-centeredness, and any other self you can think of. I needed to be reined in, Johan. Not given the reins."

"But you had your church council to help out there. Surely you would have discussed your program with them?"

"What was there to discuss? They knew I was doing my job, so they simply left me to it. I devised my own schedule, and then informed them. After my illness, they literally took a back seat."

"I can understand that. They probably wanted you to be able to pace yourself."

"Pace myself! I didn't know the meaning of the phrase. And because I was now certain of my call to be in the Sovereignty, I felt I had to strive in order for God to bless me. I reasoned that because I didn't have the time or energy to spend with Him, He would accept my gift of hard work. What it boiled down to was that I wanted the gift of the Spirit without the Giver."

"I think your assessment is far too harsh, Dr. Murray."

"Oh Johan, if only you knew! Take the Transvaal, for instance. They made far too much of me. Think of what that does to a young man's ego."

"But they loved your sermons. You also made great headway there as a pastor and a leader."

"That is true. But power is dangerous for a young person, Johan. And unfortunately, the situation in both the Sovereignty and the Transvaal encouraged strong leadership. The Boers there were used to men like Andries Pretorius and Hendrik Potgieter issuing commands. So when I adopted a strong leadership style and threw my weight around—albeit in a respectful way—I was applauded for it."

"Didn't your father try to rein you in, Dr. Murray?"

"Of course he did. But what does a young man do when he wants to go his own way?"

"He keeps his plans to himself."

"Exactly Johan."

Andrew Murray closed his eyes and groaned. Oh, the deceit of youth! And oh, how true the saying that pride cometh before a fall. But in my case it was more of a crash down—not once, but twice. It forced me to look squarely at my walk with the Lord and what I should be doing about it. And on both occasions, it came when I least expected it to."

He was about to say something more, when his daughter Annie poked her head around the corner and announced that lunch was ready.

"Well, I suppose we'll have to leave that story for next time."

He leant heavily on the armrests of the wicker chair and

pulled himself upright. I was on the verge of helping him, when Annie shook her head to indicate that I shouldn't. When he was ready, his eyes met mine, and he broke into a knowing smile.

"Ah, Johan, pride even niggles at one in old age. I'll have to give it its marching orders one of these days. Come, lunch awaits."

If you enjoyed this book, and think it worth sharing, please take a moment to write a short reader's review on Amazon. It will go a long way in helping to make Andrew Murray's story known to a new generation who may be inspired to read his insightful devotional works as well.

You may also like to read the second novel in this series. It is titled *Andrew Murray: Destined to Win* (ISBN 978-0-9925671-5-6) and covers the years 1850–1856. Here is a short summary in point form:

A true story of battles, blessings, betrayal, and breakthrough
- **Learn** of the battles fought and lost against the Basuto chief Moshesh.
- **Observe** the brinkmanship at the Sand River Convention, where independence was granted to the Transvaal.
- **Follow** Andrew Murray to England, where he preaches at Surrey Chapel.
- **Sail** down the Rhine with him on his way to meet Professor Beck, who introduces him to the works of the early Christian Fathers.
- **Accompany** him to the Herschel Estate in Cape Town, where he courts the girl of his dreams.
- **Feel for** him as his heart is broken and he realizes how miserably he has failed to progress in his spiritual walk.
- **Rejoice** with him when his dreams come true and he learns to win through a closer walk with God.

Olea is presently writing her third novel in the 'Destined' series, which will be titled *Andrew Murray: Destined to Wait*. It is due out in 2019.

Her fourth and last novel in this series will be titled *Andrew Murray: Destined to Lead*.

Notes

1. Priscilla J. Owens wrote the chorus "We Have an Anchor" in 1882. The composer was William J. Kirkpatrick. This chorus fitted in so well with this story, that I couldn't bypass the opportunity to use it. As a child I attended Three Anchor Bay Primary School—directly opposite Three Anchor Bay. And when the storms raged, we would always sing hymns associated with the sea during assembly. For those who don't know the tune, you can find it here: http://www.hymnal.net/en/hymn/h/331#1

2. It is not recorded on which sailing ship Andrew and his brother John returned to South Africa. What we do know is that J.J. Freeman of the London Missionary Society also sailed to South Africa at the end of 1848. Because he later met up with Andrew while he was crossing the Orange River, and subsequently entered into a correspondence with him, I decided to place Andrew and John on board the *Lady Flora* with Mr. Freeman. A free download of J.J. Freeman's book: *A Tour of South Africa* is available here: http://www.unz.org/Pub/FreemanJJ-1851

3. Uncle William's real name was Georg Wilhelm Stegmann. He became very friendly with Dr. Adamson of St. Andrews Presbyterian Church. As they worked very closely together to evangelize the Muslims who lived at the foot of Schotsche Kloof, it is almost certain that they were neighbors there. Within three years, Georg Stegmann had converted 1000 Muslims. Later, he would move to Craig Cottage in Kloof Street.

4. On page 85 of Johannes du Plessis's biography of Andrew Murray, he states that Willem Pretorius was a deacon. But this was not the case. Church records show that he was an elder. The induction service took place by Drs. Philip Faure and William Robertson on 6 January 1849. At that event the following men were inducted:
W.S. Pretorius (elder)
J. van Zyl (elder)
J.D. Griesel (deacon)
P.W. Coetzer (deacon)
A.J. Erwee (deacon)
J.P. Maree (deacon)

5. In Johannes du Plessis's biography of Andrew Murray, he states on page 77 that Sir Harry Smith told Andrew that he was to go to Bloemfontein. Du Plessis obviously took an educated guess as to what might have happened. But church archives show that Andrew's appointment was only made after Drs. Philip Faure and William Robertson had returned home from Graaff-Reinet. The evidence suggests that Andrew's appointment would have played out in a similar way as told in this story. As far as Andrew's brother John was concerned, his appointment needed to be endorsed by Sir Harry Smith because the Government was paying his stipend. But it would have been arranged by the Presbytery of Graaff-Reinet and the Synodical Committee beforehand. Dr. Abraham Faure would have then sought Sir Harry Smith's approval. That being said, Sir Harry did have a stick and carrot mentality. He could change his mind on a whim, especially if he thought that the Boers of a particular congregation were not "behaving" as they ought.

6. In a letter from Mr. Stuart to J.J. Freeman, he tells the latter: "I reckon the number of game in my district at one million head. What a heart-stirring thing it is to let your horse have the reins while he dashes up to some four thousand graceful antelopes!" (J.J. Freeman p. 231). A free download of J.J. Freeman's book: *A Tour of South Africa* is available here: http://www.unz.org/Pub/FreemanJJ-1851

7. The wolf Andrew Murray is referring to here is *Lycaon Pictus,* known as the African Painted Wolf, the African Wild Dog, or the African Wolf Dog.

8. Not long after his arrival, Dr. Frazer went hunting across the Vaal River. Bishop Gray, who also met him over dinner along with Andrew Murray, tells us that Frazer was imprisoned by the Boers for presuming to cross the Vaal without their permission. A description of the Bishop's tour is given in: Project Canterbury, Church in the Colonies No. 27. Diocese of Cape Town, Part II. *A Journal of the Bishop's Visitation Tour through the Cape Colony in 1850.* You can view it here: http://anglican-history.org/africa/spg27.html

9. Bishop Gray of Cape Town tells us that while on tour through the Orange River Sovereignty in May 1850, he was told (probably by Andrew Murray with whom he had dinner) that Smithfield was promised the full amount from the sale of their town plots. Of particular interest is the fact that Sir Harry Smith would not provide a stipend for a Church of England minister in Bloemfontein, despite Bishop Gray's earnest request for funds. A description of the Bishop's tour is given here: http://anglicanhistory.org/africa/spg27.html

Glossary of Terms

Ach!: (*Ag* in Afrikaans): An interjection used by Dutch and Afrikaans speakers

Afrikaner: Those who were born in South Africa and spoke Cape Dutch (Afrikaans today)

Boer: A farmer. Also used to denote those who spoke Dutch

Boerbeskuit: A rusk used for dunking in coffee or tea

Consistory: Church Council of elders and deacons. Also used to denote the vestry

Consulent: A minister from a neighboring congregation who administered Holy Communion

Dominee: The equivalent of Reverend in English

Drostdy: Magistrate's court and administrative center. Could double as home of the landdrost

Groote Kerk: Great Church situated at the top of Adderley Street

Holland: This namewas always used to denote the *Netherlands* amongst Afrikaners during Andrew Murray's day

Impi: Zulu regiment

Inspan: To harness horses or yoke oxen in a team to a vehicle

Katel: Bench made of wood and wickerwork. There were usually two to a wagon

Kleinbaas: Small or deputy boss. Used by servants to address sons in the family

Koeksisters: A syrup-coated doughnut that is plaited

Landdrost: Equivalent to a magistrate
Liefie: Lovey
Liefling: My love
Melktert: South African milk tart
Meneer: Mr.
Mevrou: Mrs.
Môre: Good morning
Oe!: An interjection
Oom: Uncle. Also used as an honorific when addressing an older person
Ouma: Grandma
Oupa: Grandpa
Outspan: Unharness horses or unyoke oxen from a vehicle
Overvaal: Used by Dutch speakers living across the Vaal River to denote their territory
Predikant: Minister
The Resident: The commanding officer of a territory
Schoft: The distance travelled before horses or oxen were outspanned. The duration was usually three hours, covering fifteen to eighteen miles for a horse-wagon, and nine to ten miles for an ox-wagon
Stoep: Veranda.
Volksraad: People's council
Vuilbaard: Dirty beard—the nickname for a male lion